'writing that leaps off the page in its lacerating forcefulness... a classic British gangster novel that evokes and matches some of the best writing in the genre' — Vic Buckner, *Crime Time*

'*The Drop* is overflowing with the grit that defines the very best of British gangster fiction' — Mike Stafford, *Bookgeeks*

'Howard Linskey does for Newcastle what Ian Rankin has done for Edinburgh' — Sam Millar, *New York Journal of Books*

'a brutal, hard-hitting debut which opens up Newcastle's dark, violent underbelly like a freshly-sharpened stiletto' — Simon Kernick

'a razor-sharp debut and Linskey is sure to be at the forefront of Northern crime writing in 2011. A writer to keep an eye on' — Nick Quantrill, *Harrogate Festival website*

'a very successful first novel' — Chris Shepherd, *newbooks magazine*

'Plainly put *The Drop* is a brilliant slice of modern Brit Grit' — Brian Lindemuth, *Spinetingler Magazine*

'A fast-paced, hard-boiled tale that zips along' — *The Crack*

'Linskey has a knack of expressing a mindset with clarity, humour and realism which along with the earthy vocabulary combines to create a marvellous tale' — *Crimesquad*

'A cracker of a tale unrolled with great understatement but loaded with verve and pace. The backdrop is brutal, harsh and downright fatal for some, the characters jump right off the page, and I found the book difficult to put down. No Exit Press has found a real winner' Adrian Magson, *Shots*

'An absolutely cracking debut novel' — *bestcrimebooks.co.uk*

'A deftly written crime thriller, which really shows off Linskey's skill at storytelling' — Luca Veste, *Guilty Conscience*

'Brilliant. Gangster writing at its best' — Paul Cleave, winner of the Ngaio Marsh Award

Critical acclaim for *The Damage*

Think *Geordie Shore* meets *The Wire* and there's a TV masterpiece out there waiting to happen' — Peter Millar, *The Times*

'Vicious, violent and unashamedly amoral' — Geoffrey Wansell, *The Daily Mail*

'One of the *Times* Top Crime & Thriller Summer Reads ' — Peter Millar, *The Times*

'An incredibly enjoyable read, *The Damage* is an excellent novel which sets Linskey up as someone to watch out for' — Luca Veste, *Crime Fiction Lover*

'Brilliant stuff' — Ian Ayris

'A hard hitting crime caper which will leave the reader desperate for the next instalment' — GS, *crimesquad.com*

'Bristles with machismo, offers frequent violent thrills and ends with a taut finale. *The Damage* is *Casino* to *The Drop's Goodfellas*' —Mike Stafford, *Bookgeeks*

'A colourful array of characters who spout some of the sparkiest dialogue around. More please!' — *The Crack*

'*The Damage* is gripping. I finished the book in one sitting ' — L J Hurst, *Shots*

'An intense and riveting sequel' — *Publishers Weekly*

'The King of Northern Noir... Taut. Tough. Terrifying. *The Damage* is a deeply atmospheric, in-your-face tale of immorality, seediness, violence, and murder, scintillating with menace from start to finish' — Sam Millar, *New York Journal of Books*

THE DROP

HOWARD LINSKEY

NO EXIT PRESS

First published in 2011 by No Exit Press,
an imprint of Oldcastle Books Ltd,
P.O.Box 394, Harpenden,
Herts, AL5 1XJ

www.noexit.co.uk

A CIP catalogue record for this book is available from the British Library.

ISBNs
978-1-84243-394-2 (original paperback)
978-1-84243-434-5 (epub)
978-1-84243-452-9 (mobi)
978-1-84243-435-2 (pdf)

6 8 10 9 7 5

Typeset in Garamond MT Std size 12.5/14pt, by Suntec, India
Printed and bound in Great Britain by Cox & Wyman, Reading, Berks

For Erin & Alison

ACKNOWLEDGEMENTS

I would like to thank the following for their faith and unflagging support during the writing of this book; Adam Pope, Andy Davis, Nikki Hurley and Gareth Chennells.

Sincere thanks to my publisher Ion Mills, at No Exit, for believing in *The Drop*. Thanks also to the whole team at No Exit, in particular Annette Crossland, Alan Forster for the cover design plus Claire Watts, Chris Burrows, Jolanta Kietaviciute and Alexandra Bolton for their hard work on my behalf, and also my anonymous copy editor – you know who you are.

A very big thank you to my Literary Agent, Phil Patterson at Marjacq, for his sound advice, editorial assistance and general good company, all of which is very greatly appreciated by me. Thanks also to the incomparable Isabella Floris at Marjacq for her amazing efforts in foreign markets and also to Luke Speed and Jacqui Lyons. Thanks also to Simon Kernick for taking the trouble to read *The Drop* and for his kind words thereafter.

Finally and most importantly a huge thank you to my loving wife, Alison, and beautiful daughter Erin for their amazing support and for putting up with me and all of this writing. This one is for you!

PROLOGUE

....

L ook at her. Go on, look. Take a good, long look. Beautiful isn't she; standing there by the swimming pool; five feet six inches of slim, tanned, hard-bodied, healthy young woman. I mean, what's not to like about Laura?

Look at the way the water slides reluctantly from her hips as she climbs out of the water in that tiny black bikini. She turns and grabs the long, dark hair that trails down her back then squeezes the water out, before combing it back with her fingers, making it hang straight. Then she looks up and smiles at me. She's got a good smile, warm and naughty and it's making me wonder what my chances are of peeling that little black bikini off her just one last time before we have to fly home again.

She's bright too, a lawyer and it's always useful to know one of those, particularly in my profession. She knows what I do for a living, well mostly, and it doesn't bother her. I mean, it's not as if I'm a gangster exactly, not really. I don't go telling her the details of my day but she knows I work for Bobby Mahoney, so it's obvious I'm no chartered accountant.

We've been together more than two years now, and I am beginning to think she might be the one. We'd been bickering a bit lately, a lot actually if I'm honest, but I reckon we were just over the honeymoon period, that's all. We've both been working hard and we needed a rest. This holiday could have been make-or-break but it's been great; lots of late nights, long lie-ins, lounging by the swimming pool, then back to the hotel for some of that lovely, unhurried, afternoon sex you only ever seem to get when you're on holiday. If only life was like this all the time.

And Laura is loyal, which helps. Loyalty is a rare and underestimated commodity these days. At least it is in my game. You want my opinion? You can't put a price on loyalty. So I have landed on my feet with Laura, no one can dispute that. Even Bobby thinks she's alright, for a posh bird.

It's funny now, looking back on it, how I had no inkling, no instinct whatsoever, while I was lying there by the pool, soaking up the sun that hovers over this part of Thailand like it just loves the place and never wants to leave, that everything was going so badly wrong back home while I was away. I can honestly say that, right then, I really did have no idea just how much shit I was in.

ONE

Finney was there to meet us at the airport so I knew, as soon as I saw his pug-ugly, scarred face that it had all gone tits-up.

I spotted him easily. He towered over everyone else; the relieved parents collecting back-packing teenagers, the mini-cab drivers on autopilot, holding up their cardboard signs with the names of self-important businessmen hastily scrawled on them in biro. We were tired by now. The plane from Bangkok to Heathrow was bang on time but the connecting flight back to Newcastle arrived an hour late, which tells you everything you need to know about this country.

Laura hadn't noticed Finney. She was too busy restoring her lifeline, as she called it, attempting to wrestle her mobile phone from her handbag while simultaneously dragging the smallest of our two cases, mine obviously, along behind her on its squeaky wheels. I could hear them squealing in protest with every step, because they were full of handcrafted, wooden nick-nacks she'd insisted on buying but had no room for in her own case. That was full to bursting with the clothes she'd packed in Newcastle but hadn't worn on the holiday because they were too bulky for the heat. 'Why do you need three different dresses for every day we are out there?' I'd asked her before we left, as I sat on her case and tried to flatten it. Now, I was dragging Laura's case behind me, feeling no happier for being right.

Ten days later, we were back in Newcastle and the look on Finney's face told me. I was in trouble.

There was no greeting, no small talk from the big man, all I wanted to know was why he was standing there, his huge frame dwarfing those flimsy, metal barriers at the arrivals gate, gnarled fists bunched like he was about to start a fight.

'What?' I asked him simply.

'Bobby needs a word Davey,' he said in that unmistakeably nasally Geordie voice of his, which had been caused by the iron bar that broke his nose years ago. I was reliably informed that it was the last thing the guy with the iron bar ever did.

'Now?' And he just nodded.

'What is it?'

He looked over at Laura, who was still a few yards behind me but preoccupied by voicemails from her girly mates and her bloody mum.

'It's the Drop,' he said and I immediately thought, oh shit.

Laura didn't take the news well. 'He needs to see you now?' she asked, as if I'd been called in at late notice for a shelf-stacking shift at the Co-Op. 'Christ David.'

I realised she was jetlagged but then so was I, and I could have done without the grief, because she was embarrassing me a little in front of Finney. I might have been a new man compared to most of our mob but, if she carried on like this, the word would go out that I was pussy-whipped.

'You know who I work for.' I hissed the words at her and was relieved when she fell silent. Finney lifted Laura's case into the boot of her Audi and I added the other one. She didn't thank either of us.

'You don't know when you'll be back?' she asked, though she already knew the answer to that stupid question.

'No,' I said through gritted teeth, my mind already on Bobby Mahoney and the reasons why he had sent his top enforcer out to the airport to bring me in. Why did he not just leave me a message, or send some low-level member of the crew with a car, unless this was serious and I was somehow to blame for it? What the hell had gone wrong with the Drop? Was it light? Had Cartwright gone completely out of his mind and skimmed off the top. No, he'd have to be mad. It would be spotted immediately. So, if not that, then what?

We waited till Laura drove away with a face like thunder, then walked over to Finney's 4x4 and climbed in. He drove us out of the car park and away.

I had a little over ten minutes to get to the bottom of what was going on before we were back in the city. I hung on for what seemed like an eternity then finally asked, 'So, you going to tell me what this is all about or do I have to guess?'

'I'm not s'posed to say. It's…'

'Don't be a total cunt.' I was deliberately talking down to him, like he was being a complete wanker for holding out on me like this, which he was. I only had a short drive to convince him he could safely let me know what had happened. 'I'm not going to let on, am I?'

It was a bit of a risk talking to a man like Finney like that and he gave me a look. We both knew he could have ripped my head off my body without even breaking sweat. He was a huge guy with a barrelled chest and fists like mell hammers. His face was marked with the scars from a thousand fights, all of which I am willing to bet he won. Put it this way, I have never heard of anybody beating Finney, not once, not in the illegal, bare-knuckle boxing bouts where he came to Bobby Mahoney's attention in the first place, not inside, when he got his ten stretch, commuted to six, and certainly not on the streets. Nobody has ever taken down Finney on the streets. He is the firm's main muscle and I take him anywhere where there might be even a hint of trouble. People soon stop giving me jip when he walks in.

He didn't say anything at first, just watched the road ahead. Then finally he quietly told me, 'It's the Drop.'

'Yeah, you said,' I replied irritably and while I was racking my brains wondering what could possibly have gone wrong, he added, 'It didn't happen.' And I am not afraid to tell you that, right then, the blood in my veins ran to ice.

TWO

....

Bobby Mahoney has meetings in lots of different places. He has to; in the back rooms of the pubs he owns, or the spa he has a stake in, or down at the Cauldron, the first club he had before he went on to control an empire. It's safer that way and makes it hard for the local plod or SOCA to get anything on tape. We sweep every location twice a week obviously, we're no mugs - and Bobby Mahoney isn't some John Gotti figure, shooting his mouth off all over Tyneside until they get enough to put him away for life. He doesn't piss about does Bobby and it's part of my job to make sure he never takes chances.

I'm not too surprised when Finney tells me we are meeting at the Cauldron. It's a sort of home from home for Bobby and I suspect he views it sentimentally, like some huge retailer who returns to his first corner shop every now and then to recall the good old days when he had nothing but naked ambition. Well, that and, in Bobby's case, the proceeds from the robbery of an armoured car which his fledgling crew turned over back in 1973. They stormed in with stocking masks over their faces and sawn-off shotguns, which they brandished under the noses of the unarmed security guards. Those guys were paid a pittance and were hardly going to act the hero.

That's how you got started in those days. You'd take out a wages van to secure the funds to start you off. It was the first step on the ladder. Nowadays if we need to be more liquid we talk to venture capitalists. It's a funny old world.

No one but a complete numpty would take out a security van these days. There's nothing like as much cash about for one thing, everybody gets their salary through BACS transfer and the wage packet stuffed with tenners is a distant memory. Police intelligence is a lot sharper as well, gangs get spotted early, their members put under round-the-clock surveillance and, if they do make a move, they get taken out by police marksmen with itchy trigger fingers, who all think they're Al Pacino in *Heat*.

We watched one botched armed robbery unfolding on Sky News a few weeks back, at least the aftermath of it. The cops weren't content with arresting the dumb shits, who hadn't realised things had changed since the days of Regan and Carter and a gruff shout of 'you're nicked son'. As soon as they pulled a handgun on the security guard they were dropped, calm as you like, by snipers they never even saw, leaving passers by to catch images of their bodies on mobile phone cameras, so they could sell the grainy footage to the 24-hour news channels. It seems we are all journalists these days. Everybody knows you can get a few bob for footage of blood on the walls of your local building society.

Bobby watched it all with interest before pronouncing, 'aye, things have definitely changed since my day,' before taking a sip of his whiskey and adding, 'course, we weren't fucking amateurs.'

Back in Bobby's younger days, the proceeds from one or two vans would set you up with a controlling stake in a club and enough readies to invest in slot machines, stolen booze or fags and old-fashioned, honest-to-goodness whoring. As Bobby told me, 'men have needed women since time began but it's still illegal thank God - and long may that continue, or they'd be offering you one when you went for your groceries at Tescos,' and he mimicked the sing-song voice of some simple-minded checkout girl, "That's ninety quid sir. Oh, got your loyalty card have you? I see you've enough points on there for one fuck, two blow jobs and a tit-wank. Would you like them now while the wife gets your petrol?" and he'd laughed, "do you think they wouldn't do it if they could" They sell everything from TVs to insurance and you can buy a vibrator on every high street these days. Where would we be if they really let retailers sell sex, eh? I've made more money out of massage than I have out of armed robbery. It just takes a bit longer, one hand job at a time.'

Finney and I were back in the city way too soon. It was the start of an October weekend and people were out and about, forgetting their cares for a few hours in the pubs and clubs of the Bigg Market and the Quayside; dozens of lasses done up to the nines and lairy lads out on the prowl looking for their one-night-Juliet. The bridges on the Quayside were all lit up, so the evening's revellers could tell which direction they were staggering.

I'd been thinking about Bobby's violent start in life for a reason. He was still a hard bastard. If he felt aggrieved, he was not afraid to use some of that famous ruthlessness on any man, even one of his trusted lieutenants. I was worrying quite a lot about that in fact, because this time the trusted lieutenant was me. I am not as used to violence as the other guys in his crew. They've all been around a lot longer and they've had to scrap their way into his outfit. They all got their hands dirty at one point or another, but me? I'm a lot younger and I'm strictly white-collar, an ideas man. I have made Bobby Mahoney a lot of money over the years and he always made sure I got my slice but none of that matters now. The Drop didn't happen and frankly, I admit it, I am shitting myself.

'Not a fucking word to Bobby, you hear me Davey?' cautioned Finney, 'no matter what he says.'

My name is David Blake but most of the firm still call me Davey, even though I grew out of it years ago.

'I said, didn't I?'

We parked outside the dirty, red-brick, windowless façade of the Cauldron, a stone's throw from China Town and a goal kick from St James Park. It was Friday night, just after traditional pub kicking-out time and the punters were already massing outside to get into the Cauldron. It's not our coolest spot but it's cheap and has a pretty loyal following. They were queuing two or three deep; teenage girls dressed in skirts so tiny they looked like they were fashioned from their grandad's hankies. Their tight shirts were buttoned or tied just far enough up the middle to leave an acre of bare, white-fleshed cleavage spilling out over the fabric. Christ, I thought, they must be freezing. Then I realised how old that made me sound. The young don't notice the cold. I remembered my poor, late ma saying the same thing to me every time I left the house without a coat on. 'You'll catch your death one day, you will.'

Finney chucked the keys at one of the bouncers and he moved the car off the double yellows. The other one hastily unclipped the red, velvet rope that was meant to give the place a veneer of class and stepped back out of our way to admit us. We walked passed the lass who took the money, Julie I think her name was, and she smiled at me. I found myself wondering if she would testify if I didn't make it out of the building alive. Would she fuck.

The thought kept going round and round in my mind; the Drop didn't happen so, right now, I was about as popular in Newcastle as Dennis Wise. I was already wishing I was on the return flight back to Thailand.

We climbed a steep flight of stairs covered in sticky, lager-encrusted, maroon carpet and I got a brief glimpse of the dancefloor ahead of me with the 80's style smoke machine billowing till the place looked like it was on fire. The club was slowly filling up with pissed-up, randy young blokes and bored-looking but equally drunk lasses. They were gyrating to Rihanna's *'Disturbia'*. For some reason it sounded jarring and ominous, the bass thumping at probably the same rate as my heart, but I knew that was just my overwrought mind fucking with me.

I caught the eye of one girl in particular. I don't know why she stood out but she looked desolate. She was sitting on her own and had more than likely just realised her friend wasn't coming back for her, probably getting her tits felt in the taxi rank outside. She'd soon be on her way back to some apprentice sparky's flat because he'd told her he played for Newcastle reserves. I looked into her doleful, hurt face and wanted to tell her 'pet, you think you've got problems?'

It was two more flights to the inner sanctum and when I got there Bobby was sitting behind his big, solid oak desk, waiting for me. There were a couple of senior members of the firm there with him; Jerry Lemon, as usual in a T-shirt, all bare arms and prison tatts, filled with so much pent up aggression I was always expecting him to have a heart attack. Standing next to him was Mickey Hunter looking uncomfortable in a supposedly smart jacket, a tie strung so loosely round his neck you could see the top button of his shirt. I wanted to march up to the big fellah and pull it taut so he didn't look like such a scruff. He obviously felt obliged to dress smart in Bobby's nightclub but it just didn't suit him. He ended up looking like a manual worker forced by his missus to wear a good suit at his niece's wedding.

Even our bent accountant Alex Northam was there, in a tweed suit that was far too old for him. He was one of those middle-aged guys who can't wait to get old so they can tell everybody how far back they go.

I'd known these guys for a long while but they all avoided my gaze now. I wondered if any of them had put in a good word for me or if they couldn't wait to dance all over my grave. No honour among thieves.

While not quite as violently psychotic as Finney, Bobby Mahoney was still a man to be reckoned with, even in his late fifties. He might have had the grey hair and lined face of a man contemplating retirement, but you could still put him in a room full of twenty-year olds and I'd bet he'd be the only one left standing at the end.

He didn't look pleased to see me.

'Alright Bobby?' I said, knowing that he wasn't.

'Where the fuck have you been?' the big booming voice silenced every one else immediately. It was so sharp it made Northam twitch in alarm.

'Thailand.' I told him as defiantly as I could manage. Rightly or wrongly, since I'd done nothing wrong I was gambling that my best form of defence was a little bit of defiance, mixed with a healthy dose of bemusement. 'Why?'

Bobby climbed to his feet and came out from behind his desk. Jerry Lemon and Mickey Hunter parting like the Red Sea so he could get at me. My mouth was dry and I didn't like the way his enormous fists were balled up. I was preparing myself for a bad beating.

'What happened to the Drop?' he asked me outright.

And this is where it got difficult for me, because I wasn't supposed to know it hadn't happened but Finney knew that I knew and he was standing there with me, so I had to be convincing. If I started looking shifty because I was denying all knowledge of what had happened to the Drop then Bobby might start to wonder why and draw the wrong, dangerous conclusion.

'I don't know, I was away. I've been on holiday remember.' Then I acted like it was just sinking in, 'what do you mean "what happened to it?"'

'You were responsible for the Drop!' the volume rose to a dangerous level. He crossed the floor towards me and the others started looking elsewhere; their shoes, the framed prints of half-naked Pirelli calendar girls on the walls, anywhere but at me, 'don't take me for a cunt Davey,' he hissed at me when he was right up close.

The situation was serious enough for me to immediately stop acting defiant. 'Yeah, I know Bobby, but I was on holiday so Geordie Cartwright said he'd do it,' I said this quietly, hoping to calm the big man down, 'just like he always does when I'm on holiday. He said he'd clear it with you and he'd take Maggot down there with him.'

He walked right up to me and stopped just in front of my face, so he could take a long look at me to see if I was lying. They say Bobby Mahoney can smell a lie. 'Well he didn't fucking clear it with me and he didn't take Maggot with him.' He was up so close to me I could smell the stale tobacco on his breath.

'You've spoken to Maggot have you?' I asked.

'Oh yeah,' said Finney wryly, 'we spoke to him alright.' By his tone I realised they must have put the fear of God into the poor bastard to make sure he was telling the truth. Finney was famous for his powers of persuasion, his trademark weapon of choice being a nail gun. He had a fondness for putting nails through people's hands, leaving them stuck to their kitchen tables, garage doors and, in one memorable case, the skull of a deceased accomplice.

'You didn't ring me,' I offered, surprised that this was not the first thing he'd thought of. I didn't have a fancy mobile with an international connection but I wasn't hard to trace.

'We phoned the hotel you gave us,' said Jerry Lemon, 'they said you weren't staying there,'

'That's bullshit,' I said, 'I was there. I've been on the same fucking resort for ten days. Laura brought back half the gift shop. Course I was fucking there.' And then a thought suddenly struck me.

Laura.

Laura made the booking.

Oh Christ.

'So, what's happened then?' I asked, looking to deflect them from the subject of my strange absence from the hotel register. For a second, I thought Bobby was going to belt me and when Bobby Mahoney starts belting people he doesn't stop. Believe me, I've seen it. It takes Finney and all his mates to drag Bobby off once he's started and by then it's usually too late.

'Nothing happened!' he snarled, 'the Drop certainly didn't happen and Cartwright's disappeared.'

'Shit!'

'Yeah, shit's the word. A whole heap of shit and we are all in it, particularly you. The first I hear about it is when I get a call to tell me the Drop's late. The Drop's never late so I know something's wrong straight away and I look into it sharpish. Turns out nobody can find Cartwright and nobody can find the money. Only thing anyone knows is it didn't fucking get there. So my question, once again, is where the fuck have you been?'

I am bright enough to realise that he is not talking literally. I know if I even say the words 'holiday' or 'Thailand' again I am liable to get a beating that would not entirely be undeserved. 'I'm sorry Bobby, I really am. I fucked up,' he doesn't seem to know how to react to that level of honesty. He's clearly not used to it. 'I should have made sure the Drop was in safer hands than Cartwright so you had nothing to worry about.'

'I'm not worried about Cartwright. I've known him for years and he's fucked either way son. It looks like someone's killed him and taken my money. That's my guess and, if it's not that, it means he's so stupid he's stolen it himself, and *I'll* bloody kill him. Don't worry about Cartwright, worry about yourself because the Drop is your responsibility. I thought I'd made that pretty clear. Now you get out there and you find Cartwright or you find his body. I want to know who's behind this and I want my fucking money back – then I am going to let Finney cut whoever's responsible into tiny pieces while they are still breathing. You have got two days to sort this mess out. I want my cash back on this desk on Monday morning. Nobody takes from me, nobody, you know that!'

Christ, my heart sank on hearing that. I already knew my chances of finding Cartwright, or his rotting carcass, and Bobby's money by Monday were slim to none, but I was definitely not going to tell Bobby Mahoney that right now. If I did, I reckoned he would have killed me, so I took the path of least resistance and bought myself some time.

'Yeah Bobby I know that. Leave it with me. I'm on it.'

'Go on then,' he said and I didn't wait to be told twice, 'and take Finney with you.'

Finney lumbered after me, which I could have done without. I needed some time on my own to think, but now I'd got Finney with me I was going to have to start making enquiries, darting round the city on a Friday night like a lunatic. Jesus, where would I even begin?

'Where to?' asked Finney as soon as we'd left the room. I was starting to get the funny feeling he was secretly enjoying this. The 'whiz kid', as he used to refer to me when I first joined the team, had been firmly put in his place and was clearly shitting himself at the prospect of a good kicking or worse. I had no idea 'where to'.

'Simple,' I said with as much nonchalance as I could muster under the circumstances, 'known associates,' he frowned at me like his simple brain couldn't quite digest the concept, 'Cartwright's nearest and dearest. We quiz them all. Let's get the car.'

I was keen to halt his questions about my plans. I didn't have any.

THREE

....

When we were back in the car Finney asked, 'where first?'
'Jesmond,' I told him, thinking on my feet, 'there's a side
street just off Osborne Road. Cartwright shacks up there with
his bird, what's-her-name, Amanda something, the one who
used to be a stripper way back when?'

'Mandy McCauley,' he told me. I was surprised he knew her
full name. 'Used to take it all off in a back room at the Sunbeam
Strip in the eighties before they closed it down. I couldn't believe
it when Cartwright took her on full time.'

'Why, what's wrong with her?'

'You mean apart from showing her growler to every man
in Newcastle?'

'Yeah,' I said, 'apart from that.'

'Well she shagged virtually the entire crew,' he told me, 'no
actually, I tell a lie, she *did* shag the entire crew. If you hadn't
have been in short trousers back then you'd have got your end

away too. If she turned up anywhere with George after it was like…' he seemed lost for a suitable phrase.

'An old boyfriends' reunion?' I offered.

'Yeah, well no, not really. None of us ever took her out. You didn't have to with Mand,' and he chuckled, 'she didn't seem to mind. Though, to tell you the truth, it was like chucking a Smartie tube up the Tyne Tunnel.' Finney laughed harder, 'I dunno,' he said reflectively, 'maybe he felt sorry for her.'

'Or maybe he just had a bigger cock than you,' but he didn't laugh at that. Instead he just pressed the accelerator more firmly and we sped closer to Jesmond.

Whatever looks Mandy McCauley once had, she'd lost them. The woman that answered the door in her dressing gown might have taken her clothes off for money twenty years ago but these days you'd have paid her to leave them on. She was an overweight, badly made up specimen with a cig in her nicotine-stained hand trailing smoke up into her bloodshot eyes. 'Finney,' she said unhappily, 'and you,' I wondered if she'd forgotten my name. She took a deep breath and when she spoke once more her voice was harsh, 'what have you done with him you bastards!'

She eventually let us in, once I'd persuaded her we were looking for Cartwright too. The house was shabbier than I would have expected, the white flock wallpaper in the hall turning brown and peeling in a corner.

'Wipe your fucking feet,' she ordered.

'Watch your dirty mouth Mandy or you'll get a slap,' Finney told her. It was moving to see these two lovers reunited. 'Now where is he?'

We followed her into a grubby little front room with a high ceiling, a three-bar electric heater and a large sofa that sagged under my weight when I sat down. When Finney sat next to me I swear I felt a spring snap under him. Mandy sat on a battered armchair and crossed her legs primly, which to me seemed like locking the door after the entire stable has bolted, 'I don't know,' she said with some feeling, 'I thought he was with you or… .'

'You thought we'd hurt him?' I said reasonably.

She flicked her cig into an ashtray, set it down and pulled the sleeves of her dressing gown taut so they half covered her hands. It wasn't cold in the room. It was a nervous gesture 'I s'pose.'

'Well, you would,' I said, 'if he's not been around. How long has he been missing?'

'Three days,' and saying it aloud set her off. Her lip quivered and the tears formed, 'Geordie's never been away for more than a night, not ever.' North east men christened George are always known as 'Geordie' and George Cartwright was no exception.

'When you last saw him where he was he off to?'

'The office. He said he had to see the accountant then he had a trip but he'd be back that night, late.'

'Collecting the Drop,' said Finney almost to himself. Cartwright would have collected it from Northam, our bent accountant. He was just like a real accountant. The difference was he knew where all the dirty money came from and he never, ever wanted your signature on anything.

'Only he didn't come back, did he?' she said accusingly.

'Was he okay when he left?' I asked her, 'not upset about anything, worried?'

'No'

'Not acting different in any way you can remember?'

'I've just told you!'

'Mandy,' warned Finney. I got the feeling he would have liked an excuse to belt her one. Maybe he was still smarting about that cock joke.

'It's alright,' I assured him, 'I think we're done. We'll get in touch with you as soon as we find him Mandy. You make sure you contact us if you hear from him. You've got the number for the club?'

She nodded. We were leaving when she suddenly said, 'has something bad happened to him?' looking like she was going mad with worry. Her eyes met mine imploringly. There was love there, for Cartwright, somewhere deep down, beneath all the fake toughness that comes from a fucked-up life, 'tell me the truth.'

'The truth?' I asked and she nodded, 'I dunno Mandy. I really don't.'

We headed back into the city and I had a bit more time to think. I stared out of the window as the concrete walls of the underpass sped by. I'd known seeing Mandy was likely to be a dead-end but I had to check her out in case she knew something, though I was no nearer solving the mystery of George 'Geordie' Cartwright's disappearance than before. I couldn't fathom it. Like Bobby had said, he'd known Cartwright for years and he didn't strike me as being a man who was dumb or greedy enough to steal from his employer, particularly an employer like Bobby. But, if it wasn't him, then who would have the temerity, the sheer fucking brass balls to take money away from Bobby Mahoney. If it was someone who knew about the Drop, and there can't have been many, then it made even less sense. You wouldn't want to steal that money believe me. Not for all the shit it would land you in.

Bobby was right though, which didn't make me feel any better. It was *my* responsibility to make sure the Drop got there. I'd been careless, and now I was in deep, deep trouble. How the fuck was I going to find Cartwright and get the money back? It would probably be easier to raise the money for the Drop myself by Monday - and that would still be impossible, even with my talents.

Bobby was right in another way too. Nobody took from him. If somebody got away with that he was finished. The message it sent out would be clear. Bobby had turned into a soft touch, somebody who could be taken on or taken out by an ambitious rival. He simply couldn't afford for that to happen. So he had to get the money back and punish the person who'd stolen from him. The punishment would have to match the crime and stealing the Drop was one down from raping his late wife's corpse, so the thief was going to wind up dead - but not before Finney had spent a long time making him see the error of his ways. Suddenly I was terrified. If I couldn't find Cartwright, I couldn't retrieve the money and I couldn't discover who was responsible, it was going to be me staring into the business end of a nail gun, because Bobby would have to show the world that somebody had paid for ripping him off.

'Pull over,' I said to Finney in a panic.

'What? Now?'

'Just pull over!' I managed to get the passenger door open just in time. I leaned out and sicked up the horrible airline meal they'd given us, all over the side of the road.

'Jesus,' hissed Finney, 'mind my upholstery!'

FOUR

As soon as we hit the Bigg Market, I tried to light a cigarette but my hand was shaking so badly the match burned down to my fingers and I had to start again. All around me in the square, drunken youngsters were propelling themselves towards the next night spot, some more steadily and silently than others. Close by, a girl fell on her arse and her friends shrieked with laughter. She cackled along too because she wouldn't be feeling that bruise until the morning. In a doorway of a pub that had long since closed, a very pissed-up teenager was trying to pull a couple of young lasses by dancing in front of them, even though he could barely stand by now. He tried a couple of moves then stopped, his head lolling like a Thunderbird puppet.

The girls thought it was hilarious, 'Eeh,' said one, 'you'll get all the ladies tonight with those moves.' They both laughed at him and walked away, leaving him staring uselessly into the space they had just occupied like he couldn't quite work out where they had gone.

There was a lot of noise, a lot of shouting, most of it good natured. One young couple were having a violent row about something or nothing but there was a good deal of laughter coming from the long queue of early-darters at the taxi rank. I reckoned Finney and I were the only sober people in the Bigg Market by this hour.

Finney asked, 'Where now?'

In an uncharacteristic move, I told him, 'fuck knows,' and immediately regretted saying it. Finney had already seen me so frightened I was throwing up out of his car, so I had to at least look like I wasn't entirely losing control. I'd blamed that on dodgy Thai food but he hadn't looked convinced. 'Everywhere.' I told him emphatically, 'he drinks round here, always has, never liked the Quayside, it's too modern for him. Speak to everybody. We need to know when anyone saw him last.' I was already thinking that if Mandy didn't know where he was then nobody would. I was worried he'd left the country along with all of Bobby's money. 'Some of his pubs will be shut by now but we'll go to all the ones that stay open late, speak to the lads on the door and the bar staff, ask them if any one has seen Geordie Cartwright.'

'Right,' he said.

'I think we should split up. We'll cover them twice as fast,'

He looked at me, 'not trying to run out on me are you?'

'Do I look that fucking stupid?'

As soon as Finney left me, I rang Laura. Her mobile trilled for what seemed like an age. Where was she? It was normally stapled to her ear.

While I waited for her to answer I ran the whole saga of the hotel back through my mind. Laura had offered to make the booking, 'I'll do it David, you've already sorted out the flights, found all the nice restaurants and changed the currency, so I'll do this.' I'd been touched that she appreciated my efforts and was looking to lend a hand, not taking me for granted.

Of course, when weeks then dragged by and, guess what, the booking had not been made, I was starting to feel very differently about her offer. All I heard was 'I'll do it later, I'm tired,' as if I wasn't, or 'work has been a bastard this week', as if I spent my days auditioning teenaged porn stars.

I could have picked up the phone or gone on the web and sorted it in minutes but no, she wouldn't let me do that either, even though I offered to take the task back off her hands. It eventually became a cause of real friction between us. Every night I would bring up the subject and every night I would chose a different way to raise it; jocular, teasing, impatient, pissed-off, very pissed-off, then finally up to Def Con Two. It was only then, when I was literally screaming at her, 'why can't you just make the fucking booking?' that she finally snapped.

'Alright, alright, stop bloody going on and on about it! Jesus!'

'I would stop going on about it if you would just bloody do it. You're like a teenager who won't tidy her room!'

She stormed off and did the job on the internet in all of about twenty minutes. It was a lot longer than twenty minutes before she spoke to me again.

Trouble was, when Laura had first said, 'I'll book the hotel,' I distinctly told her to make the booking in both our names.

When Laura finally answered her mobile I asked, 'It's me, when you booked the hotel, did you book the rooms in both our names like I asked?'

'Eh? Er, I don't know, yes, I think so, why?'

'You think so or you did so? This is important.'

'I can't remember,' she wailed, 'you'd been shouting at me. I don't know and I'm very tired. Where are you?'

I ignored her question, 'you don't know?'

'No, I don't know, which bit of that last sentence did you not understand?'

'I could have been killed tonight because you didn't do what I asked. Bobby was trying to find me and when he phoned the hotel they had no record of me staying there. He didn't think to ask if they had a Laura Collins in their hotel because he probably can't even remember your surname. Jesus, I don't understand you sometimes. It was the only thing I asked you to do!'

'Oh shut up David,' she shouted, 'stop exaggerating. Your boss is not going to kill you.'

My God, was she deliberately trying to wind me up? 'Have you forgotten who I work for?!'

'No! I haven't!' she shouted, 'in fact I am sick of hearing about it!' That was a bit rich, since I had to listen to every banal detail of her working day the minute she walked through my door each evening.

'You stupid bitch!' I screamed at her. My answer was the dead sound of her mobile being switched off, 'Laura? Laura!?' I didn't know why I was still shouting at her. She had already gone.

I'd had a shit evening. By now we were well into the early hours and getting nowhere. Finney and I had spoken to everyone and come up with zilch. My eyes were burning with tiredness. I was just starting to contemplate getting home for a few hours shut-eye to shake off the jet lag and start afresh in the morning, when the mobile began to vibrate in my jacket pocket. It was Vincent phoning from Privado.

'I'm sorry to bother you so late man,' he said.

'I'm not sleeping.' I told him, 'what is it?'

'Well... I'm afraid... ' he seemed reluctant to come to the point.

'Go on.' I prompted him.
'... it's your brother like.'

This was the last thing I needed. I persuaded Finney to drop me at Privado and leave me to it. I could always borrow Vincent's car or get a cab if I needed one and I didn't want Finney to see Danny in one of his states. Vincent was waiting by the door for me when I arrived, which I appreciated. He was either a very good bloke or he hadn't heard about my fall in prestige now that I was the man who'd cost Bobby Mahoney a small fortune. He led me into the place.

Privado was a low-rate, lap dancing bar just off the Quayside that Bobby controlled. It was pretty busy. It looked like the credit crunch wasn't stopping men from coming in here and parting with large amounts of cash for a quick flash of a girl's tits. The blue lighting was so subdued you would have had to squint to see anything though, even when the lass pressed herself right up against you, but they still turned up. There were half a dozen girls in the room, dressed in, or slowly removing, their bra and pants. The men looked drunk, sitting on their own around the leather seating that lined the bar's walls. The girls made them sit on their hands so they didn't get tempted to touch what they were supposed to just be looking at but that clearly hadn't stopped Our-young-'un from disgracing himself. They straddled the men, perched on their knees and gyrated while they draped their long hair in the guy's faces or rubbed their breasts together a couple of millimetres from their slavering mouths. The routines were all pretty similar but the men didn't seem too bothered by the lack of variety.

I saw one girl I recognised. Michelle had just climbed off a guy's lap then bent down in front of him so he could stare at her arse. She gave her bum a half-hearted smack, but her eyes told me how bored she was. Who was she trying to kid, I thought, but then I saw the look on his face. His mouth was open wider then a guppy's and his eyes looked like they were about to roll right up into their sockets. Clearly he thought this whole spectacle was an unrestrained display of raw, female sexuality, not the student-loan-busting source of revenue that Michelle viewed it as.

It took a while to cross the floor while the girls were doing their thing. I had to virtually step over one of them as she writhed on the ground. The music ended as I passed Michelle, just as she whipped her bra off so she could do the second of the fish-faced bloke's two dances topless. That was the deal; two dances for twenty notes, twenty quid spunked in around six minutes. At that rate he would be a couple of hundred quid down in around an hour, excluding tips. For the same amount he could have had full sex with one of Bobby's escorts, which made more sense to me, but I guessed he was too shy for that.

The second song was Khia's 'My Neck My Back' and Michelle bent down again to show him everything Khia was singing about. He stared at her arse once more as she peeled her knickers off. She looked up as I walked by, smiled, blew me a little kiss and gave me a wave, which he didn't spot. He didn't seem to notice Michelle wasn't giving him her undivided attention but then he wasn't looking at her face.

Michelle was a nice girl and certainly a looker. She was around twenty with long, dark hair and a cracking figure, but I couldn't understand the appeal of all this myself. I'm no prude but this didn't seem to be one thing or the other. If you needed sex and were prepared to pay for it, then have sex. Don't piss about in a lap dancing club. I didn't sleep with Bobby's escort girls and I didn't need to pay for it either, even before Laura, but I didn't have an issue with people who did. It seemed to me that all the guys in here were cowards. They wanted it but they weren't prepared to properly go for it. This was safe, it was sanitised, it was a tease but that's all it was. They'd still leave here frustrated. Like I said, I just didn't get it.

Vincent took me through an unmarked, metal door into a dimly lit corridor. The door swung shut behind us and the music was immediately muffled to a low drone in the background. We were headed for a back room and before he opened that door he spoke to me in a low whisper.

'We had to put him in here. I hope that's alright with you. He was a bit worse for wear when he came in, noisy like, disturbing the other punters. I sent a girl over to give him a couple of dances on the house, on account of him being your brother and it calmed him down for a while but when she took her top off he just grabbed her tits and she screamed blue murder.'

'Oh Christ.'

'The bouncer came right over and your bro got a bit aggressive but our doorman didn't hurt him. I made sure of that but we couldn't let him stay in there. I hope you understand.'

'Of course Vince,' I told him.

'We gave him a bit of a talking to, made him a strong cup of coffee and locked him in there to cool off then I called you. Nobody else knows anything about it and I've told the doorman to keep his trap shut. Of course there were a lot of punters in there so… ' he shrugged, meaning that word could still get back to Bobby if I was unlucky and my luck seemed to be in short supply tonight.

'Thanks Vincent, I appreciate you handling it like you did and I'm sorry for the trouble he caused you.' I took out my wallet and peeled off ten twenty pound notes and handed them to him, 'give this to the lass.' I knew Vincent would give her whatever he thought she'd accept to keep quiet about having her tits groped in public and he would keep the rest and that was fine by me.

'Hey, no problem,' he said pocketing the cash, 'he's your brother. You don't have to apologise for him. He's still a bloody hero an' all. I haven't forgotten that. I know he's had his problems.'

I patted Vincent on the back and he unlocked the door and left me to it. Danny was sitting on the kind of cheap, red plastic chair they use in school dinner halls. He was still very drunk and swaying a bit, his coffee cup was full to the brim on the table in front of him. His lank hair hung down over his eyes because his head was bowed but I couldn't tell if it was shame or if he had fallen asleep in his seat. He heard me come through the door and his head shot up.

'Oh I'm sorry bro'. I'm a fucking wreck, I'm really sorry.' He was slurring but at least he wasn't violent drunk and he knew he'd done wrong. I was relieved. I didn't want to end up scrapping with my older brother. Even in this state he could still kick me all round the room.

'That's alright Danny,' I told him, 'though I doubt that lass'll be going on a date with you any time soon.'

He grinned like a schoolboy then. 'She had a cracking pair of top bollocks,' he said, 'I couldn't resist. You should have seen them man.'

'What makes you think I haven't seen 'em?'

His smile went broader then, 'aye, you probably have an' all you dirty bastard. Bet you get to shag all of Bobby's birds. Does Posh Spice know?' and he laughed, as he always did when using his nickname for Laura. I don't think he'd ever used her real name. It was always Posh Spice or Posh Knickers and occasionally Tara Palmer Topbollockson, which was his favourite name for her but he was far too drunk to attempt that just now.

The door opened then. It was Michelle, back in her bra and pants, giving me an apologetic smile. 'Sorry,' she told me, 'I was just checking to see if you were alright like,' and she went a bit red in the face, which was strange for someone who could take all her clothes off in a room full of strangers without blushing.

'We're good thanks,' I told her.

'Smashing,' she said, 'sure you don't want a cup of tea or anything?'

'He's got a brew, thanks. I'm fine.'

'Right,' she said, 'okay.' And she hung on for a second. 'I'll leave you to it then,' and she gently closed the door behind her.

'Fuckin' hell young'un, you could have been in there man. Don't worry, I wouldn't tell Poshy.'

'Come on,' I told him firmly, 'let's get you home before that other lass sues you for groping her.'

'She wouldn't get much,' he said calmly, 'I've got nowt.'

'I know Danny,' I said, 'I know.'

I decided Our-young-'un was sober enough to bundle into a cab. I'd always called him Our-young-'un even though he was years older than me. I couldn't remember why. I got him back to his flat; a rented shit hole in a high rise, which he wouldn't let me buy him out of. He hadn't got an income except his giro and the few bob he got each month from some sort of invalidity payment from the army. I helped him out when I could, slipped him a few quid every time I saw him and I really didn't mind because he'd had a bad time of it. He wouldn't let me do more than that though, and I reckoned he spent virtually every penny of it on booze and the horses he backed that won nowt for themselves, except a short trip to the glue factory.

His crack-head neighbours left him alone because I made sure they knew whose brother he was but if I tried to do more, he just laughed and said, 'you're my younger brother, you're not supposed to look after me. It's s'posed to be the other way round!'

I helped him in through the doorway and got him to lie down on the couch then I made more coffee but not before giving the two mugs on his draining board a proper wash. He was out of milk again, so I made the coffee black.

'You should get yourself a bird,' I told him, 'you need a woman to clean up this shit tip. She can put some milk in the fridge while she's at it.'

He laughed again, 'Nae bugger'd have us,' and I'm afraid he had a point there, 'I don't have a fancy job working for Bobby Mahoney, yer knaa.'

I brought the coffees into the tiny lounge and set them down on his rickety, little coffee table. He had an old TV in there with a battered PlayStation rigged up to it. He was always playing those war games where you have to shoot robots that look a bit like the Terminator, which I found strange, considering that the war he'd been in had clearly messed with his mind. Last time I was round, I gave him a few cartons of fags, some games for his play station and an iPod.

'How are you getting on with that iPod?' I asked him.

'It's great man,' he told me, 'thanks.'

'So have you actually downloaded some tracks then?'

'Downloaded?' he asked me doubtfully. He clearly didn't realise you had to do that.

I laughed, 'You've not taken it out of the box have you?'

He looked hurt. 'Aye, I have and like I said it looks great. I just haven't had the chance to do the downloading thing yet. Jimmy will help us like. He knaas everything there is to knaa about computers.'

'Jimmy? I'm sure he does. He probably has a Dragon 32.' He didn't have a clue what I meant and I knew he'd never get round to using that iPod.

He didn't have much of anything if the truth be told, except a couple of photos from his days in the Paras; one with him in uniform, with a blacked up face from the camouflage paint, holding an SLR, standing next to three other mates he had lost touch with over the years. He was smiling like he might have been fairly happy back then but I doubted it because I knew when it was taken, some years after he got the Campaign medal that he kept in his drawer. It was the South Atlantic medal and it proved my brother did a minimum of thirty days of continuous or accumulated service, between seven degrees and sixty degrees south latitude, between the 2nd April and the 14th June 1982. In other words he fought in the Falklands War. I refuse to call it the Falklands Conflict, people got killed, his friends got killed, so it was a war.

I'd seen my brother's medal many times, held it reverently in my hand when I was a tiny wee lad. Even today, I can still recall the chest-bursting pride I felt, knowing my brother was an elite member of the 2nd battalion of The Parachute Regiment that took Goose Green. It was undoubtedly his finest hour. Trouble is, the rest of his life has been an absolutely unrelenting torrent of shit. He's had every bit of trouble going; a shite marriage and a worse divorce, run-ins with the police, fights, drinking, drugs for a while but, thank Christ, we got him out of that world before it took a hold. When he left the Paras he worked a bit, casual stuff, labouring mostly but even that seemed to just tail away after a while. He went from being one of the most reliable men in the whole British army to a fellah you couldn't trust to turn up at a building site two days running. He doesn't talk about his war but something bloody awful must have happened to him there because he has never been the same since. I don't ask him about it. I just try and keep him out of trouble.

I was a bit pissed-off with Danny because he had gone wandering into one of Bobby's places and groped a lass when he should have known a lot better than that, even when he was completely off his face. And his timing was impeccable. I needed that kind of hassle on top of my troubles with Bobby, Geordie Cartwright and the Drop like I needed a frontal lobotomy. But he's my brother and he is, and always will be, a fucking hero. Nothing can change that.

It had been a long night. I contemplated phoning Laura but to be honest, right then, I didn't need the grief I'd get from her. She'd have fallen asleep in front of the television by now, blissfully unaware of the fact that her boyfriend was already a dead man walking.

FIVE

....

When he woke up in the morning, Danny wandered in and found me still lying on his couch and said, 'eeh young'un,' like it was all suddenly coming back to him, 'I'm sorry. I was off me tits.' Then he scratched his crotch, offered me a cup of tea, which I declined because he still hadn't got any milk, or teabags for that matter, and then he thought for a while and said, 'do you think I should send that lass some flowers? To say sorry like?'

'No Danny,' I told him firmly, 'I don't.'

Laura went a bit nuts when I finally called her in the morning and I got a lengthy version of the time-honoured where-the-fuck-have–you-been speech that lasses have been delivering to their men folk since Moses first went out on the lash.

I felt a bit bad, particularly after I'd called her a stupid bitch for forgetting to put my name on the booking. She had clearly not grasped the seriousness of the situation she'd put me in but then how could she?

'Look I'm sorry, I am, but it got so late there didn't seem any point in phoning or texting you. I'd have woken you up.'

'Woken me up? Do you think I sleep when you're not here? I was worried sick David.'

I had to bite my tongue so as not to say 'well, why the fuck didn't you call me then?', because I realised this would just escalate things. Laura was spoiling for a fight and it was a bit sad how we had got right back into our old, bickering habits again just 24 hours after such a wonderful holiday. It was, however, the least of my worries right now.

'Look it's complicated alright? It's not as if I was out having a few drinks with the boys. I've got a problem.'

'What kind of problem?' this is the type of stupid question I wouldn't have expected from Laura and I didn't say anything, just exhaled wearily down the phone at her. 'Alright, okay, I know you can't tell me,' she moaned.

'You don't want me to tell you, believe me. It's not about shutting you out, not letting you in, not trusting you or any of that utter bollocks, it's just that I *cannot* tell you.'

'Okay, okay,' she said making the two words sound like the absolute opposite of their meaning, 'it's fine,' another lie. The word 'fine' never means fine to a woman. 'I'll see you back at the flat,' and she hung up on me before I could say anything else.

'Bitch,' I hissed into the phone even though, or perhaps because, I knew she couldn't hear me. Christ, where was the girl's imagination? She knew the circles I moved in. The very fact that I even bothered to tell her there was a problem should have alerted those highly-educated brain cells of hers that I was in deep, deep shit. Women come home every night and go through their entire day, telling their men every trivial bloody problem they've encountered, so they can get some weird kind of catharsis from reliving the whole damned thing. Men aren't like that. We like to switch off and forget our troubles, so me saying 'Laura, I've got a problem' is like watching a drowning man frantically waving with both hands. It's a sign I thought she might have picked up on.

I bought my bro a fry-up in a greasy spoon near the station. Then I gave him a few quid and left him to it, knowing he'd mooch round the pubs for a few hours and hoping he'd keep out of trouble. Then I phoned Sharp.

He picked me up outside the Royal Station Hotel and I quickly climbed into his old VW. I'd hung back a bit, playing it safe, in case anyone spotted us.

Sharp was just north of thirty but he looked older, mainly because he was the only man I knew who still thought a moustache was a sensible choice. We drove out of the city for a while, not saying much until he pulled up in a tiny industrial estate, which was totally empty as it was Saturday morning.

'So,' he said, 'must be pretty serious for me to risk picking you up in broad daylight in the city on a match day.' He seemed a bit narked but I wasn't going to allow that.

'You get paid enough to justify a bit of weekend work.'

He spread his palms, 'I'm not complaining. What can I do for you boss?'

'I have a problem,' I said, 'a missing person,' and I told him about Cartwright going AWOL, though I left out the bit about the Drop going missing with him. The fewer people that knew about that the better.

'You want me to find him for you?'

'It's what you're good at it isn't it?'

He nodded, 'that and other things,' he thought for a moment, 'and when I find him? Call you or deal with it?'

'Call me. I need to talk to him before any decision is made on the man's future.'

'Okay.'

I spent the next fifteen minutes telling him everything I knew about Cartwright that might help him to track the man down. 'I'll be looking for him as well, so if you hear about someone asking after Cartwright it's probably me.' That bit was true but that morning I'd also phoned Palmer and set him on the task as well and I didn't want Sharp and him getting in each other's way.

'You're out on the streets for this one?' he seemed genuinely surprised, 'what's he done?' I didn't say anything. 'Hey, it's none of my business but you must want him bad, that's all.'

'We do.'

'And you sure you don't want me to just… '

'Not until I've spoken to him,' I told him sharply, 'did you not just hear me?'

'Hey, no problem, it's cool.'

I must be slipping, because I didn't see the uniformed bobby who came walking up to the car from behind and tapped on the window.

Sharp let the electric window wind down and the uniform said, all sarcastic like, 'would you two lover boys like to tell me what you're doing out here?' and he nodded at the empty office opposite, 'casing the joint are we gents? Well you can forget about that now.'

Sharp raised his hand to the window and showed the uniform his warrant card, 'DS Sharp,' he said firmly, 'you just compromised a confidential meeting with a major criminal source,' which even I found amusing but I didn't crack a smile.

'I'm really sorry Detective Sergeant,' and the uniform didn't look so smug all of a sudden, 'but I had no way of knowing… '

'Fuck off,' Sharp interrupted him, 'go on, fuck off, now.' And he did, sharpish.

'Fucking uniforms,' said Sharp, 'really piss me off,'

'You were one too,' I reminded him, 'once.'

'Not for long,' he said quietly, 'I knew the real money was in plain clothes.'

'I'm curious,' I told him, 'were you always bent, or did you only cross over to the dark side when you realised how far a policeman's pay goes?'

He chuckled but didn't really answer the question, 'well, I do have a wife and kids... and a mistress... a girlfriend... and a couple or three floozies when the mistress and girlfriend are busy.'

'Expensive.'

'Yeah, all of them. Believe me.'

'Well, let's make sure we don't kill the golden goose then, shall we? Find Cartwright for me and find him quick.'

'I'll do my best,' he assured me, 'there is one other thing you should know.'

'Yeah?'

'My new boss,' he told me, 'he's got a hard-on for Bobby.'

'Really?'

He nodded, 'He's a careerist, my new DI he knows the quickest way to the top is a high profile bust. There'd be nobody bigger round here than Bobby Mahoney.'

'True.'

'That doesn't worry you?'

It did but I wasn't going to tell him that, 'Should it?'

'Dunno, he's a determined little shit. He's got a picture of Bobby on the office wall with arrows going down to other pictures of Finney, Jerry Lemon and Mickey Hunter. It's like something out of one of those Mafia films where the FBI are trying to take the whole family down, you know.'

'Yeah, I know. Is my picture up there yet?'

'No but it's only a matter of time.'

I'd never heard Sharp talk like this before. He seemed resigned. 'You're worried aren't you?'

'Bit,' he said, 'he's a quick one this bloke. Not like the others. He's ambitious, you know, wants to be a Chief Super one day.'

'Well, he won't be the first to try will he?'

'No, nor the last.'

'What's his name?'

SIX

That afternoon I decided to check out all the small, low key boozers in the Bigg Market and the Quayside. There weren't too many left that had that combination of decent ale and 80's music that Cartwright favoured but I went in them all, starting in the Quayside and working my way up the hill and through the Bigg Market, right up to Newcastle's ground. I started early, as soon as they opened, because it was match day and they'd be filling up before you knew it.

From my own knowledge of the man, he had half a dozen regular haunts, all of which looked likely to close down at any minute, judging by the number of old blokes that were slowly nursing pints that could keep them going until closing time. I don't mind these old-man pubs myself but they don't make any sense financially, not when a bunch of teenagers can spend more in five minutes than some bloke in a flat cap is willing to part with in four hours. They were a relic of a bygone era, about as relevant to the modern age as pit boots and football rattles. I walked in one and, no word of a lie, they were playing Dean Martin. While Deano was singing *Little Old Wine Drinker Me*, I spoke to some of the old gadgies, then the landlord and bar staff. They all knew Geordie Cartwright of course but couldn't shed any light on his whereabouts. Nobody had seen Cartwright since the night before he'd calmly announced to his missus that he was off to meet Northam before going on a trip.

When I reached the top of the town, I walked right up to the ground and looked into the Strawberry. When I was a kid, the closest pub to St James Park used to almost always have its broken windows boarded up. Now it had a roof terrace; a sign of the times. It was fairly quiet as it was still early, just a few die-hards in there, sipping beers and craning their necks to watch the wall-to-wall Sky coverage. Anyone who didn't have a ticket for the game could wait here until Jeff Stelling announced the inevitable black and white collapse.

The bitter taste of my pint rejuvenated me. I figured I'd start again and do the rounds of all the pubs and clubs Cartwright didn't drink in just in case it turned out that he did drink in them after all. I knew I was clutching at straws but that was what drowning men did. I went from the Strawberry to Rosie's, my own preferred pre-match venue. Most of the crew had a couple in one or other of these pubs before the game, and I half expected Cartwright to be sitting there with a pint in his hand but then, if he had been, he would have been a dead man. There was no sign of him of course and no fresh sightings either.

I called in at the Newcastle Arms then outside Faces a teenage girl in a bikini, with goose bumps on her arms, stuffed a leaflet into my hands promising me 'live entertainment'. An obscure former Toon 'legend' was due to talk to the fans and there would be more girls in bikinis plus a couple of strippers. With football, beer and half-naked girls on offer I would have been surprised if I hadn't spotted at least one of our lads in there, so I walked in. The music was pumping and it was pretty dark. I ordered another pint while I waited for my eyes to adjust to the gloom and then I spotted Billy Warren heading towards me. He fought his way through a crowd of football fans ogling a blonde stripper with a boob job that made her look like an adult Barbie doll.

'Good to see you man,' he told me like I was a long lost friend. He offered me a cold and pasty hand which I shook. He looked terrible. I didn't know how much of his own product he was using these days but he definitely had the undernourished look of the professional dope head.

'How's business Billy?' I had to shout it into his ear to make myself heard.

He raised his hand and wobbled it from side to side, 'Same old, same old,' he said, 'it's all gone a bit credit crunch thanks to K.'

'Ketamine?'

'Yeah, time was when everybody did a bit of blow, which is pretty pricey so it had more profit. Now they all want Ket, which is cheaper so...'

'Less profit.'

'Exactly,' he said it like I was the Brain of Britain for working that out. 'Can't blame 'em I s'pose. K is half the price of coke. Twenty quid a gram these days so all the young 'uns want it instead of blow.'

'Yeah but vets use it don't they?' Call me old-fashioned but I wouldn't take something that's used to tranquilise horses.

'I s'pose,' he admitted, 'but it works for people too. It gives them that nice boozy high without the paranoia, know what I mean?'

I did and I didn't. Drugs might be the foundation of our business model these days but they left me cold. I liked to stay in control and most coke heads I'd met had a pretty thin grasp on what constituted reality. I'd heard about people taking Ketamine and floating off to happy land. It was meant to be the recession-busting drug. Why go out when you can just invite your mates round, take some K and sit there giggling at each other? To me it just sounded boring. Booze was more my thing. I liked to go out.

There was a brief burst of applause for the blonde with the boob job as she finished one dance and began another. She wasn't my type. I preferred the natural look, 'What have you heard about Geordie Cartwright?' I asked Billy.

'The last time I saw him was a few days back, he was in City Vaults,' he replied a bit quickly.

'Yeah?' I wondered why he didn't ask me why I was asking. Maybe he thought that was my business.

'Yeah, he was at the bar, talking to some Russian bloke.'

'A Russian bloke,' I asked, 'you sure?'

'Well, he sounded Russian, yeah I'd say so. I dunno, I s'pose he could have been Polish or something, how should I know, but he looked like a Russian.'

'And what did this guy look like, apart from Russian?'

'A big fucker, about six-foot-five. A beefy bloke with a shaved head,' and he laughed, 'he looked like something James Bond would have to fight.' And he grinned and waved his hands around in front of me like he was doing martial arts.

'Okay,' I said, trying to disguise my very obvious interest in this development, 'and what were they talking about?'

He shrugged. 'Fuck knows, I wasn't really paying attention. I just ordered my pint near them, said hello to Cartwright and left them to it.'

'Did it look like they knew each other well then?'

'Well it looked like they hadn't just met but I dunno. Maybe the bloke was on his holidays and Cartwright was just chatting to him.'

'On his holidays? In Newcastle?'

'I dunno, maybe he was a football fan or something.'

'I repeat, in Newcastle?'

'Yeah, well, I dunno, right. All I know is Cartwright was talking to a Russian bloke and they seemed pretty pally. That's all I know mate. What can I say?'

'That's alright Billy. No bother.'

'Was that useful like?' he asked hopefully.

'Who knows mate, who knows?' I drained my pint. 'Enjoy the match.'

He snorted, 'doubt it.'

Normally I would have gone to the match. Usually, only the cast iron guarantee of a threesome with Cameron Diaz and Kylie Minogue would have tempted me to give up my place and, even then, I'd have been checking text messages for the score while they were going down on each other. But this wasn't usually. I didn't think Bobby would want to see my unpopular face in his executive box today. He'd want to know I was out there pounding the streets looking for Cartwright and, since I'd already tried that and got nowhere, except for the strange tale of a big Russian, drinking pints with our missing friend, I picked up my car and set off up the A1.

I'd not had the Merc CLS long but I was getting used to it. It had every feature going and looked pretty cool in black with its matching leather interior. In fact I was more chuffed with it than I let on. Anyway, it made short work of the A1, which was quiet now that half the city was at the match. Before I knew it I'd left the city's houses and high rises behind me. People who've never been up here still think the north east is one big slag heap or derelict pit site, but a fair bit of it is countryside, stretching out for miles either side of what used to be called the Great North Road, in a sea of green.

When I reached the farmhouse, I walked up to the door and rang the bell. No answer. The place was looking a bit dilapidated these days. It had been a working farm once but the owner pissed away the family legacy with the usual money-shredding combination of gambling and booze. When he eventually took a shotgun to himself, the land was bought by an adjacent farm. Our old associate Mark Miller bought the house for a song because it was surplus to requirements.

I asked him once, 'doesn't it bother you that the bloke blew his brains out in here?'

'No man, not me,' he said, shaking his head and its accompanying long mane of greying hippy hair, tied back in a pony tail, 'don't believe in ghosts or any of that bullshit.'

I rang the bell again and again. Still no reply, so I called his mobile.

'Where the fuck are you?'

He laughed, 'my studio.'

'You mean the cow shed?'

He laughed again, 'it's not a cow shed. It's a custom built, state-of-the-art, professional, photographic studio,' then he whispered, 'come round David. It'll be worth the walk.'

SEVEN

....

I went down the side of the house and crossed a small patch of rough ground. The door of the so-called studio, an enormous metal-roofed lock-up that looked like a World War Two era Nissen hut, was unlocked, so I pulled it open and went inside. The entrance way was a dark corridor. All I could hear up ahead was the staccato click-click-whir coming from deep within the darkened room then a high pitched whine as if a flash gun was charging up again. I walked towards the big studio lights, passed metal shelves filled with car parts and tools set aside for DIY and gardening. There was a big, old-fashioned steel girder supporting the roof and the flash from Miller's camera was rebounding off it. I turned into the large, open area of the studio where Mark 'Windy' Miller worked and, seeing me, a stark naked young girl squealed.

I got a quick flash of her pale body as she jumped down from the sofa Miller had her standing on. She grabbed a white towelling robe and clasped it tightly to her in an effort to avoid any more of her intimate bits being placed on show to a complete stranger.

'Come on Kayleigh,' he told her, like she was the worst kind of prude, 'you've got to learn to be less body conscious than that.' I was trying to take in the fact she was actually called Kayleigh. No prizes for guessing what band her dad was into back in the 80s. 'This here is David Blake. He's not just an old friend, he's a professional photographer too. Aren't you mate?'

'Absolutely,' I said.

'So he's seen it all before, hasn't he?' she hesitated, keeping the robe pressed tightly against her young body, but her eyebrows knitted together in a frown that told me she was unsure how she should be behaving. 'Hasn't he?' he repeated. Mark tutted at her like she was being a silly girl then asked patiently, 'what would Keeley Hazell do?'

She smiled then, blushed, giggled and finally dropped the robe, standing in front of me in all her Page-three-hopeful, naked glory. 'That's better,' he told her and, all of a sudden, she seemed to be enjoying the exposure. She blew air out of the corner of her upturned bottom lip, disturbing a wisp of blonde hair over her forehead, put her hands on her hips and stood straight so there wasn't an inch of her I couldn't see, then she did a self-conscious little wiggle from side to side. 'Good girl,' he told her then turned to me, 'I think Kayleigh here has got everything it takes to go all the way.'

'Undoubtedly,' I told them. She beamed at us both, the silly cow.

'And he ought to know,' said Miller and somehow we both managed to look serious. 'Nearly done mate, why don't you just take a seat for a minute.'

I waited till he shot another roll of film while young Kayleigh stood there and posed. She tried to look serious, then pouted like a naughty schoolgirl, then adopted what she presumably thought was a coquettish pose and all on Miller's instructions. He asked her to raise an arm, cup a breast, roll her nipples between her fingers to make them hard then stick out her tongue at the camera and laugh like he was the funniest guy she had ever seen. He even got her to bend forwards over the arm of the sofa so her bum was up in the air and her face was practically buried in the cushions. That way she couldn't see he was no longer looking at the camera, just pointing it at her bare arse. He shot pictures one-handed while winking at me, silently laughing and giving me the thumbs up.

'Thanks love,' he said when he was done, 'you were brilliant. I tell you what, that Keeley Hazell will be shitting herself,' she laughed as she pulled up her knickers and put on her jeans. When she'd gone, he said, 'that last roll was just for you, you did realise.'

'I guessed as much. Interesting hobby you've got there Mark.'

'Hobby?' he asked, 'bit more than a hobby. It brings in the money, which is always much needed round here I can tell you. I can't retire early on what Bobby pays me you know.'

'Yeah? How much do you have to shell out to get a lass like that stark naked then? And what will you get for the photos?'

He laughed, 'No mate, you've got it all wrong. I don't pay them. They pay me.'

'You're joking?'

'No, think about it. There are hundreds of young lasses all over Newcastle who've got big tits and they all think they're going to be the next big glamour model but they don't know how to go about it. Then they see my advert in their local paper; 'professional modelling portfolios artistically created to your specification', a snip at just £350.'

'Three-fifty?' I whistled.

'I know,' and he chuckled.

'And has young Kayleigh got what it takes?'

'In my considered professional opinion?' I nodded. 'Has she fuck. Got legs like a giraffe, she's too top-heavy in the breast department, they'll be sagging before she's twenty and she has a smile like a frightened rabbit caught having a dump in the woods.'

'Yet you told her she was gonna be a star. Shameless.'

'Who am I to destroy a young girl's dreams? That'll come soon enough. At least this way she'll have something to show her grandkids.'

'A bunch of pictures with her arse in the air?'

'Yeah,' and he put on a dumb voice, 'I used to be a mod-dull.'

'Looking on the bright side, she gave you a cheap thrill at least.'

'Oh yeah, definitely but she don't mind,' he laughed, 'she did at first but I said I was gay.'

'Unbelievable.'

'I told her I'm immune to fanny. "Think of me like your family doctor," I told her and she took her clothes off, easy as you like.' He clicked his fingers to illustrate how quick she'd been to shed her knickers in pursuit of fame. 'Ironic isn't it. Some poor young bloke'll blow a month's wages tonight, buying her drinks so she'll let him put his hand up her top. Look at me, I'm just an old git yet I saw the lot - and *she's* paying me!' and he laughed like it was the best joke ever, and maybe it was.

As soon as I told Miller why I was there, he stopped laughing, 'I heard about it,' he admitted as he handed me a mug of tea. We were sitting at a table in the studio. 'Been worried. I know it sounds a bit lame but me and Geordie Cartwright go back a lot of years. He's a good lad. We used to take our boys to play football on Sunday mornings. He'd be there in all weathers,' he shook his head as if he couldn't believe what the world had become. 'So what have you heard?'

'The same as you,' I said, 'Cartwright's gone missing.'

'With some of Bobby's money,' he added, so the word was already out. Shit.

'Yeah,' there was no point denying it.

'Jesus,' he said.

'Won't help him if he's taken it,' I assured him.

'It's got to be a misunderstanding,' he said with conviction and I just looked at him. 'I know but he isn't like that is he, not Cartwright? He wouldn't do it, wouldn't have the nerve to cross Bobby.'

'That's what I thought,' I assured him without pointing out that the alternative was probably worse for Cartwright, as it was more than likely he'd be dead already. At least if he had stolen Bobby's money he had a chance of getting away with it; a very small chance but a chance nonetheless.

'What have you heard about Geordie and this Russian?'

'Come again?'

I shrugged, 'I heard he'd done some business with a Russian, that's all.' I was stretching it a bit but I wanted to see how it would play, 'wondered what you knew about it?'

'Sorry mate,' he said simply, 'not heard that one,'

Miller was pretty helpful though and I didn't leave empty-handed. He gave me a sizeable list of names to look up and places to check. Surely one of them would have a lead on Geordie. The drive out here had been worth it.

'Good luck,' he told me, 'and I mean it. Geordie Cartwright's a gent. I hope he's alright.'

'So do I Mark,' I said, 'so do I.'

I spent the rest of the day and most of the night getting round Miller's names with Finney. It was the same wherever we went. Nobody had seen Cartwright. Nobody knew what he'd been planning. We were drawing a complete blank.

More in hope than expectation, we called in on Jerry Lemon. I thought he must have heard something. He went back as far as any of Bobby's crew, had known the big man for years, Cartwright too. He was one of Bobby's originals. Unfortunately he was also a complete tosser but I was hoping loyalty to Bobby might prompt him to help me. I was badly wrong.

Jerry operated out of a pool & snooker hall, imaginatively named 'Lemons'. There was a big wooden sign over the front door which had two crossed snooker cues and two lemons painted on it, above his name. Clearly Jerry was a marketing genius.

'What the fuck do you want?' he said loud and aggressively and a lot of people in the room started to pay attention, which was exactly what the big mouth had intended. The great man was holding court. He was dressed in a style of bleached jeans that went out of fashion around 1985 and a T-shirt with no arms that showed off his bulging biceps and fading tatts. He went back to his shot, missing an easy pot into the middle pocket, which made me realise he was pissed.

'A quiet word, if it's alright with you.'

'No, it's not alright with me. Can't you see I'm playing pool? I thought you were supposed to be the clever one Davey. If you want to say something to me, say it now, I've nothing to hide.'

The place was half full of the old villains and apprentice wannabes Jerry liked to have hanging round in case he could find a use for them. He was a regular Fagin and his tales of the old days always had them hanging on his every word, which he loved.

'I never said you did Jerry. I wanted to speak to you about our mutual friend,' I wasn't going to mention Cartwright's name out loud in here.

' "Our Mutual Friend", that's Dickens that is,' he was very pleased with himself, 'bet you didn't think I knew that. Well, you're not the only one round here who's read a book. You mean Cartwright I suppose. How long has Bobby given you to find his money eh, until Monday wasn't it?'

'Jerry,' I said his name as a warning.

'Don't you try and shut me up in my own place,' he told me, straightening and pointing his cue at me, 'you've got no chance. You don't know what you're doing, you never have done. If you did you wouldn't be down here wasting my time, you'd be out looking for the real guilty party.'

'I know you don't like me much these days Jerry, but can we not put that to one side while we try to find Cartwright?'

'Correction,' he told me, 'I have never liked you son. I don't even know who you are.'

'You've known me for years.'

'What do I know? That your name is David Blake and you appeared out of the blue one day and next thing I know you're part of the crew. You set yourself up fair with Bobby while we weren't looking. You kissed his arse and all of a sudden you'd risen through the ranks while better men made their money the hard way, on the doors of Bobby's clubs. Well, we don't want any of that whiz kid stuff around here. Cartwright's gone missing? Tough, that's your responsibility, you find him. The Drop's gone? Tough, it's your fault so it's your arse on the line and when Bobby finally realises you're all mouth and no action, no one will be laughing harder than me. You're a plastic gangster and you're going to get what you deserve boy. Your big words and your bullshit won't help you. You're shitting it aren't you? Well you should be, you cocky little fucker. You're gonna learn what it means to be a face in this city. It's not just about wearing a sharp suit and getting the best table in the restaurant. I'll bet Finney here can't wait to get to work on you. Isn't that right Finney?'

It would have been better for me if Finney had said something at this point, anything really - though I was actually hoping he would tell Jerry Lemon to shut his big mouth - but it didn't happen. His silence told me everything I needed to know about the accuracy of Jerry's little prediction. Everyone was waiting for Bobby's cocky young protégé to come crashing down.

'Thanks Jerry,' I told him quietly, 'you've been a big help,' and I walked towards the exit, all the while wondering if he was going to break his cue over my head. Finney ambled after me. It must have looked like I was being followed by the Grim Reaper.

When I reached the door I turned back. Jerry Lemon was still watching me intently, every eye in the room was on me. I gave him what I hoped looked like a faintly amused, half smile. 'I'm glad you like my suit Jerry.'

EIGHT

Eventually Finney left me on my own. So I went for a couple of drinks in Akenside Traders, right at the bottom of the hill on the Quayside. Miller was sitting at a table when I walked in. It could have been a coincidence but he knew I called in there for a pint sometimes, mainly because the place had nothing to do with us, so I wondered if he was hoping to bump into me. Maybe he had something else to tell me?

I walked over to the long bar, bought myself a pint and got him his usual diet coke before joining him. The place was pretty busy and it was a young crowd but we had a quiet table in the corner, 'don't know how you can be in a pub and not drink,' I told him.

'You get used to it,' he said calmly, 'I like the craic in pubs but I got to the stage where I didn't like what the booze was doing to me. It made me into an angry person, so I stopped.'

'Just like that?'

'Just like that,' he confirmed. I admired him for that because he would have had to put up with a huge amount of shit from the lads for drinking pop in a pub but he had stuck to his guns, 'been four years now.'

'I'll drink to that,' I said, sipping my bitter, 'what brings you to town?' I nodded at a group of twenty-something lasses on a night out, 'looking for more gullible girls to photo in the buff?'

'I pop in often enough. Got to make a couple of collections for Bobby later,' Miller picked up protection money and loan repayments where real muscle wasn't required, amongst other things. He was a veteran of the firm, who did the low–risk stuff for Bobby but it gave him a decent enough income, 'I thought I might see you down here.'

Before I could ask him what was on his mind we were interrupted by a silver-haired old lady who'd come into the pub dressed in her Sally Army hat. She was selling 'War Cry' so I dropped a quid in her collecting tin but turned down a copy of the magazine.

'How can you believe in religion or a god if you take just one minute out of your day to think about the universe?' Miller asked me as he watched her doing the rounds.

'Most people don't take a moment to think about the universe mate,' I told him, 'most people are unthinking morons. They need to believe in a god because if they didn't their whole meaningless existence would come crashing down around them. It would make them realise how bloody pointless they are. Not you though eh?' I asked him, 'you were always the philosopher in Bobby's crew, the thinker. You were the only one I ever caught buying the *Times*.'

'One doesn't *buy* the *Times*, dear boy,' he told me in a voice that was almost Oscar Wilde, if he'd been raised in Gateshead, 'one *takes* the *Times*.'

'Does one?'

'Yes, one does,' he said, 'and if one does, one will have read their fascinating piece on the stars recently. Not the Hollywood variety. Apparently there are one hundred billion stars like the sun in our galaxy that are likely to have at least one planet capable of supporting life. And there are one hundred billion galaxies in the universe, so that means there are… '

'A fuck of a lot?'

'A fuck of a lot, thank you, of planets that could have life on them but we won't get to see any of it because the nearest star from ours is hundreds of thousands of years from here at the speeds we are currently capable of. Now, when you consider the vast scale of our galaxy and the ludicrously huge size of the whole universe, you'd have to be completely puddled to believe there's a god up there somewhere who gives a tinker's toss about you and yours on planet earth,' he raised his glass of coke and clinked it against my pint, 'life is a load of random shite and all of us are just spinning helplessly round the sun. When you can confront that fact head on and still keep your sanity, well, then you are a man my son.'

'I knew you were a fucking hippy,' I said, 'and it may be random shite to you but I have to put some sense into it all and quickly. I've got to find Cartwright and I have a funny feeling that, alive or dead, he is still on this planet.'

'That ought to narrow it down then, eh?' he said cheerfully.

We had a couple more drinks, him sticking with his coke and me sipping more of the local bitter. People carried on getting bladdered around us.

Sitting with Miller reminded me of my early days working for Bobby. He was a veteran back then but he'd been alright when others had treated me with suspicion if not downright hostility, 'You know, you're one of the few from the old crowd who doesn't treat me like a leper,' I told him.

'Well, they don't always get it, that lot. I don't think they understand what you do for Bobby, but I can see it David,' and he thought for a moment. 'They probably can too, they just don't want to admit it.'

'Maybe, but whatever the reason I've always found it easier to deal with you, which is why I didn't bring Finney with me when I came out to see you earlier.'

'Finney?' he looked a bit alarmed, with good reason, 'why would you bring him?'

'I don't think you're telling me everything Mark.'

'How do you mean like?'

'About Cartwright,' I said, 'everyone I speak to says he's not the sort of man to get mixed up with anything that's likely to piss Bobby off but we know he lied about the Drop. He said he was going to take Maggot with him but he didn't. Now that's strange behaviour for a man like Cartwright; a quiet, unassuming bloke who seems happy enough with his missus and his football, and a few pints at the weekend, so what the hell happened? You knew him as well as anyone. So what are you not telling me?' he hesitated then, his eyes moving from me to the floor and back again, 'you'd be better off telling me Mark, you know I'll find out sooner or later and I'd rather hear it from you. You're protecting him aren't you? What is it?'

He let out a deep sigh, 'there was something but if I tell you, you have to go easy on him.'

'No promises and no ifs. You're going to tell me or I'll phone Finney and he'll ask you.'

'There's no need for that but please, I'm asking you, can you see what you can do for Geordie if it does go tits up like?'

'I'll do my best,' I told him, knowing that my influence wouldn't count for much if he'd screwed Bobby.

'Gambling,' he said simply.

'Gambling?' I was stunned, 'Geordie Cartwright? Are you sure?'

He nodded reluctantly, 'been doing it for years man, low key at first. I mean he was losing but all gamblers lose don't they, whether it's football, horses, casinos, the house always wins.'

'So what happened?'

'It's the same sad and simple story. He started small, he mostly lost but he had a few wins. The wins just made him feel like he should have had a bit extra on the horses that came in. So he started betting more, only he wasn't very lucky.'

'How much was he in for?'

'He's been losing twenty or thirty grand a year for a good while now.'

'Shit - and he isn't our biggest earner.' I was taken aback that I didn't realise one of our main men was pissing his earnings away like that down at the bookies, 'it would explain the shit hole he lives in,' I was annoyed at myself. I should have known. I should have been to his house before and checked him out. Here was a guy handling large amounts of the firm's money and he was blowing thirty large a year on horses and football matches and I knew nothing about it.

'Yeah,' he said hesitantly, like he didn't really want to go on, 'but he could just about cover that. I mean you know what we've always been like; money's easy come, easy go in our game. You can bury that sort of thing in accounts without the wife knowing. I mean we are not exactly PAYE are we.'

'No, we're not. So what happened?'

'Spread betting happened. It was new, not so long back. If you did well you could make big money in minutes but if you fucked it up or you're just plain unlucky then you can be thousands down before you know what's hit you.'

'I wouldn't go near it myself. People betting fortunes on the number of throw-ins in the first half of a game.'

'Yeah, well he lost alright and he lost pretty big; have-to-tell-the-wife-before-you-lose-your-house big.'

'How much?'

'Sixty.'

'Sixty grand. Shit.'

'That's not all. He met some geezer down the pub who does spread betting on shares so then he got into that, trying to recoup his losses. He was putting a thousand pounds a point down, so if the share price went up a penny he was quids in and they did go up at first...'

'Then it all went pear shaped. How much was he down when he finished?' I asked.

'Two hundred and thirty grand.'

'Fucking hell,'

'Yeah, cleaned him out mate. All the savings, everything he'd put away for that retirement pad in Spain. He had to take a second mortgage which he couldn't afford.'

'So he was fucked,' I said, 'unless he could find some money from somewhere and the only easy money going was the Drop - and with me on holiday he had his chance, didn't he? To do one with the money.'

'You're putting two and two together and making five. I still don't buy that. He wouldn't just fuck off and leave Mandy. He's hopeless without her, like a little kid,' he shook his head for emphasis, 'they've got a boy, he's grown up now, but he's not going to abandon his family is he? He's not leaving her with all that debt and no house. Come on.'

'Maybe you're right but something's happened. Perhaps Geordie Cartwright didn't leave his clothes on the beach, but people do. Every day, people you wouldn't expect just walk out of the door and never come back, leaving their family wondering what's happened.'

The table rocked then, as a young lad who'd had one too many climbed out of the seat next to us and blundered into it on his way to the bog. A little of my beer got spilt and Miller's coke would have been upended if he hadn't deftly snaked out a hand and caught the glass before it toppled over. The young lad wasn't a bit apologetic. Miller's placid countenance didn't alter much but I could see a change come over him. His brow furrowed into a frown as his eyes locked onto the offending teenager, 'steady son,' was all he said. He said it softly but his confident gaze was enough to wipe the smile straight off the youngster's face. The lad was probably expecting to see fear in Miller's eyes, not the self assurance of a man who had held his own around villains for thirty years.

'Sorry mate,' said the teenager and he looked worried. Miller accepted his apology with a little nod and let him go.

'Boys playing at men,' he told me as he watched the lad make himself scarce, 'a sniff of the barmaid's apron and they can't handle it.'

When he turned back to face me he said, 'I'm sorry, I know I should have said summat about Geordie and his betting earlier but I thought you'd reckon he'd just nicked the Drop and I really don't believe he's that stupid.'

'No but he's stupid enough to lose two-hundred-odd grand betting on share prices he knows nothing about. Look, at least you told me now and that's the main thing.'

'What are you going to do?'

'Keep looking for him. I've got to go on doing the rounds with Finney until we get the full story and find our man.'

'Finney?' he asked doubtfully.

'What's that supposed to mean,' I retorted, but he didn't want to say. 'Come on, out with it.'

'Just be careful mate,' he warned me, 'you said yourself, guys like Finney and Jerry Lemon, they don't really get you. I'd say they wouldn't pause for the length of a heartbeat before selling you down the river. Just watch your back with Bobby when men like them are talking to him. Look out for yourself that's all.'

I wondered if he'd heard about my falling out with Jerry Lemon. It hadn't been long but bad news travels fast in this city,

'Cheers mate. I appreciate that,' I told him, 'but I can take care of myself.'

I got an Indian takeaway and grabbed a cab from the rank outside the Akenside Traders. It weaved its way out of the Quayside but not before the driver slowed to let a hen night cross the road in front of him. I'd already seen half a dozen hens that evening; little groups of lasses dressed as soldiers, policewomen or cowgirls in pink Stetsons; now a dozen young girls were done up like burlesque dancers from the Moulin Rouge; all fishnets and red basques, with cleavage hanging out all over the place. One of them waved at me through the windscreen and did a little dance in front of us twirling a feather boa while her mates pissed themselves laughing.

'Amazing, isn't it?' commented my driver, 'if you asked wor lass to dress like that in the bedroom she'd call you a dirty bastard and tell yuz to fuck off but if it's a hen night and all her mates are doing it then all of a sudden it's 'girl power'.'

He had a point.

I got in late with my lukewarm takeaway in a leaking carrier bag. Laura was in bed. I still hadn't seen her since the airport.

I'd have probably sat on the couch with my dinner in my lap but, as usual, I couldn't get my arse near it for cushions. What is it about women and cushions? Instead of chucking them all on the floor, I sat at the kitchen table, poured myself a beer, had two forkfuls of Chicken Bhuna then my mobile rang. It was Sharp, my bent DS.

'There's something you need to see.' He said and he sounded rattled.

'What is it?'

'Can't say, just come to the last place and we'll take it from there.' His voice was grim so I agreed and he hung up.

I took two more mouthfuls of curry and a big bite of

Peshwari Naan, put my jacket back on and left the rest of my dinner congealing on the plate.

I had to get one of our crew to pick me up and drive me. The last thing I wanted was to be done for drink driving on top of everything else. I got him to take me to the spot where DS Sharp had told the uniformed copper to fuck off. His Range Rover was parked there and he flashed his lights once. I got out of the car, let my driver go and climbed in next to Sharp.

'This better be good,' I said, knowing Sharp wasn't prone to this kind of melodrama.

'Depends on your definition of the word,' he said grimly.

I already had a bad feeling about it.

NINE

....

Cartwright didn't look too pretty under the torchlight. He'd only been lying there for three or four days but a rat had already messed with his face. It had taken the flesh off his cheeks leaving two obscene-looking holes where the skin had been and had a go at his throat too.

George Cartwright's body was lying on the cold concrete floor of a disused factory, the derelict sight of a minor manufacturing company that went bust years back. The factory was open on both sides and all that was left was the metal skeleton of the building, which had huge holes in its sides and roof. A cold wind was whistling through it that night and there were puddles on the floor where last night's rain had come in. What was left of George's face was white, his eyes open, staring up at us. It made me feel sick right down in the pit of my stomach to see him like that. I had spent a lot of time with Geordie Cartwright over the years. We'd drunk together in the pubs when things were going well and we'd shared a car countless times when we'd taken the Drop. Now here he was lying dead in a disused factory, his stone cold body open to the elements, where any scavenger could crawl in and take a bite out of him.

I kept picturing Geordie's face before it had been messed up. I could remember his laugh, his soft spoken Geordie accent, the conversations we'd had about the future, his dreams of that retirement home in Spain. Well, he had no future now. It was all over for Geordie Cartwright.

'What happened Geordie,' I asked him, 'what did you get yourself mixed up in?'

As I gazed down on his mutilated face, I couldn't get the other nagging thought out of my mind; how this could just as easily have been me lying there. If I'd not been on holiday when he was lifted, it probably would have been me.

'Are you alright?' asked Sharp, his tone suggesting he was a bit rattled by the spectacle himself. I knew what was worrying Sharp. Despite the mess the rats had made of Geordie's face, the cause of his death was clear to see. There was a bullet hole right in the middle of his forehead. It had gone in, neat as you like, and it looked professional. Most probably it was the exit wound that had attracted the rats. Half of the back of Geordie's skull had been blown off and there was blood and brain matter all over the concrete floor behind him.

This was an execution, pure and simple. They had brought poor Geordie Cartwright out to this cold and lonely spot, probably put him down on his knees, , then pressed a gun right into his face so he could see it and pulled the trigger. He must have realised what was coming when they drove him out here. I couldn't imagine how scared he must have been or what had gone through his mind at the end. I wondered if he had pleaded for his life.

'Yeah,' I said, 'I'm alright,' and I suddenly felt my sadness turn to anger. The sheer fucking nerve of this was breathtaking and the complete lack of mercy shown to Geordie Cartwright made me resolve to be just as pitiless if I was ever in a position to let Finney off his leash. 'Fuck!'

'This is bad,' muttered Sharp unnecessarily, 'very bad. Is it going to be a war? You don't need a war. *We* don't need a fucking turf war.'

'I don't know yet, do I? It depends on who it is. If it's a lone operator or a couple of freelancers, we'll find them and...' I didn't need to finish the sentence.

'And if not? What if it's someone who thinks he can take out Bobby, someone who wants to be Top Boy, then what?'

'Then he's a dead man. You don't mess with Bobby Mahoney, you know that. How many times has he proven it? Time and time again, for more than twenty five years.'

'I know,' he said unhappily.

'But what?'

'This feels different somehow, more professional.'

'What's professional about putting a bullet through someone's forehead,' I said, even though his thoughts mirrored my own, 'anyone can do that. They didn't even get rid of the body properly. You found it in twenty four hours.'

'I've been thinking about that,' he said, 'why leave a body out in the open like this, in a Police no-go area that's crawling with gangs, unless you want it to be found?'

I'd thought about that too. I figured somebody was sending us a message.

'Word on the street is; Cartwright disappeared with some of Bobby's money,' he said, 'a lot of Bobby's money.'

'Word travels fast,' I said, exasperated that the whole damn city seemed to know what was going on, except me, 'good.'

'What?'

'Sounds like somebody's been talking, bragging about taking on Bobby, stealing from him and getting away with it, which means we'll hear who it is soon enough and we'll lift him. End of problem.'

'Maybe.'

'You know that's how half the young villains on Tyneside get taken down. They can't resist blabbing about what they've done. They think it gets them respect.'

'Yeah, you're right there.'

'I know I am,' I snapped. I didn't need him to tell me. I walked away from Cartwright's body and Sharp followed me across the cracked concrete floor of the warehouse, stepping over puddles. Most of the roof had caved in years ago, leaving it open to the elements and I shivered.

'How did you find him?' I asked.

'I put the word out I was looking for George Cartwright, unofficial like. I said there was a couple of grand in it if anyone found him, alive or dead. I assumed that was okay.'

'Yeah, no problem.' That was pennies in our game.

'A few hours later, I get this call. It seems the Western Boyz discovered him when they were patrolling their patch.'

'Shit name for a gang. They sound like a bunch of queer cowboys.'

'This is their area apparently. It's a no-go zone for civilians and uniforms keep away from it as well.'

'That's good, should make it easier for my lads to get rid of the body. No one would take their dog for a walk down here.'

'Not unless they had a death wish. The Western Boyz called me first. They're good lads, know the score.'

'Good lads?' that was an unusual description.

'For drug peddling, robbing, raping scum bags," he shrugged, "it's all relative. We meet worse believe me.'

'They'll get their two grand. I'll sort it. Cartwright's body will be gone in an hour. Tell nobody about this and tell the

Western Boyz to keep it schtum too. If they do we might be able to use them again, put some money in their pockets from time to time. Would that appeal to them?'

'I'd say so,' we walked back to his car and got in. 'What the fuck was Cartwright doing with Bobby's money in the first place and how would they know who to hit?' he asked reflectively, like he wasn't expecting an answer and, to tell you the truth, that was what was worrying me the most right now. Even Sharp didn't know about the Drop. He didn't know how much it was or who it was for, let alone the fact that Cartwright and me were both responsible for delivering it. Only a handful of people in Bobby's organisation knew about it, which meant we had a rat - and a high level one at that.

'Sharp?' I called to him as we were climbing into our cars, 'tell no one about this. I want it buried.'

'Okay,' he said, 'what are you going to do?'

As soon as I could, I called Bobby.

'We've got a problem,' I said.

'Go on.'

'We found our rep,' I was speaking in that guarded way he preferred over the phone. We treated every conversation like it was being taped or someone could be listening in, 'it turns out he hadn't resigned.'

Bobby sighed, like he'd known it all along but didn't want to believe the truth.

'Someone's retired him?'

'Yep.'

'Right,' he said suddenly, a flash of anger in his voice now he had proof that one of his men had been killed. 'Find out who and sort it,' before reminding me, 'that's what I pay you for,' then he added the single word, 'Monday,' as if I needed reminding of the deadline.

Laura was still asleep when I got in but I knew I wouldn't be able to rest if I'd wanted to. The whole thing was going through my mind, over and over again but it boiled down to very simple questions. Who has done this thing and why? I'd gone through everybody I could think of. I'd started with the main players in cities within striking distance of us, the family firms who controlled large patches of Glasgow, Edinburgh, Manchester and Liverpool, but surely they had enough on their plate without starting a war with us over our city. I put myself in their shoes, dispassionately weighing up the risks and advantages of launching an attack on a rival family in a city I didn't know and I came to the conclusion I wouldn't risk it myself, not for millions. It was too dangerous, too likely to threaten their current empires and would just result in tit-for-tat killings with no side fully destroying the other. It would be messy, bloody and expensive and it might just give the police all of the evidence they needed to put everybody involved away for years.

I poured myself another beer and thought about the smaller local crews that operated under our noses and, if not always with our outright permission, a tacit understanding that as long as they didn't tread on our toes, they had a right to earn a living. Had the leader of one of those crews suddenly become too ambitious? It was possible, natural even. That was how Bobby became Top Boy - by being more ruthless than the guy who was in his way. There must have been a day when Bobby looked around him and suddenly thought 'I want to be the man. I'm good enough, hard enough and I'm going to make it happen. Men will die as a result but it's a price I'm willing to pay'. And he did pay that price, displacing the guy at the top by killing him and all of his main men, with Finney's help of course. But that was twenty-odd years ago now and the world wasn't quite the same. You had to be a very political animal to cope with life at the top these days. That was what the Drop was all about, after all. You had to understand politics, big business, the legit world as well as the criminal one, you had to feather nests and keep the money flowing, you needed bent coppers and shady politicians, dodgy journalists and crooked accountants. You had to know when to scare people and when to pay them off. It was a tough job running an empire and somehow I couldn't see any of the local hoodlums having the grey cells to even attempt it.

So, who then?

I was lying in bed that night next to Laura, not sleeping, when suddenly in a flash of realisation it hit me – the reason that Bobby should trust me. It was a risk phoning him in the middle of the night for a meet but my instinct told me it was the right thing to do. It might have been late but he wouldn't be sleeping either. I knew him too well. He'd be up and pacing, churning over all of the same thoughts in his head that I was having.

Sure enough he answered his mobile on the first ring. He sounded guarded, defensive.

'Yeah,' he said impatiently.

'I want a meet,' I told him.

'What? Now?'

'No not now,' I told him, 'tomorrow, as soon as you can do it. There's something I need to tell you.'

There was a short pause on the line while he digested this. 'Right,' he said, 'meet me at Frank's in the morning.' We agreed a time and I rang off. I went back to bed then and slept like a baby.

TEN

We were both naked, lying face down on two massage tables, a pair of soft white towels draped across our arses to preserve our modesty. Tina and Susan, the two fittest young lasses in the place, no coincidence there, were expertly kneading the tension out of our necks with their soft, oiled hands and it felt good, really good.

Bobby was on form considering. Maybe he had already stopped suspecting I'd ripped him off, now that I had found Cartwright's body, but most likely it was just for appearances. That's why he was having such a good craic with the girls. When things were bad in your business you carried on like everything was rosy. Some people call it fiddling while Rome burns. I call it common sense, because if people started to lose confidence in Bobby's ability to control things then he was as good as dead already.

'You know this is about the only legit massage parlour I have any involvement with,' he told Tina who chuckled at this.

She was in her mid twenties and a trained therapist, masseuse and a holistic white witch, or whatever it is they like to call themselves these days when they graduate with their certificates in that alternative therapy shit.

'That's right pet,' she told him confidently, 'you won't get any hand jobs here,' and the other girl laughed, 'well,' she added cheekily, 'mebbe's on your birthday,' and that set all of us off laughing.

'He's 29 today as it happens,' I said and that prompted more laughing but there was no phasing Tina.

'In that case you're on,' she said. She paused for effect then told us, 'I'll go and fetch Gary. He's the hand job expert round here.'

'And you can fuck right off,' said Bobby but he was still laughing. I've seen Gary, the in-house male masseuse and if he isn't gay, he should be. Personally I couldn't give a fuck who anybody shags, as long as it isn't children, but I wouldn't be comfortable getting a massage from any man, especially Gary. I reckon he'd enjoy it more than I would.

The massage Tina's mate was giving me was excellent. It was just what I needed and chilled me right out, unwinding all the knots of tension in my back and neck. 'Frank's', named in honour of Bobby's personal favourite Frank Sinatra, was a gym and spa that Bobby had a share in. His fellow investors may or may not have been fully aware that his stake was based on ill-gotten gains but they didn't seem to care and it was a legitimate form of income, which supported our story that Bobby was, to all intents and purposes, a successful, local businessman.

When Tina was done, Bobby said, 'leave us to it pet,' and the girls disappeared. We wrapped the towels around ourselves and I followed Bobby out into the steam room to talk business. I closed the door tightly behind us and we almost disappeared in the vapour, but I could still make out Bobby's face as he sat opposite me on a little wooden slatted bench. He was wearing that frown again.

'What you got to tell me?'

'Not much,' I replied, 'just the reason why you should start trusting me again.'

'I'm listening.'

'It's not enough.' I said.

'What isn't?'

'The money,' and I made sure I looked him right in the eye when I said this, 'the amount that's gone missing wouldn't be worth the risk for crossing you. Let's put aside for one minute the fact I've known you since I was a nipper, let's ignore the years of loyal service shall we? We both know that right now that doesn't mean much. Someone has ripped you off and it could be anybody, including me. If I was you, I wouldn't trust me either. Maybe I've got money worries you don't know about, debts or perhaps I just want a bigger house. Maybe my bird's been bending my ear about it.'

'Go on,' we were staring each other out at this point.

'Or look at it another way. What if I'm just too ambitious? You've said no to a couple of my ideas this year so perhaps I think you're slipping and I could do a better job than you as the boss. Suppose I can't be bothered to wait till you retire to someplace hot and I want you out of my way.'

'Fuck me,' he told me with something like astonishment, 'you tell it straight don't you?'

'Don't kid me you haven't had those thoughts in the last few days.'

'Maybe I have.'

'Course you have. You're trying to work out who's brave enough or stupid enough to move against you by stealing the Drop, but my point is, the Drop isn't large enough for me to chuck in a good screw with your firm. Think about it, if I was going to rip you off, it would have to be big, really big. We both know I'm a clever cunt and I wouldn't want to be looking over my shoulder for the rest of my life waiting for Finney to turn up and put me in the ground. For that, it would have to be millions and I would never be able to sleep easy at night if I left you breathing.'

'Jesus,' he said, clearly shocked by my lack of tact but I could see he understood my point.

'If I was working with Cartwright I'd have had to split the Drop and there'd be fuck all left for either of us, so let's assume that's why I topped him. If I wasn't working with him I'd have to kill him anyway, but we both know I'm no killer and I can prove I was in Thailand when he was last seen, so I must have paid someone and the same logic applies. I'm not going to give the job to a couple of crack-heads and watch them balls it up, so it would have to be a professional and they aren't cheap. Same problem, I'm a young man, I'd be on the run and I'd have sod all left to retire on.'

'Fair enough,' he said. The sweat was pouring down Bobby's face and I could feel drops of it sliding down my torso. They had the heat up high in the steam room today.

'Besides, you know I could earn the same money in two good years with you so why would I jeopardise that? You taught me to pay top men well enough so they don't even think about betraying you.'

Bobby looked at me for a long while without saying anything. Then he looked away, like he was thinking. In my fevered state I was starting to wonder if I'd gone too far and he was going to suddenly lose it and smash my head in on the floor tiles.

'I'm sorry,' he said finally.

I wasn't expecting that.

'Come again?'

'For not trusting you.'

I let this sink in for a bit then said, 'you shouldn't trust me,' and he looked me right in the eye, 'you shouldn't trust anyone Bobby, not right now.'

'You're right Davey,' he said, 'but you are the only one who ever tells me that, which is why I do trust you.'

He was looking straight at me again in that unflinching way he had of sizing people up, 'you can forget tomorrow's deadline.'

I nodded gratefully. I felt the pressure visibly lift until he jabbed his finger at me and said, 'but that doesn't mean you're off the hook. That money was still your responsibility and Cartwright was one of your boys, so it's still your neck…'

He didn't have to finish.

'Course,' I said, 'I'm all over it, believe me.'

'Good, you should be,' he didn't look much happier now that he'd stopped suspecting me of personally ripping him off. I guess he had the same problem; someone had done it and we still didn't know who, 'and I've got a job for you.' He finished.

'What kind of job?' I didn't know why but I was suddenly worried he was going to ask me to kill somebody to prove my loyalty. It was an absurd notion but I got a little surge of panic anyway. The heat in the steam room was making me feel weak and I wanted to get out of there.

'The Drop. I need to make good on the Drop. I want you to deliver it and I want you to take Finney, just in case.'

Just in case someone tries to kill me or just in case I try and run off with it, I wondered, probably both.

'When we realised it hadn't reached him I managed to buy us some time but it did not go down well,' he continued, 'so I've put some extra in there to sugar the pill. Northam will let you have it when you turn up with Finney. Make sure you hand it over to Amrein personally and whatever you do make sure he understands we are back in control.'

'Of course,' I said. He was teaching me to suck eggs but I understood. He was stressing out, making sure no detail was left to chance. I'd have done the same in his shoes. 'I'll get it there, no problem.'

'Good, make sure you do.'

I spent Monday morning at our restaurant in the Quayside. I knew I'd get some peace there. I sat at a table before it opened to the public, making calls, sending members of our crew out on errands, following up leads and leaning on people, anybody I could think of who might know anything about Cartwright, however trivial. My meeting with Bobby had bought me some time but I knew I couldn't relax, not until I'd got his money back, every penny.

The sun came out, shining through the big open windows, bathing the place. It was a lovely spot and Bobby hadn't skimped on the décor; bright white linen tablecloths topped with outsized wine glasses and expensive flower arrangements, welcomed the diners, who could sink into soft leather banquette seating and chose from a wine list that had more pages than the phone book. This was about as classy as we got.

The place opened up around me and people started to wander in. It was quite busy for the beginning of the week; mostly business lunches by the look of it, but there were one or two well-heeled couples and some ladies who lunched.

I took calls from our guys as they reported back to me. Nobody had come up with anything new. No one knew anything about this mysterious Russian. One of the waitresses brought me a plate of halloumi and chorizo, some foccaccia and hummus and a glass of Sauvignon. She was a pretty little thing, neat in her crisp, white blouse, short black skirt and dark stockings, with her honey coloured hair tied back, not much make-up, natural looking, the way I like them.

'Chef thought you might fancy a plate of something, Mister Blake?' she said, then she smiled, 'the wine was my idea.'

'Tell the chef he's a mind reader,' I told her, 'and you're a darling.'

She gave me a big smile before she walked away. It was a nice little spread but I made sure I got through it quick before any of our crew caught me eating 'poncy foreign food'. Most of our lads thought lasagne was exotic. Me? I'm different. I'm interested in good food and decent wine. One day, I'll have enough money to open a restaurant like this myself, somewhere classy with a good chef and a respectable wine list, that you wouldn't be ashamed to take your other half to on her birthday. Until that day though, well, as they say, this beats working for a living. Well, usually. Today was a bit different of course.

I was just finishing my lunch when in walked DS Sharp followed by a man I'd never seen before. He was a short, rotund guy in a long, black overcoat with a cheap grey suit beneath it, the collar of his white shirt slightly frayed. He was obviously one of those men who never looked entirely comfortable in a suit - that fact alone would probably prevent further promotion.

Sharp pointed me out. The shorter man walked up to me determinedly.

'David Blake?' he asked me, 'Detective Inspector Clifford,' he added sternly, with the unmistakeable accent of East London. He made sure he showed me his warrant card, holding it high enough for the other diners to satisfy their curiosity. It was a form of harassment I was used to and I was hardly going to be embarrassed by it, 'you've probably heard, I'm the new kid on the block,' I thought that was an odd description for a middle-aged man with a receding hairline and a straggly little moustache that contained a greasy fragment of his breakfast. What was it with these two and their 'taches?

'No,' I said, as if his arrival was of no consequence to me whatsoever.

'Detective Sergeant Sharp you do know,' he told me.

'We've had the pleasure,' we all shook hands. 'Inspector,' I said giving him my best hundred-watt smile, 'would you like to join me for some lunch, your colleague too of course? This Sauvignon is excellent,'

'No thank you Mister Blake,' he said, like I had just offered him an all-expenses trip to the Bahamas in return for forgetting a murder I'd committed, 'do you have somewhere for a private conversation?' A bit rich, considering his very public entrance.

'Of course,' I assured him, 'always happy to assist Northumbria's finest.'

I led them into a poky little office out back and we sat around a desk normally used by the restaurant's bookkeeper, 'how can I help?'

'By dispensing with the usual bullshit,' he told me. He was leaning forward in his chair, an excitable sort who couldn't wait to tell me what was on his mind.

I decided to play the genteel, slightly-incredulous suspect, the kind you might see on an episode of *Inspector Morse*. 'I'm not sure if I follow Inspector.' Sharp smirked slightly.

'Heard of the Marshall brothers?' he asked, 'Don't answer that, course you have.'

'I think I may have read about them in the newspaper.'

'I'll bet you did,' he nodded emphatically, 'A lovely bust, that one. They'd ruled half of Manchester for donkey's years, then, one day we took down one of their dealers for the third time. I mean, he was looking at more Porridge than Ronnie Barker.'

'Use that joke a lot do you?' I asked him.

He ignored me. 'So he lays down for us and starts bleating; names, dates, places, money, grams and kilos. Yeah, they were shifting kilos, the cocky buggers. He gave us a name and we busted him, that bloke gave us a name and we busted him too, and so on, all the way up the big, long, greasy pole right to the very top. You see, nobody wants to be the only one doing life. You'd have to be a right mug, so you sneak on the guy who's giving you orders and taking home more money than you for less risk, in theory,' he added the 'in theory' like it was darkly significant, 'there's a kind of resentment that we find quite easy to tap into. Before you know it we'd got all the lieutenants, knocked them down one by one like dominoes, till the Marshalls had no one left to do their dirty work for them. Then we came after the brothers, see. Did you hear what they got in the end?'

'Ninety-nine years.'

'You do remember,' he said triumphantly.

'Of course, he had a good eye for the headlines the old "hanging judge". I thought at the time it was quite a coincidence how his carefully considered sentences all added up neatly to ninety-nine years.'

'Terry Marshall got thirty-two years,' and he whistled like he was impressed, 'minimum recommendation was twenty-five. The judge may have liked headlines but he had a good sense of humour an' all. There's Terry standing in the dock at his age and he says "I can't do all that time" meaning he is going to be long dead by the end of his sentence and do you know what the judge said. "Do your best," and DI Clifford laughed until he almost choked. "Do your best?" You should have seen the look on poor Terry's little face. I mean imagine it, you've robbed and thieved and battered and murdered till you are at the top of the whole shitty pile and how do you spend your last days; sharing a tiny cell for twenty-three hours a day with a mugger and a rapist until you finally die. He's got to be asking himself every hour of every day what was it all for?' he paused to let that sink in, 'that's how it ends for people like him - but it doesn't have to be like that for everybody who works for the top boys.' He leaned forward like he was sharing a conspiracy with me. 'You know Bobby Mahoney is on a list don't you? I mean right at the top of that list, along with a few cockneys, a couple of Scousers and some Jocks I could mention.'

I tried to look blank, 'New Year's Honours?'

'SOCA's hit parade.'

SOCA or the Serious Organised Crime Agency, was created with the merger of the National Crime Squad and the National Criminal Intelligence Service, to become an organisation the tabloids had taken to referring to as the British F.B.I. They were meant to tackle drug barons, people traffickers and large scale money laundering.

'It's like top of the pops,' DI Clifford continued, 'only you don't want to be in their chart and I wouldn't be surprised if Bobby isn't number one with a bullet. The man most wanted. You know they have a list of all the major players in organised crime right across the country and they are gunning for them all. They are going to get them too. You know who's in charge at SOCA, the former head of MI5, Britain's Counter Intelligence service, the spooks. They fought the cold war, the IRA and Al Qaeda so they are going to make mincemeat of your lot.'

'So why are you even here?' I asked, 'if they are that good, you can just sit back and relax and watch while the show happens all around you.'

'I am here to offer you a way out. Your only way out, come to mention it. Cooperate with me and when the wheels do come off, as they will, spectacularly, you'll have at least one friend who can put a word in for you when it matters. Otherwise you'll be just another pretty boy getting gang-raped in the showers at Strangeways.'

'Cooperate? How exactly?' I asked him calmly.

He straightened, full of adrenalin now. He was doing a selling job on me and I could tell he was pretty sure I was interested, 'tell me what you know and maybe it will be easier for Bobby if his local nick does the arresting. I might even be persuaded to bust him on lesser charges just as long as it takes him off the streets. We could focus on his role in the vice game and play down his little drugs empire?' He said that last bit like I should be impressed he knew we were shifting drugs. Well whoop-tee-doo. He folded his arms smugly and sat back in his chair.

'Know what I think?' I asked him, 'honestly want to hear it?'

'Go on,' he urged me.

'You've got nothing and you're shit scared. You're worried that SOCA are going to carry out some huge bust up here on your new doorstep and you'll be left standing there like the ugly bird at the party no one wants to dance with.' He seemed a bit taken aback to be spoken to like that.

'How long have you been a DI, Clifford? A bit too long I'd say, from the look of you. Bet you were the star Detective Constable weren't you, but then most of them are fucking numpties. Maybe you were even a fast-tracked DS but somehow it hasn't happened for you has it? You were standing on the dockside in your cheap suit and you've missed the boat? And what's all this 'we'? *We* busted the Marshall Brothers, *we* brought them down. The guy who really made that bust is well high up in the funny handshake brigade by now. He's probably Assistant Commissioner, at least. Am I right? And you, you're stuck up here in the grim old north, miles from home. Bet the wife hates it and secretly hates you too these days. Frankly Clifford, you look tired. You're classic heart attack material. I can smell the desperation on you from here. I reckon you'd give someone a blowjob if they made you Superintendent. Well I could make you a Chief Super overnight, so are you going to suck me off now or what?'

He didn't say a word. He just sat there trying to rein in his fury. I think he was actually trembling with rage at that point. I wondered if I was about to be on the receiving end of a bit of good, old fashioned Police brutality.

'It's alright Clifford,' I told him, 'you don't have to worry, you're not really my type. Now why don't you fuck off out of my face and take the other Chuckle Brother with you. My wine is getting warm.'

He pointed his finger at me as he rose from his seat, 'you won't be laughing.' he said, jabbing it at me, 'you... won't... be... fucking... laughing... ' it wasn't exactly Noel Coward but I was surprised he could string the words of a sentence together the way he looked. I guess I'd touched a nerve. I don't normally like to rattle the cages of the local law enforcement and I try to keep it from turning personal. They've got their job to do and we've got ours and I never want to give them any more incentive to come after us than they've already got, but this cocky fucker needed taking down a peg for thinking he could turn me into a grass. I reckon he'd be up half the night churning my words over in his head, wondering if they were at least partially true.

Clifford walked out, leaving DS Sharp to trail after him. Sharp went a bit over the top, turning back to me, and shouting, 'we'll be back!' but I supposed he had to play the part.

ELEVEN

It was dark and cold and threatening rain as I climbed out of the car outside my apartment. I couldn't wait to get inside in the warm but then Vince called, 'I'm at Mirage. You need to come down here and see something.'

'Now? It's not my brother again is it?'

'Not this time.'

'It better be important Vince, it's late and I'm knackered. I'm not coming down there if some prat's glassed someone on the dance floor. You can handle that.'

'No it's not that,' he assured me, 'I wouldn't bother you with that.'

'Well what then?'

'It's hard to explain over the phone,' he said, 'you're better off coming down here, believe me.'

'Okay,' I said, 'I'm on my way.'

I climbed back into my car.

I called Finney and picked him up on the way over to Mirage. It was a venue we had a full share in, part bar, part nightclub. The idea was to get the young 'uns into the bar with cheap happy-hour offers then, when they were pissed and happy, encourage them to pay to get through a set of double doors into the night club. The music was good, the crowd wasn't too rough and we made decent money out of the place. Obviously our own boys manned the doors on both the bar and the club, so I couldn't imagine anything that could have gone seriously wrong in there.

'You don't think one of Benny's lads has gone ape and killed some muppet do you?' asked Finney.

'I hope not,' I said, 'the paperwork would be a nightmare. They'd close us down for sure.'

The place was still open when we got there and fairly busy for a Monday, late evening, but there was no one on the door and that was more than a bit strange. I told a barman to fetch Vince and we waited for him to make an appearance. I clocked Finney looking up at the big screen where they were showing videos on MTV.

'Look at that preening prat.' He didn't bother to disguise his disgust. I looked over to see what had offended him.

'What's wrong with him?' I asked.

'What's wrong with him? To start with his shorts are at half mast. How can he walk in them? I've not seen shorts like that since Stanley Fucking Matthews. He's got a dog lead round his neck and a plaster on his face. What's he done? Cut himself shaving? There's bum fluff on his lip and he's wearing a hat I wouldn't have on at the beach. Who is he? He's a disgrace.'

'That's Nelly.' I told him.

'Nelly? For fuck's sake,' he snorted, 'I used to have an Aunt Nelly,' he jabbed a sausage-sized finger at the screen, 'and she was probably harder than him.'

She probably was, if she was related to Finney.

When Vince showed up I asked him, 'why is there no one on the door?' in reply he simply jerked his head to one side to indicate we should follow and took us behind the scenes to the little office with the CCTV monitors in it. 'You need to see this,' he said, pushing a button to play a scene he had obviously set up for us.

We watched in silence as a grainy black and white image appeared. We got a bird's eye view of the lobby between the bar and the club. There was, as always, one of our girls standing behind the counter waiting to take the entrance money. Nearby, in front of her counter, stood the huge, hulking figure of Benny Evans and one of his lads, looking like a couple of sentries on guard duty. They had on the regulation uniform, black shoes and trousers, white shirt, black leather jackets. They were all bloody enormous guys on our doors but they needed to be, to deal with the tanked up specimens we were serving.

The image on the screen kept changing, flashing back and forth between the door of the bar where, sure enough, two more of our lads were standing right where they should have been, and the lobby of the club.

'So far, so normal,' said Vince.

'Just what are you showing us here?' I asked but before he could answer the scene outside the bar changed. It all happened so fast. There was a blur of movement as two big, heavy-set guys with shaven heads literally ran into view and went straight for our doormen. Our two guys were caught by surprise but they were used to dealing with dirty fighters. It made no difference to the outcome though, as blow after blow rained down on them. It took them all of their guts and strength just to stay on their feet, let alone fight back. Before they dropped, and they did drop, two other blokes - the same types, big buggers with close-cropped heads - went flying between them and on into the bar. You could just make out some frightened punters in the background stepping out of their way.

They disappeared from view but came back into it straight away, as soon as the screen changed to the scene in the lobby by the club doors. Nobody had raised the alarm with Benny and his man. It had all happened too fast for that. The two new guys went straight for Benny and his bloke and the scene repeated itself. It was a carbon copy of the fight outside, with the addition of Kathy, our poor cash-desk girl, ducking under the counter and, though we didn't have the benefit of volume, more than likely screaming her head off in the process. Our lads were well surprised but at first they held firm. Fat lot of good it did them. Their only reward was a serious pummelling. When they finally fell to the ground, the shaven heads waded in with their boots, and as soon as all four lads were out cold, the shaven heads turned on their toes and marched off. The whole thing took less than two minutes. It was amazing. If it had not been our lads on the receiving end I'd have probably been seriously impressed.

'Fuck me,' said Finney, 'where did those twats come from?'

'No idea,' said Vince, 'it happened just like you saw. They came in, they decked all four of our lads and gave them a proper kicking, then they left, didn't take a thing, didn't say a word, just did what they came here to do and went. Our boys are all in hospital. I sent Kathy with them. That's why there's no one on the door.

'I'll make a call,' I told him, 'get you someone down here. I doubt they'll come back again tonight but in case they do... '

'What good will it do?' He asked me. 'I'm not being funny but you saw that... '

'We'll make sure the next lot have baseball bats,' said Finney.

'Fuck that,' I told him, 'I want them armed. Those guys weren't just a bunch of arm-chancers or local lads with a grudge. Someone was sending us a message.'

'Yeah, probably best to be tooled up after this,' Finney conceded.

'Have you ever seen Benny Evans take a beating like that?' I asked him.

He shook his head, 'I've never even seen him take a beating.' He banged his fist down on the desk, 'I don't care how hard they are, I'll fucking murder them. All of them, personally.'

'Give me that tape,' I ordered.

'What are you going to do?' asked Vince

'Show it to Bobby.'

'He'll have someone's eyes for this,' said Finney.

I took the tape up to Bobby's house. It was a big mansion style building in Gosforth. The posh-end as he liked to call it. He'd come a long way since he was a youngster. The house lay behind two massive wrought iron gates.

Bobby poured us both a drink, 'you can come through, Sarah's at her mate's house.' Sarah Mahoney was the one person who could wrap Bobby round her little finger. She was twenty years old, had gone off to college a year early and was now graduated, back home and living with the old man again. Her graduation picture held pride of place on his mantelpiece. She was still beautiful, even in that ridiculous get-up they make you wear when you pick up your certificate. I think Bobby was delighted she was home and he was in no hurry to move her out. His missus had been dead nearly ten years now and he'd shown no interest in replacing her. He had women when he wanted them of course, but nothing permanent. Like every dad I've ever met, he thought his girl was the most special thing on the planet. Bobby would have done anything for his daughter, anything.

He watched the tape silently then asked me, 'what the fuck does this mean?'

'I think someone is testing us, sending us a message. They are trying to say they can take over whenever they like.'

'That's bullshit.'

'I know but I think that's what they are telling us.'

He thought about this for a moment, 'Who has got the balls to come after us like that?'

'What about Anderson? There was that row in Ibiza.'

'Nah, he wasn't too happy about it but he's got too much on his plate for this. His accountant's not as slippery as ours. Now he's got ARA all over him 'cos he can't explain how he's got the house, the cars and all the bling with no visible means of support.'

ARA was the Assets Recovery Agency, tasked under the Proceeds of Crime Act with confiscating the ill-gotten gains of career criminals. Sensible people always had legitimate businesses to demonstrate where their income came from, which is why Bobby owned pubs, clubs, restaurants, a catering company, a property agency, even a couple of newsagents, anything with legitimate turnover that we could use to launder cash.

'Didn't he have anything legit?'

Bobby shook his head, 'stupid bastard was still signing on in Toxteth.'

'That is sticking two fingers up at the man,' I said, 'queuing up at the dole office with your Rolex and a wodge of drug money in your back pocket.'

'He'll need benefits by the time they've finished with him. They filmed him secretly for one of those uncovered, fly-on-the-wall documentaries,' and he shook his head, 'I tell you, if that Macintyre bloke came near me looking to make a name for himself I'd stick him in the boot of his own car, lock it and push it into the Tyne, I really would.'

'I know you would. How about our friends in Glasgow?' I offered, 'the Gladwells?'

Bobby thought for a moment, 'too old, maybe ten years ago but not now. We've had our scrapes me and Arthur Gladwell but we always sorted them in the end. Imagine the stress of being the Top Boy in Glasgow for that long.'

'There's a lot of competition.'

'They're fucking psychos up there. Remember, it was us that built the wall, to keep those buggers out.'

'I'll have to remember to tell Laura that. Her old lady's a Scot. So you don't think it's him?'

'Gladwell? No, too old, too busy and he's got enough on his plate keeping his boys out of trouble.' He's got four sons. Remember we met the eldest and his shrew when we went up there a couple of years back to sort out that construction scam? What was her name again?'

'Martine,'

'You called her Lady Macbeth.'

'With good cause,' I assured him, 'but not to her face. She was as sour as a bag of lemons that one.'

'Imagine fucking that,' and he whistled as if he was contemplating the demands of the SAS selection process.

'Tommy Gladwell must have done it, at least a couple of times. They've got two kids.'

'He's a twat that bloke.'

'Known as 'wee Tommy Gladwell from what I remember, even though he was fat and forty by then.'

'He's like all the Gladwell lads, carries on like he's hard as nails but he can't shit without his old man's permission and now he's got his wife involved in his business, imagine that,' he clearly thought that was taking feminism a step too far.

'London then?' I suggested.

'Met's all over it. You've got Super grasses and SOCA, the ARA and not to mention all the competition, Albanians, Russians, Yardies and Turks. Who'd have time to come up here?'

'Maybe they think it'd be easier?' he gave me a filthy look, 'I'm not saying they'd be right mind but, you know, with some people, the grass is always greener,'

'It's possible,' he conceded then reconsidered, 'no, no, you're telling me that some fat cockney twat's gonna come all the way up here, shooting his mouth off, while we let him get away with taking over the place? Nah, I can't see it, can you?'

'I dunno,' I said, 'it happened to the football club.'

He laughed so hard at that I thought he was going to choke. 'Who then?' I urged him when he'd calmed down.

'What about closer to home?' he asked.

'You mean our crew or beyond?'

'Either.'

'Our mob? Only one man with the balls and the brawn and, how can I put this nicely? I can't. He's not got the brain.'

'Finney? I know and he's loyal, at least he always has been and we pay him a lot. I mean what's he going to spend it on? He wouldn't make a boss and I can't see him working for anybody else after all these years. So, not Finney, anyone else?'

'I've thought about it, obviously I have. I've thrown out all my preconceived ideas about these men we've been close to for years but even then I just can't see any of them having the capability or desire to be the boss.'

'What about Jerry Lemon?'

'What about him?'

Bobby shrugged, 'he's been with me all this time,' he said, 'maybe he wants to be Top Boy?'

'I thought about it,' I said, 'but honestly? No, I can't see Jerry Lemon wanting to take you out of the equation. He's loyal enough and sensible. He knows he's making good money right where he is. So, no, I don't think so.'

Bobby chuckled, 'that's what I like about you son,' he said, 'I heard all about the way he spoke to you down at the snooker hall, 'course I did. He treated you like a cunt but when you get the chance to whisper in the bosses' ear about him, maybe get him on my bad side, you play a totally straight bat. Did it even cross your mind?'

'Yeah,' I admitted, 'but only for a second. So Jerry Lemon doesn't have me on his Christmas card list, so what? If he's bitter about something that's more about him than me.'

'Trouble with Jerry, he's old school. He doesn't like you because he reckons you've never paid your dues. You've not killed men for the firm, you've never been inside or had to punch your way out of the gutter like he had to, like I had to. We both had to fight on the streets every day when we were young, fight for everything, and you didn't, but that isn't your fault and it doesn't make me come over all sentimental for the old days, because they were shite. Jerry had a very hard life when he was a nipper and it's affected him, but basically he's a good bloke. I've told him right enough that you've put money in all of our pockets one way or another. He's admitted to me privately that the stuff you do keeps us all out of jail but don't expect him to give you any credit for it.'

I nodded, 'it's no big deal,' so Jerry Lemon had a hard time when he was a nipper. My heart bled for him.

'And the new breed?' he asked, 'Monk and JD?'

'JD doesn't know what day it is. He's been enjoying too much of his own product. Monk's lads are making their living from house breaking with violence and his main muscle got eleven years not long back.'

'What for?'

'Broke into some poor couple's home and accidentally woke them up, decided he might as well rape the wife while he was there, knocked her old man senseless first though, then tied him up and made him watch. Police arrived while he was still on top of her.'

'Christ almighty,' said Bobby, 'is there no fucking decency in our game any more?'

'To tell you the truth, I have been through every name I can think of; every apprentice hard-knock and wannabe villain who might have heard of you and thought they could do a better job but there's nobody in our bloody league, not even close.'

'Whoever it was, they knew about the Drop,' he said, 'and not many do, even in our outfit.'

'I've been thinking about that as well,' I said, 'we've been sloppy; you, me, everybody. There's six people who've been down south with that money in the past two years. It only takes one of them to boast to a mate or tell some bird they're shagging and word can spread like the clap. Soon a whole bunch of people know Bobby Mahoney sends money to a top level fixer every month.'

'You're right,' he admitted, 'it pains me to admit it but you're right. So what are we going to do about it?'

'We are going to keep asking people until we hear something useful. We are going to stay sharp and make no mistakes, we are going to tighten things up and make sure there are no more fuck-ups. We are going to ride this one out and we are going to win.'

'You sound like the boss already,' he said, 'you sure you don't want my job?' he frowned at me, but I knew it was a wind-up.

'No,' I said, 'I have a better quality of life than you do and I don't need the stress.'

'Thanks a bleeding lot.' He smiled.

We talked some more about business and I was pleased to be back going over the detail again. Eventually, he said, 'you're still coming to our Sarah's 21st right?'

'I was planning to,' I said, 'as long as you still want me there.'

'Course,' he said, 'but do me a personal favour Davey. Stay off the sauce and get her and her daft friend home at the end of the night. They want to go off to some club after the meal and she won't want her old man there with her,' he stopped looking at me then. Instead he studied a space on the wall just over my left shoulder and said, 'with all that's been going on, I want to be careful, you know,' I did know. He meant if someone wanted to hurt him, really hurt him, they could go after Sarah. 'Look after her for me.'

'Sure,' I said straight away and he nodded like he was

genuinely grateful.

'One other thing,' he told me, 'you've not got any answers yet, so it's time you went to see Kinane,' I'd known this was coming and been dreading it but I nodded like it was a sensible idea. 'Get down that gym of his and find out what he knows. He must have heard something.'

'Okay Bobby,' I said.

'And take Finney with you,' Christ, that's all I needed. Finney and Kinane in the same room together. Having them both in the same city was scary enough.

TWELVE

Kinane's gym was called, The Cronk, in tribute to Emanuel Steward's original, justifiably famous, Kronk gym in Detroit; a place where hard men entered and champions emerged; Gerard McClellan, Dennis Andries, Michael Moorer and Thomas 'Hitman' Hearns, to name just a handful of them.

The only thing that emerged from Kinane's version was a little drug money and some unquestioning muscle, capable of guarding the door to a club on a Saturday night.

'Stay in the car.' I told Finney.

'What? You're fucking joking aren't you?' he growled.

'It was four years ago and I wasn't involved remember. He has no argument with me.'

'Aye, well, maybe but you tell him I'm out here and I'll rip his arms and legs off if he dares to show his face. Any time he wants. He just has to come out and say the word.'

'I don't doubt you would, which is why you're staying in the car. We haven't got time for all that macho shit right now. We're here to find out who killed Cartwright and that's all.' He was pissed off at me because he genuinely wanted an excuse to have a crack at Kinane but I was not having that.

I'd never been in the Cronk before. It was a real throwback. Talk about no frills. The entrance was bare except for a framed photograph on the wall, taken about twenty years ago, which constituted the gym's hall of fame; a 24 year old bare-chested fighter with an IBF Cruiserweight belt fastened proudly around his waste. Glenn McCrory is still the only world champion boxer the north east has ever produced, our very own great white hope.

The only other decoration on the walls of the Cronk was a big fist-shaped hole where someone had taken it out on the plasterboard. I walked past McCrory and on through a door that took me into the main gym.

The smell of sweat hit me as soon as I walked in. The gym was a big, open room with breeze-block walls and a dusty wooden floor. There were eight or nine tough looking men in there pumping iron or shadow boxing. Light shone down on them from a row of old windows set high up in the walls. I knew Kinane had three grown-up sons and, sure enough, some of the guys in there looked like younger, slightly smaller versions of him. They were still pumped up like it was a full-time occupation to look ripped.

There were no fancy touches here. No modern weight-lifting machines, it was all just free weights, as if anything else was an affront to manhood. A big guy was lifting what had to be in excess of three hundred pounds, the veins on his neck and face standing out with the strain. He was making a noise like he was struggling to finish a shit. He completed his lift, bringing his weights up to his chest then over his head before letting them slam back down again on the floor with an almighty crash. I felt the vibrations through my feet even though I was yards away.

Joe Kinane wasn't hard to spot. He was a massive bloke, about six-six with hands like shovels and a chest like the bonnet of a Transit van. He was in the ring, supervising a muscular heavy-weight who was pounding a bag being held by a little bloke who had to be in his mid sixties. Every punch landed with such force it threatened to lift the old trainer off his feet. It made me wince just watching it. Kinane glowered at me when I walked into the room. He broke away from his fighter, stepped out of the ring and crossed the floor to meet me.

'David Blake, what the fuck do you want?'

'It's good to see you too Joe,' I told him, 'I need a word, if you could spare me a minute of your time.'

He said nothing to me just turned to the young boxer, 'take a break,' before adding, 'five minutes.' The big lad didn't argue. The old guy looked mightily relieved.

We walked to a small office with a timber and glass front that seemed to have been added to an inside wall of the old gym as an afterthought.

'He looks useful,' I offered.

'Know fighters do you?' asked Kinane, knowing I didn't.

'Nope,' I admitted, 'but even I can see he was knocking seven shades of shite out of that bag.

'That lad will be a British champion one day,' he told me as if it was an undisputed fact.

We sat on stained office chairs that must have been bought from a liquidation sale or sold off by the police from their retrieved stolen goods stock. The place was a dump, and I could tell in his face Kinane knew this and was bothered by it now that I was here.

'I take it you are still working for the old cunt.'

If anybody else had said that I would have had Finney break their arm on principle, but Kinane was a special case, so I confirmed I was still working for the "old cunt", 'you know I am.'

He nodded slowly, 'so what brings you here? None of my business has anything to do with him. I'm legit. I train fighters, they box and sometimes they go on doors.'

'Bobby knows how you make your living,' I told him and I decided against telling Kinane that Bobby permitted him to earn that living, even though we both knew this was true. I could see no point in riling Kinane. Not when I needed his help. 'He knows about your fighters and your doormen,' I told him, 'he also knows about the coke deals, the Es and the protection your boys have been offering the heroin dealers on the Sunnydale estate.'

Kinane looked a little pissed-off at this last nugget of information but it was my job to know these things. 'Bobby's got nowt to do with those high rises,' he told me, 'never has done.'

'Which is why it doesn't trouble him,' I have had many a long discussion with Bobby about the potential gold mine in the Sunnydale estates, the most inaccurately named collection of high rises in Newcastle, provoking images of country fields and sunshine that are in stark contrast to its burned out cars, derelict flats and a dealer on every corner, but he has a real downer on the idea. He doesn't like heroin. He thinks it's risky and could end up putting him inside for life, which I understand and he doesn't want to deal to the kids on those estates, which is noble enough. My argument is there's always someone dealing there anyway, always has been, always will be, so it might as well be us. That way, it's organised, there's less anarchy, you know the purity level of the product on the streets and you don't get users OD'ing all the time because someone didn't know how to cut it right. There'd be no stupid feuds between rival dealers either, because they'd all be working for us and the income was about as regular as it gets. Anyway, he won't have it.

'Then why are you here?'

'Cartwright.'

'Oh,' he said, 'people are talking about that.'

'I'm sure they are,'

'I did wonder if that was why you came,' then he frowned, 'Bobby doesn't think that I... ?'

'No, no, of course not,' I lied. Bobby clearly did wonder if Kinane might be behind his problems and with some justification. They'd had a big tear-up, over lord knows what, about four, maybe five years ago now. To be honest I can barely remember the details myself after all this time but the hurt and the hate was still fresh on both sides. At the end of it all, Kinane was banished from the inner sanctum of our firm in disgrace, like Lancelot being kicked out of court by King Arthur for shagging Guinevere. Only he stuck around, stayed in the city and eked out a living in Newcastle. He could have made a big name in any other city in the country but he was one of those blokes who wouldn't know what to do with himself if he didn't live here.

'I'm getting round everybody,' I told him, 'so I thought I may as well come and see a man who knows. You always knew everything that went on in this city Joe. We worked together often enough for me to realise that.'

'When you were a snot-nosed kid you mean?'

'When I was a snot-nosed kid,' I agreed, not rising to it.

'Well,' he concluded, 'you're not a kid any more, one of Bobby's main men, so I hear. I have heard that much.'

'And what have you heard about Cartwright?'

'Nowt, but I'd be surprised if he's done a bunk. I'm assuming he's not the only thing that's gone missing or you wouldn't be half so bothered.' He'd obviously heard there was money involved but didn't want to admit it. My silence told him everything he needed to know. He frowned, 'Cartwright's not the kind of bloke who would steal from a man like Mahoney, for what that's worth, so I doubt he's gone voluntary like.'

I took a risk then, without really knowing why.

'He didn't,' I said, 'he's dead.'

'Jesus,' the big man seemed affected by that news. He would have known Cartwright well, 'and you don't know who's done it?'

I shook my head and waited. The look on his face told me there was something.

'It might be nowt.'

'Go on.' I urged him.

'One of my boys was out a few weeks back and he saw Cartwright in a bar in the Bigg Market. He was talking to an Ivan.' So someone else had seen them.

'A Russian? Was he sure?'

'Well my son doesn't speak the language but yeah he reckoned it was a Russian. I s'pose he could have been from anywhere round there. Anyway he was a big fucker apparently, looked like he was in the business.'

What had George Cartwright been up to? 'Thanks,' I said, 'it might be something,'

'Yeah, well, that's for you. I wouldn't tell Bobby fuck all but you were alright, even when me and Bobby had that row.'

'That was between you two. It was none of my business.'

'I know but the rest of the crew treated me like I'd shagged their sisters after that. And that cunt Finney… ' he froze then as if he suddenly realised Bobby wouldn't send me down here without some muscle to back me up, 'he's not out there is he?' his eyes narrowed, 'because if he is he can come in here now and I'll show him who's the real hard man.'

'I don't doubt it,' I said, 'which is why I told him to wait in the car. Just leave it Joe. I know you hate him but I haven't got time for that right now.'

Remember when you were a kid and you used to play that game with your mates where you're wondering if Superman could fight Captain Marvel or who would win between Godzilla and King Kong? Well, there is not a man in Bobby's firm who hasn't silently wondered who would win if Finney and Kinane came to serious blows. I feel certain whoever finally lost that one would be a dead man and the other wouldn't be fit for anything much afterwards.

I changed the subject, 'tell me about your boy, your youngest. I hear he's in some bother.'

As I'd hoped, this took his mind off what he'd like to do to Finney. 'GBH,' he said simply.

'Chip off the old block.'

'I tell him not to get involved but some big tosser had a few drinks and fancied himself. Our Gary broke his jaw, a couple of ribs and an arm. He's in court next month.'

'I've got some bent law working for me. I'll get him to do some digging on the other bloke if you give me a name. By the time he's finished, your innocent victim will be lucky to escape jail time he'll look so crooked.' I took a business card out of my wallet and gave it to him, 'a friendly solicitor, very clever. She'll make it look like the most honourable case of self-defence the jury can imagine. Give her a call.'

'Thanks Davey,' he said.

'But this is on me,' I warned him, 'if Bobby ever finds out I'm using a family lawyer to help your boy, I'll be in the shit, so it goes no further, you hear.'

'Yeah, cheers man,' he pocketed the card gratefully and to my surprise he handed me a cheap business card with the name of the Gym and a boxing glove on it and his mobile number underneath. 'When you hear what happened to Geordie Cartwright. Let me know like,' I assured him I would.

As I was leaving he said, 'don't trust Finney, he's a snake that one. He might look dumb but he's not. He's clever, in his own way, sneaky like.'

I smiled, 'I don't trust anyone.'

It had been worth it to come here. Hearing it from Billy was one thing. He could have been wrong, pissed, high or just plain lying to me but now we'd got it from two sources. We'd had two definite sightings of Cartwright in a pub discussing business with a foreigner. What was going on? What the fuck was Geordie Cartwright doing talking to a Russian in the Bigg Market?

THIRTEEN

‘He mention me?’ asked Finney when I climbed back into the car.

‘Nope.’

‘Good job an’ all,’ he said, turning the key in the ignition and revving the car for no good reason. ‘Where next?’

‘The accountant’s.’

‘I hate that slippery fucker.’

‘Me too,’ I said.

‘He acts like his shit don’t stink.’

‘At least we agree on that,’ and he gave an affirming grunt.

‘Coffee, gentlemen?’ asked the lady receptionist in a voice that you could have cut glass with. She was acting as if Finney resembled a respectable member of the upper middle-class customer base she was used to greeting, rather than the violent criminal low-life he obviously was.

'No thanks,' I said and Finney shook his head.

'Another cup Mister Northam?' she offered.

'No thank you Barbara,' he covered his empty cup with his hand, 'I've had an elegant sufficiency.' When Northam said this, Finney gave him a look like he'd just caught our accountant sodomising a minor.

Alexander Northam's small accountancy firm was on the second floor, over an estate agent in Grainger Street, slap bang in the middle of the city. He wasn't entirely crooked, there were legitimate clients too, but none of them put as much money through him as we did. Despite this he had the manner of a city banker and usually looked at us as if we were something he'd picked up on the bottom of his shoes.

'Excuse me gentlemen,' she was using that word again. Finney peered at her as if he suspected she might be taking the piss but she was oblivious. She merely smoothed her skirt with the palms of her hands and bent to clear away the cup, 'I'll be outside if you need me Mister Northam.' And she left us to it.

'Doesn't she know your first name?' I asked. He gave me a withering look and ignored me. 'Nice couch,' I said, 'must have cost a pretty packet,' I patted the soft Italian leather and we sat down uninvited. As usual, Northam didn't look too pleased to see us. Having Finney in his well appointed office, all teak and leather furnishings, must have been like having a naked hooker at a WI meeting.

'Yes, well, it did but then one has to maintain a veneer of prosperity, even in these testing economic times. There's a crisis of confidence out there - or don't you read the newspapers?'

'I read them,' I assured him, 'all of them. And you reckon a leather sofa and a few old books are going to fool people into thinking you know what to do with their money?'

'Did you come here to talk about my new couch Blake?' he asked testily, 'I rather doubt that.' He was a Geordie born and bred but he didn't want to be. He'd spent his life trying to shed the accent. He folded his arms, which made him look like he was wearing a straight jacket made of Harris tweed. Northam was a heavily balding man in his late fifties, who couldn't summon up the nerve to shave off the last thin wisp of combed-over ginger hair that rested on his head like a Brillo pad.

'I've come to talk to you about the Drop,' I informed him.

'Thought as much,' and his expression was almost a smirk, 'in a spot of bother with the boss eh? Not having a good time of it right now, are we?' He leaned forward and gave me an undertaker's smile, 'I hear your brother was making a nuisance of himself at Privado the other day. Does Bobby know about that as well? I realise he was at Goose Green but the Falklands Conflict was a long time ago and it's hardly a get-out-of-jail-free-card.'

'A long time,' I agreed, 'I wonder where you were when Our-young-'un was up to his nuts in mud and bullets? Probably sitting your accountancy exams in Thatcher's Britain?' He straightened, clearly not liking my tone but he didn't have the balls to say as much. 'Bet you took a few moments out of your day to raise a glass to our fine boys in the army for showing those bloody Argies who was boss. Salt of the earth weren't they Northam, just so long as you didn't ever have to meet any of them. Funny you don't feel that way about gangsters but they tend to have more money than squaddies and that's what it all boils down to with you doesn't it, the money.'

'Is there a point to this conversation? I'm surmising there must be.' He was trying to sound unruffled but I had evidently got to him.

'Let's not fuck about, shall we Northam? Yes, I am in a spot of bother with the boss, in fact there's a good chance he will cut my arms and legs off and feed me to the pigs if I don't come up with some answers and I'm stuck for some right now, which is why I might have to resort to wondering aloud to Bobby why you ignored all of our safeguards and procedures.'

'Ignored what?' he stammered, 'but I never…'

'Yeah you did,' I said cheerfully, 'what are we not supposed to do with the Drop Northam? Think hard.'

'I don't know what…'

I interrupted him, 'the Drop does not get released into the hands of just one individual, always two. That's the rule, the golden rule, there really is only one and you either forgot it, which makes you a fuckwit, or you wilfully ignored it, which makes you a suspect, so which is it?'

'Now wait a minute…' his face flushed. He sounded flustered. He'd known he'd done wrong all along and was just hoping nobody was ever going to pull him up on it.

'No, you wait a minute,' I told him, 'I wasn't there and Cartwright didn't have Maggot with him, did he? So why let him take the money?' I knew the answer or at least I thought I did. He'd been sloppy, we'd all been sloppy this time and our bent accountant was no exception.

'He told me he was with him.' he said, his mouth going dry.

'Sorry, who told who what?' I was being deliberately awkward.

'Cartwright told me that Barry Hennessy was in the car outside.'

'So you went out to verify this?'

'Well no.'

'You looked out of the window at least, saw him sitting there?'

'No.

'Why not?'

'I didn't think…'

'You didn't think?'

'No, well why would I?'

'I dunno,' I shrugged, 'maybe because you were handing over a very large amount of Bobby Mahoney's money to one guy, even though that same Bobby Mahoney had personally instructed you never to hand over a very large chunk of his money to only one guy. That's why you might just have given it a thought.'

'I had no reason to suspect Cartwright.' he protested.

'Why? Are you two old mates? '

'No, he is not my mate.'

'Not your friend and not a blood relative or anything? He's not part of the family?'

'Don't be absurd.'

'Me, absurd? I'm not the one giving big wadges of cash out to people who are neither my friends nor my relatives. That's fucking absurd. You realise nobody saw Geordie Cartwright walk in here or leave with the cash. So how do we know he ever received it from you? How can you prove you gave him the money when we don't sign for anything?'

'Now hang on a moment.'

'No moments and no hanging on. You're forgetting yourself Northam. I'm responsible for security in our organisation, whereas you are just a fucking bean counter with delusions of grandeur.'

'Don't you talk to me like that.'

'I'll talk to you anyway I want until you start giving me some answers. We are staying here until you can prove you gave that money to Cartwright and you had nothing to do with his murder.' I didn't think for one minute he was responsible for Cartwright's death but I was enjoying watching the slimy little shit sweat.

'Murder?' that took the wind out of his sails, 'this is ridiculous,' he stammered, 'I don't have to… '

'Finney,' I said quietly and Finney rose to his feet. Northam went white. When Finney pulled a flick knife from his pocket, pressed a button and a blade popped out, I thought Northam was going to keel over right there and then and have a heart attack in his own office.

Finney took a step forward, 'Please,' pleaded Northam, 'don't,'

Finney reached behind him, plucked the soft, Italian leather cushion he had been sitting on from out of the outrageously expensive sofa and plunged his knife deep into it, until there was a huge gash in the middle of the pristine leather.

'Oh,' Northam drew his hand up to his mouth in agitation but didn't dare say a word in protest. I stood up and Finney reached for the cushion I'd been sitting on and gave it the same treatment.

'I don't know what you want from me,' Northam pleaded. Only when I was convinced he had almost soiled himself did I give him any leeway.

'Sit down Northam,' and he almost fell into his desk chair, 'now, let's start again shall we? I want you tell me everything that happened that day. What time Cartwright arrived, what he said, what you said, what he was wearing, what mood he was in, what the weather was doing outside, what you had for breakfast that morning and if you had a dump afterwards. And if you go running off bleating to Bobby about us coming here I'll drop you right in the shit with him, understand?'

Finney held up the knife.

'Yes,' whimpered Northam.

Finney folded the knife back up.

'Go on then,' I said.

Finney chuckled as we drove away, 'I enjoyed that,'

'It was a moment of light relief,' I admitted, 'and he had been holding out on us.'

Putting the fear of god into Northam had worked. He'd told us two things we didn't already know; firstly Cartwright had taken the Drop a day early and of course he'd blamed that on me. I'd apparently told him to collect it twenty four hours before it was due. Because I was on holiday, Northam couldn't verify that with me at the time so he just assumed it was legit, the idiot.

The other thing Northam remembered, when we took him through the meeting minute by minute, was that mild-mannered Geordie Cartwright had been carrying. He'd spotted the gun in Cartwright's shoulder holster when he'd leaned forward to pick up the bag.

'What would Geordie need a gun for?' Finney wondered aloud.

'I don't know,' I admitted, 'but there's a good chance he got it from Hunter.'

'Yeah, probably,' he said, 'him and Cartwright go back years, to the old days.'

Doesn't everybody in our organisation, I thought, except me.

'I'm not sure how far forward we are getting here. Every time we learn something new it just throws up more questions. Why collect the Drop early? Why carry a gun when that isn't your line of work? Why tell Northam that Barry Hennessy was waiting outside in the car when he wasn't? Unless Barry was lying when you saw him after?'

'Doubt it, we scared the shite out of him, literally.'

I didn't want to think about that. 'And Northam looked too scared to lie to us in there, so it was Cartwright telling porkie pies but why would he risk that?'

'He was on the run with it?' suggested Finney, 'he knew we'd be after him if he lifted the money so he had the gun, just in case.'

'I don't think so. He'd know a gun wouldn't do him much good and the Drop had to be handed over in twenty four hours or he'd be in the deepest shit imaginable, so what was to be gained by it? Anyway, we should go and see Hunter and I think it might be worth having another word with Barry Hennessy.'

Finney smirked to himself at that. He was clearly enjoying his day. I drove for a little while then a thought struck me, 'why does Barry get called Maggot in the first place?'

Finney thought for a moment, 'cos he's a fucking maggot,'
'Fair enough.'

Our next stop was across the river in Gateshead; the Railway
arches and an appointment with Mickey Hunter. The arches
all had solid metal doors on them, emblazoned with the names
of the small businesses that operated out of the offices and
workshops within. If you could stand the noise and vibration
from the trains that went whizzing overhead you could get a
very good deal on premises right by the city.

Hunter ran a little body shop that knocked dents out of cars,
put new bumpers and bonnets on for you if you'd had a smash, and
might stretch to a respray, if you had the cash and didn't mind him
not declaring it. There was always a demand for low maintenance,
cheap repair work and it was a lovely cover for his real business.
That's why he could afford to undercut the main dealers.

'He wanted a piece.' Hunter told me as if it was the most
natural thing in the world. He was sitting back in his chair in
the garage's tiny office, which overlooked three dilapidated
cars that were all being worked on at once by blokes in
grease-stained overalls. Our conversation was constantly
being interrupted by the high pitched squeal as wheel nuts
were unscrewed, then an angle grinder screamed as someone
sorted out some body work. Mickey wore overalls too but I
never saw him getting his hands dirty. He was a tall, stocky
bloke in his late forties and his dark hair was flecked with
grey. He was also a bit boss-eyed. You wouldn't notice at
first. It was only when he was talking to you and was meant
to be looking right at you that, instead, you suddenly realised
he was staring at a space somewhere above your right
shoulder. It wasn't his fault his eye was a bit out of sinc but
it made him look decidedly shifty nonetheless. Hunter had
been with Bobby since he was a teenage tearaway, nicking

cars, re-spraying them and selling them on. Now he was the firm's quarter-master.

'Geordie Cartwright wanted a gun?' I still couldn't believe it. I'd never even known him fire a gun much less carry one around with him, 'what kind?'

'Handgun,' he said, 'a Sig Sauer, one of those flashy pistols the cops have in the States.'

'I know what a Sig Sauer is. Did you get him one?'

'Of course.'

'On whose say-so?'

'Well,' he looked at me dumbly, 'yours.'

'Mine?'

'He said you'd asked him to get a piece in case things got a bit hairy down south like.

'He said what?'

'That's what he said. You mean you didn't… '

'No,' I said, 'I didn't.'

'Christ, I'm really sorry man,' he told the wall behind me, 'but it sounded legit. I mean I've known Cartwright as long as I've known any of you and, well I mean, why would he lie?'

'That's the big question,' I wasn't really annoyed with Hunter. It's not as if we have written orders or signed requisition sheets for his bent weaponry, and he could hardly phone me on a land line and say 'is it true you asked Geordie Cartwright to get tooled up in case you had a spot of bother with some southerners?' We didn't work like that. A lot of what we did, strangely enough in our game, was based on trust, that and the fear of a sickening retribution afterwards if you were caught doing something that was against Bobby's interests. So what would drive a mild bloke like George Cartwright to get a Sig Sauer from our armourer and collect the Drop all on his own?

'When was this? What time?'

'Last Monday afternoon... No, Tuesday; I remember because the Toon were playing their cup replay that night and we were talking about it. We didn't think they'd get a result... And of course they didn't... They were knocked out... So we were right like.'

I held up a hand, 'yeah, yeah, did he say anything else? Was there anything odd about the way he was handling himself?'

'Well he seemed a bit distracted I suppose, looking back on it.'

And I understood why he was distracted. He was scared - but what would scare him so much he needed a gun? Answer that question and we were closer to the truth. Whatever it was, the gun hadn't done him any good in the end of course. Geordie Cartwright still wound up dead.

FOURTEEN

The massage parlour was an understated little building that looked like a doctor's surgery, perched at the end of a residential street in an area that was almost but not quite the suburbs. Its frosted glass windows and discreet signage, which indicated it was the place to go to with a sports injury, was intended to ensure no one objected too much to its presence.

I didn't know what the neighbours really thought about having a knocking shop on their doorstep but they didn't make too much of a fuss about it. The whole operation was designed to be as discreet as possible, to avoid attracting the attention of the police or any self-appointed moral guardians in the neighbourhood.

To be fair, we ran a good, clean operation. All the girls were volunteers and there was absolutely no trafficking of any kind. We only put willing lasses into jobs like that. The police knew it was a brothel, everybody did, but they didn't give a shit.

I walked in first, so as not to startle Barry Hennessy, aka Maggot, but it looked like he wasn't there. Instead we were met by Elaine, our housekeeper. She took the bookings, vetted the clients as they walked in and looked after the girls, making sure they were all right, earning money and paying us our proper cut. It was 30 quid to get through the door, which included the straightforward massage, not that anyone ever wanted just that. The rest was negotiable with the girls but a basic service, including a BJ and a shag would set you back another £100, which was cheaper than dinner for two in a lot of Newcastle's restaurants these days. The girls kicked another £20 back to the house, so we took 50 quid for providing them with a safe, secure environment where they wouldn't get beaten up, ripped off or arrested for soliciting. They took home £80 a punter and with a steady stream of clients they could earn upwards of £300 a shift. Put another way, that's £60,000 to £70,000 a year for lasses who would rather be doing this than earning minimum wage on a check-out till.

The girls here weren't drug addicts or nymphomaniacs. They were paying off debts their no-account blokes had left them with, putting themselves through college or bringing up their kids, feeding and clothing them, and they were doing okay but it wasn't exactly Pretty Woman. It's not what I'd have called easy work having some fat, sweaty Herbert lying on top of you and it certainly wasn't for everyone but they didn't have to do it. They could leave whenever they liked. We never held a gun to anyone's head or kept anybody against their will and they weren't that hard to replace.

'He not in?' I asked Elaine.

'He was,' she replied, 'I'll fetch him,' she wandered away down the corridor and we watched her go. Just as she reached the end I saw Maggot coming the other way. He clocked us, spotted Finney and his eyes went wild then he turned round and pegged it. Whatever Finney had done to him last time, Maggot wasn't up for a repeat performance.

'Maggot!' I shouted, 'don't fucking run. Christ.' I took off after him. Finney was the hardest man on our books but he was no athlete. He wouldn't be able to catch Maggot when he was pegging it away like the devil himself was after him.

I tore down the corridor and Elaine flattened herself against the wall as I hurtled by. I went through a door that had a little lounge area beyond it. No sign of Maggot. Two bored-looking girls in smart black cocktail dresses were sitting there sipping tea, waiting for their next John. We didn't want them sitting round in their skimpies. It made the place look less respectable. They looked up and I was about to ask them which way Maggot was headed when, ahead of me, a door banged and I ran on down a little flight of stairs that led to the showers, sauna, jacuzzi and the tiny rooms the girls took their clients into.

'Shite.' There were too many doors, they all looked the same, white painted, deliberately neutral and I didn't know where any of them led to. Fuck it, I thought and I ran right through the one that looked most likely to be the back door.

I nearly knocked over the naked girl who was in the middle of giving a middle-aged business type a hand job on his lunch hour. Nadia looked at me like I'd gone mad. He almost had a coronary. 'Oh fuck, no please. I'm sorry. I only wanted a massage. She grabbed me. Please, let me go,' he pleaded.

'Sorry,' I said, 'it's alright, I'm not the police.'

'Shut up Tony,' she scolded him sharply, properly aggrieved at being accused of a sexual assault, 'he's one of us,' then she turned to me and hissed, 'are you going to fuck off?'

'Back door?' I gasped and she pointed.

This time I tried the door first before I opened it. When I got a crack of daylight I went through, just in time to see Maggot at the other end of the back yard, rounding the corner which would take him out and down the side of the building. Predictably he ran straight into Finney, who'd come round the front at a more leisurely pace. Maggot swore and skidded to a halt like some cartoon character in a chase scene. I half expected smoke to come from the heels of his shoes. He turned back, saw me and realised he had nowhere left to run. Maggot backed away from Finney, heading for the crumbling brick wall that covered three sides of the back yard. His eyes were darting around as he desperately searched for somewhere to go.

'What you going to do now Maggot?' asked Finney, 'shit bricks and build a wall?'

Finney saw him eyeing up the actual walls like he was about to attempt to climb them.

'Don't be fucking stupid. You're going nowhere,' barked Finney. Maggot was terrified. When I drew near I noticed for the first time that he had a large red mark in the centre of his forehead. It looked pretty permanent, the kind of scar you are never going to lose completely.

'Look at you,' said Finney, staring at the red spot he had presumably inflicted, 'you look like a fucking Hindu or something,' Finney advanced on Maggot, 'never, ever run away from me again you cunt,' and Finney gave Maggot what he would have described as 'a little slap'.

Maggot sat on the sofa, holding a damp towel hard against his right eye to dampen down the bruising caused by Finney's 'little slap' - a blow that had knocked him off his feet and propelled him several feet across the yard. We were back in the knocking-shop's lobby. The girls who did not already have clients had been told to go for a walk around the block.

I was about to start questioning Maggot when a vaguely familiar figure came into view. A pale-faced overweight bloke, dressed in a dark blue business suit and tie emerged from downstairs. He saw me, flushed and immediately looked away, keeping his gaze fixedly towards the front door. He left as quickly as he could without actually breaking into a run. Nadia, back in her black cocktail dress, was right behind him. She was quite an attractive woman for her mid-thirties and she'd kept her figure, judging by what I'd seen earlier.

'You certainly put him off his stride,' she said.

'Sorry I made you work for it,' I told her.

'He got there in the end but I'd be surprised if he ever showed his face round here again.'

'Believe me Nadia, it's not his face I'll be trying to banish from my dreams.'

She thought about that for a moment, then cackled like one of Shakespeare's witches before leaving us to it.

'What happened there then?' asked Finney.

'I accidentally burst in on them while she was pulling him off.'

'You prat,' said Finney.

'I don't know,' I told him, 'I reckon it was a blessing in disguise.'

'How?'

'Don't watch the local news do you?'

'Never,' he said.

'That was Councillor Jennings,' I said. It was always good to have a couple of friendly councillors on your books, 'and I have a funny feeling that, after today, me and him are going to be the best of mates. Particularly when I tell him about the camera and the two-way mirrors.'

'We haven't got a camera and two-way mirrors,' said Finney, 'have we?'

'No,' I admitted, 'but he doesn't know that.'

Maggot was actually physically trembling. He couldn't tear his fearful eyes away from Finney and I figured I'd get more out of him without our enforcer's malevolent presence.

'Finney, you know that pub on the corner?'

'Aye.'

'Why don't you go and have a pint in it?' he frowned at me like I was trying to hide something from him, 'I think you being here is making it hard for our good friend Barry to express himself.'

Finney wordlessly accepted the logic of this. He rose to his feet but couldn't resist suddenly pulling his arm back and pretending to throw a punch into Maggot's face, stopping the blow almost as soon as it had started. The pretend punch still made Maggot jump like a cat that's been shot with an air rifle. Finney laughed and wandered down the corridor whistling 'we'll meet again'. I waited till he had left.

'Right Magg… Barry,' I said, 'I just want a little word about Geordie Cartwright.'

'I told him everything I know,' he nodded at the door Finney had disappeared through, 'which was fuck all by the way! I don't know anything about Geordie or what he was up to. If I did, do you think I wouldn't tell him? He's a fucking animal! Do you know what he did? He's only come at me with me drill. I was in my own garage, minding my own business and he comes in, takes my drill off me and starts waving it in my face. He had me pinned to my workbench and he said he was going to drill right through my head unless I told him where Geordie Cartwright is. I said "I don't know where Geordie Cartwright is", and he did this!'

He jabbed a finger at the little red welt on his forehead where Finney had let the drill bit glance against Maggot's skull. Most people wouldn't be capable of such an act, because they'd be too worried their hand might slip and the drill would go right into someone's brains but not Finney. His hand was steady because he didn't care two fucks if it slipped and killed Maggot.

'I believe you don't know anything about Cartwright's disappearance Maggot. If I had a drill shoved in my face I'd tell Finney the truth too. I believe you. I just want to know if you had any contact with him before he disappeared, that's all.'

'No, well no, not really.' He stammered.

'No, well no, not really,' I mimicked, 'meaning yes you did. Look Maggot, I'm not as daft as I look and I know there's probably stuff you are too shit-scared to admit to Finney, in case he tries to drill you a new pair of nostrils, but this is me. I don't work like that. What you say to me stays with me and nobody needs to know it came from you, okay? But if I find you are holding out on me I will tell Finney to go round to your house and turn you into a colander. Now where was it and when?'

Maggot put a hand to his injured forehead and instinctively rubbed the red spot there, 'a few days ago. I only saw him around that's all.'

'Where and fucking when, you tool?' I told him.

His injured forehead creased as he tried to recall when it was. 'Okay, well it was in the Bigg Market and it must have been the night when the Toon lost the replay at home 'cos I remember the city was packed with pissed-off people drowning their sorrows. You know the usual "the-season's-over-in-bloody-January-again' feeling."

'I know it well. So it was Tuesday night, the place was crawling with fans. Where did you bump into Cartwright and who was he with?'

'Well, he wasn't with nobody like but he was happy as Larry. That's what I remember seeing, everybody else in the pub's acting like their mother's just died and here's Cartwright laughing and joking, buying drinks an' all.'

'He wasn't noted for that.'

'No, exactly. So I asked him, "what's gannin' doon man, you win the lottery or summat?" and he says, "aye, summat like that." '

'What else did he say?' and he gave me an uncertain look. 'Elaine!' I shouted, 'Go and fetch Finney from the pub!'

'No! Don't do that man!'

'It's okay Elaine!'

'I asked him what had happened and he just said he had a bit of business lined up. He didn't say 'owt but I took it to mean it was tax free like, yer knaa.'

'Yes, I know, a bit of freelance that Bobby needn't worry about. I take it you didn't share this bit of wisdom with Finney and Bobby because you were worried they might use a whole tool kit on Geordie?'

'That's right.'

'Except I know you Maggot, you're a crafty little fucker so you wouldn't have left it there, not if there was a chance of you making a few bob out of it as well. You'd have bought Geordie one or three drinks and you'd have got it out of him. He was in the mood to talk, boasting about it even, so a pro like you could have got him to cough in half an hour. "Eeh you're such a clever bugger Geordie, oh you're the man Geordie, ooh can I suck your cock Geordie." '

'Hey man, steady on.'

'So what was the deal and who was it with? Come on, I told you it'll stay with me. They won't know you passed on the info.'

'Well he didn't tell me what the product was but when he told me the name it wasn't hard to guess like.'

'And the name was?'

'Billy Warren.'

FIFTEEN

....

I wanted to have another word with Billy Warren anyway. There'd been something about him when I'd seen him in Faces. It wasn't that he was avoiding me or being guarded, it was the exact opposite and that wasn't right somehow. Had he been trying to knock me off track? That day, as soon as he spotted me he came over and, when I mentioned Cartwright, he'd admitted he'd seen him, then told me about the Russian. He probably wasn't lying about that, because Kinane's lad backed up his story but I reckoned he wasn't telling me everything.

'Remind me why we are here,' said Finney as I rang the bell on the front door of his Wallsend flat for the fourth time.

'I just want another word.' I told him.

Billy eventually answered the door looking bleary eyed, even though it was the middle of the afternoon. He pretended to be pleased to see me.

'I've been leaning on your doorbell you dopey fucker,' I told him.

'Sorry man, had my music on.'

'Bet your neighbours love you.'

'Yeah,' he said, 'but they're old cunts. Er… the thing is I've got a bit of company right now, you know.' He meant he was in the middle of a deal.

'That's alright,' I told him, 'we'll introduce ourselves,' Finney pushed passed him and I followed.

When we got in the flat I told him, 'nice place you've got these days Billy, must be doing alright?'

'I get by,' he said, still with the cocky smile.

'We're not taxing him enough,' I told Finney who nodded solemnly.

'Oh no,' he protested, 'don't be like that. I've got overheads and everything. I'm a good little earner, you know that. The boss knows that.'

I was glad he knew better than to say Bobby's name out loud because when we walked into the lounge there was a bleached blonde piece there. She was wearing a short skirt so tight she had to sit with one bum cheek parked sideways on his sofa. Her legs were stick-thin and she was browner than a burns victim. She looked like her make-up weighed more than she did, yet her enormous, very fake breasts stuck out in front of her like the cantilevered roof on a football stand. She looked up but paid us no attention, returning instead to her nails, which she scrutinised as if they were a crossword puzzle.

'Do I know you?' asked an obviously confused Finney because he clearly recognised her face. He seemed a bit baffled that a bird that looked like this could have any place in Billy Warren's life, even as a customer.

'Yeah, you probably do,' she said airily, which confused him even more. She was acting like she was Angelina Jolie and he was a fan.

'She's a WAG,' I told him and when she gave me a dirty look I asked, 'which one are you seeing these days love, Stevie or Gary? Or are you between careers at the moment.'

'I'm a model,' she told me, 'and an actress.'

'Yeah,' I said, 'but were you a model before you started shagging that bloke from Spurs?'

'Well *you* recognised me,' she said sharply.

I nodded towards Finney, 'just because your tits were plastered all over his *Daily Sport* for a week doesn't make you Meryl Streep, now does it?'

Finney was peering down at her now, 'oh yeah, I know you,' and he chuckled, 'you've got a right pair of thruppenny's, haven't you?' he asked her as if the evidence wasn't right there in front of them both.

'Fuck off,' she told him. This was her signal to call her latest lover's name and, right on queue, the toilet flushed noisily and out walked a familiar face to any one who had ever watched Sky Sports or bought a tabloid.

'Bloody hell,' said Finney, 'it's you.'

'Yeah,' mumbled the Premier League player who'd exposed his coke habit as he came out of Billy's toilet sniffing audibly. He was still doing up his fly and I noticed the gold rings on his fingers and the chunky Rolex that gleamed from his wrist. If you added in the diamond earring he probably had twenty grand's worth of bling on him that afternoon just to go and score some blow at Billy Warren's flat. I wondered how much he wore when he really wanted to impress. He turned to his girlfriend, 'what is it babe?'

'These two have been dissing me while you woz like nowhere.'

'Is that right?' he asked, puffing his chest out at me like the hard man he was always telling everybody he was, 'what you got to say for yourselves then?' Either he was completely insane or he was so coked-up already that he actually believed he was capable of kicking Finney's arse, 'you'd better apologise right now.'

I wondered if he'd seen something like this in a movie. If he had, things weren't going to go the way he expected. Belting some sixteen-year-old apprentice or turning a table upside down in a bar and smashing a few glasses, before the bouncers raced across to protect you from yourself, was one thing but threatening us was an entirely different matter altogether.

All I had to do was sigh and Finney moved towards him. The idiot tried to throw a punch which just bounced off Finney's advancing chest. Finney reacted like he'd been hit by a snowball. Next thing, the Premier League's finest had been spun round to face the other way, his arm pulled right up his back. He cried out and tried to struggle but Finney just tightened his grip.

'Steady man,' cautioned Billy but my look silenced him.

'Leave him alone,' screeched the WAG.

'Shut it you noisy mare,' Finney told her and she fell silent. He turned his attention back to the man he held, 'you disgusting cunt,' Finney hissed as he tightened his grip on the footballer, pulling his head back by his ear so he could speak right into it 'all that talent, all that money and what do you do? You piss it all away on coke and slags like that dirty bitch.'

'Get off me,' he was clearly terrified and even the WAG had shut up now, too scared to take exception to being called a slag, or maybe she just recognised the truth when she heard it.

'No,' said Finney, 'I'm going to break your legs, both of them. I don't think a wanker like you deserves to be a footballer.'

Our man groaned in protest as Finney picked him up and dumped him hard onto the floor. He rolled over onto his back and pushed against the carpet with his feet, scuttling backwards across it until he was pressed against the wall.

'Don't go crawling away from me you dirty junkie.' Finney told him. He raised his boot high above the guy's leg.

'Which leg first then?'

'No, no please, not my legs.'

'The right one or the left?'

'Do you even know which one's which?' I asked Golden Boots.

'No, no, don't.'

'What are you on eh? Fifty, sixty grand a week? Got to be. Tell me, tell me now!' ordered Finney.

'Sixty,' he managed to say without taking his eye off the massive boot that was hovering over those famous legs. Amazing, three million quid a year to a scumbag like this. If he wasn't playing football he would be the one selling the coke. 'How many cars have you got?' asked Finney.

'What?'

'How many?' Finney ordered him, 'go on, tell me!'

'F... Four. No five, five!'

'See he can't even remember,' Finney went to stamp on his leg again and the bloke screamed like a nine-year-old girl. Finney stopped.

'What are they then?'

'Eh?'

'Tell me what you got, those five cars. Name them or I'll break your arms too. You won't even be able to wipe your own arse.'

'A Maserati,' he squealed, terrified now, 'a Ferrari Enzo... a... a...'

Finney raised his leg again, 'a what?'

'A Lamborghini Gallardo, a BMW X5 and... and... a Bentley Continental.'

'That figures,' I said, 'break his legs Finney, he deserves it for the Baby Bentley alone.'

'No! Please!'

Finney raised his foot once more, 'disgusting,' he said again and he brought his boot down as hard as he could.

The girl squealed, the footballer screamed. Finney's boot slammed into the wooden flooring between the bloke's knees. The Bentley-driving tosser screamed again and hid his eyes behind his hands. When he finally realised he was unharmed he barely dared to peer out from behind them.

Finney wasn't through lecturing him, 'when Bobby Robson was captain of England he didn't even have a car! Now get out of here and take that minging slag with you.'

'Tell anyone about this and we'll make sure your piss is the most tested in the country,' I told him, 'and my friend here will definitely come back and break both those precious legs.'

Finney let him get up, the WAG followed him sharpish and they both headed for the door.

'Just a minute,' hissed Finney as they reached it and they both froze, 'come here.' Golden Boots reluctantly walked back over to face Finney, 'you haven't said thank you.'

'Eh?'

'For teaching you a valuable lesson,' the Premiership's finest just stared at him like a frightened rabbit, 'well go on then, say it.'

There was a sizeable pause while he tried to find the words, 'Thank you.' His voice was a high pitched squeak.

'What for?'

Another pause.

'For teaching me a valuable lesson.'

Finney nodded, giving them permission to leave. As Golden Boots walked out of the door, I told him, 'welcome to the real Premier League.'

SIXTEEN

....

When they were gone, Billy said, 'Jesus lads, he was my biggest earner.'

'Tough,' I told him, 'sit down. I want a word.'

Finney was clearly still troubled by the footballer's behaviour. 'You know who that was, don't you?' he asked me.

'Yep,'

He shook his head like the world had gone completely mad. 'Can you imagine Alan Shearer behaving like that?'

'No,' I said truthfully, 'I can't.'

I got Finney to search Billy's flat while we went over the story of Cartwright and the Russian one more time. It didn't take Finney long before he came out of the bedroom carrying a large holdall. It contained around three kilos of coke.

'Oh shit,' said Billy.

'No wonder you can afford this place Billy,' I said, 'there's got to be fifty grand's worth there. Now, how did you come by that?'

Billy was evasive at first, for all of about two seconds, until Finney picked him off the ground by his neck and pressed him hard against the wall. I watched his feet kicking a few inches from the floor and let him gasp for breath for a moment before I told Finney to loosen his grip and let him drop to the ground, where he lay choking.

'Now then Billy,' I told him, 'we know you didn't tell me the whole truth about Cartwright so explain it all to me now or I walk out of this door and leave Finney to finish you off. I'm in too much shit to waste any more time on you. You've got one chance.'

'I don't know nothing about it,' the words were strangled in his mangled throat.

'I'll leave you to it then Finney,' I said.

'Right,' he said matter-of-factly and he started to roll up his sleeves while Billy looked on horrified.

'Make sure it's not quick.' I said and walked away. I'd almost reached the door.

'Wait!' cried Billy, 'wait, wait, I'll tell you.'

We had to make the silly bastard a mug of tea to calm him down. He had to grip it in both hands he was shaking so much. At first he was so scared all we could get out of him was apologies.

'I'm sorry, I'm sorry, I was only trying to... .'

'What have you done Billy?' I asked him, 'you'd best tell us and I'll see what I can do for you. It's the only way. If you don't tell us Finney's going to kill you anyway aren't you?'

Finney nodded, 'definitely.'

'It wasn't much, honest,' he assured me, 'we was just trying to do a little on the side. A bit of business, that's all, tax free, you know. I always pay my way with Bobby but this was a chance to do something just for me.'

'And Cartwright,'

'And him too.'

'With this Russian?'

'Yeah, how'd you know that?' and he gave me a look like I was Mystic Meg or something.

'Did you introduce him to the Russian or did he bring him on board?'

'No he was Cartwright's man. I don't know how they met, honest I don't. He brought him down the pub to see me.'

'Why?'

'Because I've known Cartwright for ages and I trust him… I mean as much as you *can* trust people in our game… he's not greedy you know.'

'Not like you, you mean?'

'I was just trying to put a bit aside. I don't want to be doing this all my life do I?'

'What was the plan for the coke?'

'I'd told Geordie ages ago that I could sell a bit more than normal if only I could get a supply from somewhere else.'

'Someone other than Bobby?'

'Well, yeah. I told him we could split the proceeds if he could find me someone reliable.'

'Who were you going to sell to?'

'That dopey fucker you just scared off. All his mates are on it. Half the Premier League runs on white powder. You'd be amazed at who's doing it. They can't get a buzz from nothing else. They've got women on tap, gambling's pointless 'cos they're all millionaires by the time they're twenty, drugs is the only thing that excites them. They all want to be gangsters.'

'That's funny, most of the gangsters I know want to be footballers.' I said.

'Too right,' said Finney.

'Anyway, the bloke's a tool right enough but he's minted and he wants a couple of kilos a time so he can show it off at parties, you know, he wants to be Charlie Big Potatoes. Plus he doesn't know anything about it does he? We can cut it and pass off any old shite as the purest Bolivian and he's none the wiser. He pays over the odds because he can and he don't care. He doesn't know what a pint of milk costs so he's not going to know how much a kilo of coke is. There was going to be a big mark-up, very big. Cartwright said he could get the coke off the Russian and he'd pay him. My bit was disposing of it to my football contacts.'

'And you never thought to ask him where he was going to get the money for that amount of blow?'

'It was none of my business was it?' protested Billy, 'he said he would get the guy his money but that I had to set up the meet with our footballer for that same day.'

'So he'd pay the Russian for the coke and sell it on through you to Golden Boots straight away for a nice, quick profit?'

'Exactly.'

'Did he say why it had to be so quick?'

Billy shook his head, 'That was his business.'

'So you reckon you didn't know he was stealing money from Bobby Mahoney to fund this deal?'

"Course not!' he said, 'I would never have allowed... '

'Yeah, yeah,' I interrupted, 'so what happened?'

'Cartwright dropped the coke off like he said he would. I set up the meet but I had to call it off at the last minute.'

'Why?'

'Well it turned out our client had to play in a reserve match at short notice so he couldn't come by after all. In any case, Cartwright didn't come back,' he shrugged.

'Cartwright didn't come back,' I said, 'because Cartwright was being killed, most probably by his Russian mate.

'Jesus,' said Billy his eyes widening, 'he got killed for a few grands worth of coke?'

'No Billy,' I told him patiently, 'he got killed because of the money he was holding for Bobby, which was worth a lot more than a couple of Ks of coke.'

'Oh Christ,' he turned pale, well, even more pale, 'what can I do? Name it man, anything. What can I do to make this right?'

'Can you contact this Russian?'

'No, it all went through Cartwright.'

'I don't know then Billy,' I said regretfully, 'you're in the shit now and no mistake.'

'I knew I shouldn't have listened to Cartwright,' he was rocking back and forth on his sofa like a traumatised soldier. 'I knew it.'

I let it sink in for a while so even a man as stupid as Billy Warren could work out how much trouble he was in. When he was good and scared I told him, 'okay, you want a way out of this,' I said, 'here's what you're going to do. You are going to phone up Golden Boots and get the deal back on. Only this time you won't be making anything because Finney will be standing behind you when you hand it over. Do that and make a few more deals with the Premiership's finest and we'll see if Bobby will let you be square, eventually, as long as you keep your nose clean.'

'Yeah, yeah, of course man, anything - but how will I get him back in here after what you did to him? He was shitting himself when he left.'

'Which is precisely why he'll come back and buy your coke. Tell him Finney here is still mad at him and if he doesn't want to spend the rest of his days contemplating the tragic, premature end to his playing career he'd better turn up and do the business. It's not as if we'll have trouble finding him. Just remind him we know where he's going to be every Saturday afternoon.'

We were sitting in Bobby's office at the Cauldron. It was sunny outside but the blinds were drawn. It could have been any hour of the day or night.

'So Geordie Cartwright was freelancing?' asked the big man.

'So it would seem,'

'To pay off gambling debts?' added Bobby.

I nodded. 'I'm sorry,' I said, 'I should have known he was chucking his money away.'

'Maybe you should,' he said and he was right to. I was still kicking myself for not knowing about Geordie's little weakness. 'But these days you can lose a fortune without even leaving your house. I've heard about guys pissing away their life savings on the internet while the missus is asleep in the room next door. I never would have imagined it though, Geordie Cartwright brought down by gambling. He was a good bloke, in the old days. It's no way to end up is it?'

'No.'

'And we can't find this Russian? What about your bent DS?'

'He's on it but no, there are no leads yet.'

Bobby was swirling a scotch thoughtfully in his glass. 'What brought these people to my city? What makes them think they can take the piss out of me? Who's feeding them their information?'

'That's what we've got to find out.'

'That's what *you've* got to find out,' he told me firmly, 'and fast.'

It's three hundred miles from Newcastle down to Surrey. We spent most of them in silence. We never had that much to say to each other anyway, Finney and me. I didn't particularly like the guy but then who said I had to - I was just glad he was on my side.

The BBC news came on the radio; the usual mix of economic doom-mongering and British army casualties from foreign wars, ending with a supposedly light-hearted story about some senile, old bloke from Sevenoaks who'd managed to drive his car straight into a river and somehow survived.

Finney listened to the story with interest.

'Why would you call a place Sevenoaks?' he said, 'daft name that.'

'Because there used to be seven big oaks there.' Did Finney ever read anything but the sports pages?

'Used to be?'

'Six of them blew down in the hurricane in the 80s.'

'Really?' he seemed to find that highly amusing.

'Yep.'

'That's brilliant,' he said, 'you call a place fucking Sevenoaks and six of the cunts blow down?'

Finney drove the whole way and I was glad of it. It gave me some time to think things through, away from Bobby, away from Laura, away from the whole bloody business.

After a while I stopped churning over the mystery of Geordie Cartwright and the missing money and started mentally preparing myself for my meeting with Amrein and how I was going to explain the late arrival of the Drop.

'That Amrein,' said Finney like he'd been thinking about it for a while, 'he's on a good screw isn't he? I'm not even sure what we get for our money when you think about it?'

I grunted in a non-committal way that I hoped would satisfy Finney. I didn't want to have to try and explain to him what we got out of the Drop.

The Drop was an insurance policy. It was a bribe and a sweetener. The Drop bought influence and intelligence. It granted us permission to do business on our patch. The Drop was all of those things rolled into one and more.

The organisation we paid had been around for a long time. It had very long arms and a big reach. It didn't have a name and there were no accounts filed in Companies House. We paid cash and we always paid punctually, except for this last time.

So what did we get out of it? Well for starters, if we didn't pay they'd come after us - or at least someone else would, with their blessing. You can look at the Drop as a tax that we stumped up and if we didn't there'd be a big queue of people willing to pay it, as long as they were allowed to take on an operation the size of ours. The Drop was a considerable amount of money but it was nowhere near the profit we made on a yearly basis. If it was, we wouldn't pay it, simple as that. We'd take our chances on our own but we'd know there was a big outfit out there, devoting a lot of time and energy into bringing us down and we could do without that kind of conflict.

It was not all negative though. We got a lot out of the Drop, including some priceless information. Amrein's people had an uncanny knack of finding things out, like the name and address of a key prosecution witness in a trial for example. They could tell us if we were on the hit list of someone in authority or if we had dropped below their radar, if the police had a big investigation going on about an aspect of our business or if they were happy to leave us alone since we were the devil they knew. People don't seem to realise that a lot of organised crime is allowed to exist because the alternative would be disorganised crime, otherwise known as complete anarchy. Police forces don't like amateur gangsters killing each other every week over a bag of heroin. It makes their turf look lawless and their crime stats go through the roof, which means their top boy is never going to become head of Scotland Yard. Instead they prefer to allow somebody who knows the score to control and regulate a bit of illegal trade. That way nobody gets hurt, particularly innocent bystanders. The police hate it when some housewife or harmless middle manager gets their heads blown off because a drive-by went horribly wrong. They are less bothered when a known heroin dealer is found face-down in the Tyne if that's what it takes to keep the peace. The police are like everybody really. What they want most of all is a quiet life and we try to give it to them.

What else does the Drop provide? Influence; political and otherwise. I'm not saying that somebody goes around using our money to bribe cabinet ministers into changing the law in our favour. I'm not saying that. It's a damn sight more subtle but it probably amounts to much the same thing.

Here's how it works. Amrein's people take in a lot of money and some of it is used to make political donations to the major parties. The money doesn't go straight from Amrein. Instead it is filtered through legitimate organisations run by some quite high-profile businessmen. People you have probably heard of. They shell out enough to get the ear of the men in government; lunch with the Party Chairman, an invite to Chequers, that sort of thing. During the course of their discussions they let slip that they might be willing to increase their funding; let's say one hundred thousand pounds a year could be turned into a quarter of a million, if only the government would share that businessman's sense of priorities about the area he lives in. At which point the greedy little eyes of the party chairman light up, he leans over his glass of Chassagne Montrachet and asks confidentially what these policies might be. He is then given a passionate entreaty about how the police waste their time and resources in the north east of England. Why are they chasing a couple of big time gangsters who only seem to spend their time fighting amongst themselves? When instead they could be concentrating on other, more serious matters, such as people trafficking, which we have no interest in, or cracking down on those heroin dealers on the sink estates, or burglary, which is definitely of no use to us at all.

If it's done properly, the mug on the receiving end of this patter will walk away convinced that the legitimate businessman who, after all, has been solidly vetted in advance, has an eccentric but touchingly heartfelt belief in, for example, the provision of community bobbies, who will patrol the streets every night, catching burglars as they shin down drainpipes with bags marked 'swag' on their shoulders. Frankly, he will deduce that for a quarter of a mill in the party coffers, humouring the old boy seems a small price to pay.

A discreet missive will then go out to the Chief Constable of Northumbria Police Force, telling him that the Home

Office wishes to see an increased clean-up rate on burglaries. There may even be a follow-up phone call, containing a hint that their Chief Constable is on the shortlist the next time the Head Boy at the Met implodes and there's a vacancy. Overnight the emphasis on solving a certain kind of crime shifts. Officers once earmarked to investigate the supply of blow and Es in nightclubs suddenly find themselves stepped down and redirected to intelligence gathering on burgling crews. A few months down the line and a notorious gang of burglars is arrested, charged then convicted, receiving lengthy jail sentences for their evil deeds. The Police Commissioner will even go on television to boast of his officers' success in combating a crime he himself finds personally abhorrent. He will then do everything in his power to ensure footage of this interview finds its way to the relevant minister in Whitehall. It's all perfectly legitimate and everybody involved, kids themselves, are somehow fulfilling a public need. Meanwhile we carry on earning our living largely unmolested.

You might not believe it works like that but I'm telling you that it does. Why do you think people like Bobby Mahoney carry on operating for so long when everybody out there knows who they are?

We parked the car down by the river next to a little hotel I'd stayed in once before. Not today though. I wanted to be in and out of there as quick as you like. We walked through Shepperton. It was a small place, just a couple of pubs and restaurants, the hotel and some houses normal people couldn't afford. Not much to do but pretty enough. The place seemed to exist purely to give prosperous southerners somewhere respectable to retire to.

'It's a bit quiet,' said Finney, looking about him at all the trees that lined the route between the centre of the little town and Amrein's property.

'I don't know,' I said looking about me at the old houses bathed in a sunlight that rarely ventured as far north as Newcastle, 'I quite like it.'

You'd be forgiven for assuming a place like Shepperton is about as far removed from the world of drugs and protection money as it is possible to be and it is, at first glance, which is why we bring the Drop here. What's the alternative? Handing it over in disused factories or at the top floor of an NCP car park after dark? That's strictly for the movies. Those places are usually covered by CCTV or full of junkies shooting up. Not the kind of venue you'd choose to hand over a lot of cash safely.

Here, at the weekend, the population is swelled by amateur boatmen mucking about on the Thames, but during the week it's quiet. It was the kind of place where the vicar walked by and said good morning to strangers, somewhere there'd be a cricket match played on Sundays. I had to remind myself that we were on our way to meet the most dangerous man I knew.

SEVENTEEN

···

Amrein's house was at the bottom of a country lane. All the houses here were set back discreetly from the public road and we had to press a buzzer at the gate. I looked up directly into the CCTV camera so they could get a good look at my face, frowning impatiently as if this was a routine drop and I didn't have the time to be messed about. There was a loud buzzing sound and the gate clicked and swung in on its hinge. We walked up the long, gravel driveway and Finney looked about him at the vast expanse of manicured lawn on either side.

'Jesus,' he hissed, 'how the other half live eh? You could put a full size football pitch on that lawn.'

'I think you should suggest it,' I said.

Our destination was a huge, white-painted house at the end of the drive. It was tucked away just far enough round a natural bend that it couldn't be seen from the road. Lord knows how many rooms Amrein had. He was clearly doing pretty well for himself, on the back of us and others.

Two of Amrein's men met us at the door and patted us down, quick and professional like. They even took our keys, car keys, wallets and my silver Cross pen, leaving nothing that could remotely be used as a weapon. The only thing they didn't touch was the case Finney was carrying. He wasn't going to let go of that until he was face to face with Amrein.

We were shown into a large dining room with a highly-polished table that would have comfortably seated a dozen for dinner. Sunlight shone through the enormous French windows at the far end, picking out little specks of dust that hung in the air.

'Mister Amrein will be here presently Mister Blake,' said one of the men who'd patted us down. We stayed on our feet and, sure enough, a few moments later, Amrein himself arrived with yet another bodyguard and a third man who didn't look like muscle. Amrein was a small man in late middle age. His hair was receding around a widow's peak and he wore wire-framed spectacles on his long, angular nose. His thin, bloodless lips were pressed tightly together like he meant business. Amrein looked more like a banker than a villain. Some times I think the world is run by small men in wire-framed spectacles.

There were handshakes and I introduced Finney. If Amrein was put off by the presence of Bobby's scariest employee, he chose not to show it.

'Gentlemen please,' he said amiably as he held out a hand to indicate we should each take a seat around the table. Amrein's English was flawless, without a trace of accent. He'd been educated somewhere very expensive but he still had the look of a foreigner. Was he Swiss, Belgian, Nordic? He was impossible to place. Amrein sat with us while the bodyguard stayed on his feet behind him. Finney handed over the case and left the talking to me.

'Thank you,' he said, immediately handing the case to the bodyguard who in turn gave it to the third man. He opened it on a small table and began to silently count the contents, expertly skimming the notes with his fingertips.

Amrein smiled slightly, like I'd just given him a belated birthday present. 'Of course I don't have to mention that it is late.'

'A week late,' I admitted, 'we had a problem,' I wasn't looking to concede much more than that, 'which is why you will find an additional payment,' I assured him.

'Most gracious,' he dipped his head to acknowledge this, 'but I am afraid the issue is rather more complicated than a little… ' he seemed to be searching for the right word, '… interest. The funds were already allocated,' he told me, 'committed elsewhere. The lateness of the payment caused me considerable embarrassment. There was some… ' again he thought for a while before choosing his words carefully, '… consternation,' he spread his palms and in one gesture seemed to convey the fact that he was a reasonable man who had been placed in an entirely unreasonable position. I knew I had to walk a thin line between winning him over and acting like his poodle.

'Mister Mahoney understands your liquidity issue and he appreciates your position, which is why he sends his apologies, along with a generous commission to alleviate the inconvenience caused.' God I was starting to sound just like Amrein. We both glanced over at the man who had been counting. He finished and gave Amrein an affirmative nod, as if to confirm the generosity of Bobby's additional bung. My guess was all of it would go straight into Amrein's pocket without being kicked up to any one.

'Notwithstanding,' he said, in that lawyer-speak he favoured, 'this must never be allowed to happen again. You do understand that? Bobby Mahoney does understand that?'

'Of course,' I told him, 'that's why I am here personally. That's why Mister Finney has accompanied me today.'

'Good,' he said as if the matter was concluded, 'would you walk with me in my garden?'

I nodded, assuming he didn't just want to show me his rhododendrons. Finney and I both rose with Amrein and the bodyguard opened the French windows for us to step through. Amrein looked at Finney, 'would you excuse us for a time?' he asked. Finney looked at me for confirmation and I nodded. Amrein and I walked out onto a manicured lawn so immaculate he must have had a platoon of Eastern-Europeans attacking it each morning with nail scissors.

'There are some matters I don't like to discuss in front of employees. Ours or yours,' he told me.

'Please,' I urged him, 'speak freely.'

'I will. Thank you.' He assured me, 'the Drop has never been late before. Not once. Not in all these years,' we were walking across the lawn, heading for a clump of trees by a wall at the far end, 'of course you don't have to give me an explanation,' he said calmly but I was left with the impression that it would be much better for us if I did.

'A little local difficulty,' I assured him.

'Local difficulty?' he mulled that ambiguous phrase over, clearly unsatisfied by it.

'An employee of ours turned out to be untrustworthy,' I said, bending the truth a little.

'Mmm, I see.'

'All organisations have them,' I said, 'just as all major businesses have problems from time to time. That's not what matters. What matters is how you deal with those problems.'

'And you have dealt with this… problem?'

'It's in hand,' I assured him.

'Good,' he said firmly. 'There is one other thing; Serious and organised.'

'Expressing an interest in us?'

'Yes,' he said calmly, as if an old family friend had been asking about our wellbeing. My heart sank. One of the reasons we paid the Drop every month was to avoid the close attention of SOCA. Perhaps DI Clifford was right after all.

'They aren't even policemen,' I said dismissively, 'just glorified customs officers,'

'Technically speaking, they are not actual police officers - but that will be of little consolation to any of us if they succeed in bringing Bobby Mahoney down.' He was right and I was more worried than I let on. Because SOCA was relatively new, it was still a bit of an unknown quantity. 'We've heard they've opened another file on Mister Mahoney. They developed a strong interest in certain aspects of his business following that very public and regrettable incident in Ibiza.'

'That was more than two years ago,' I reminded him.

We'd been looking for a share of the action in Ibiza for some time. The Scousers had had the whole island tied up for years and were making a fortune. The place had a steady supply of clubbers looking for Es and blow and the customs officials were woeful; undermanned, under-resourced and frankly uninterested. Keeping it all to themselves was just being greedy, though we realised the Scousers wouldn't see it that way. We reached an accord of sorts, eventually, but not before they lost a couple of their lower level men in a very public shoot-out with some of Bobby's young turks. Apparently both sides were driving parallel at high speed along the highway, trying to shoot the shit out of each other, till one car overturned, killing the Scouse dealers. It was all very unsubtle and it took quite a bit of sorting out but we got there in the end. Why? Because of the cash and because, whatever you might see in the movies, nobody really wants to be at war. They just want the money to keep on flowing like water.

'Everybody knows what Bobby does,' I told him, '*proving* it is the issue and nobody has ever come close to that.'

'Indeed, which is why their new-found interest concerns us,' Amrein cleared his throat and continued, 'what do they have? Why are they sparing man hours when they cannot afford to waste time on no-hope investigations? In short, what have they got on Bobby Mahoney?'

'Are these rhetorical questions?' I asked, 'or are you going to tell me what you've found?'

'They have an insider,' he said, 'somebody in your business, someone who has enough information to put a case together against Mister Mahoney that will lead to a conviction, and a very long prison sentence.'

I was stunned. 'There are only half a dozen men in our organisation who could even attempt to do that.'

'Yes,' he said, 'and you are one of them.' He looked me in the eye and smiled, 'that should narrow it down for you when you begin your investigation. You are responsible for Mister Mahoney's security are you not?' I nodded, 'then you have work to do, if you are to keep him from dying in prison.'

'We pay handsomely for this kind of information,' I reminded him, 'is that all you have for me? What about a name?'

'We are working on that, I can assure you,' it was my turn to look unimpressed, 'for some time now we have been attempting to infiltrate SOCA,' he continued, 'recently we succeeded in getting a man into HUMINT, the department responsible for Covert Human Intelligence.'

'I know what it is. They turn and run sources,' in other words they recruited rats, sometimes for money, sometimes for the promise of a place on the UK equivalent of the witness protection programme. It was just like DI Clifford had described it. Most often these guys turned against their bosses because they had been caught red-handed doing something that would get them twenty years on its own. Then they received a simple choice: go down for the rest of your natural life or grass up your boss. The only trouble with choosing to be a rat is the strong chance the boss'll find out about it and shut you up forever before you get near a trial. 'So if you have discovered there's a rat, why don't you have a name for me?'

'It's not that simple, as I am sure you will appreciate. Our man must move carefully. He can't just tap into a computer file with the word 'sources' on it and look for a name he recognises. If he opens a file on Bobby Mahoney his accessing of it will immediately be logged and he will be exposed. His enquiries must be more circumspect.'

'What if these circumspect enquiries take too long? What if our rat disappears into the programme next week and Bobby is arrested the next day?'

We'd all be fucked, me included. That's what.

'I'm afraid that's a risk you must live with, for now.'

'Easy for you to say,' I said.

We had reached a glade and I noticed for the first time that, set back against the far garden wall was a little summer house. It had glass windows, an ornately carved door and a timber roof. It looked old, like it had been put up long before by a dutiful family man, so his wife and children could take afternoon tea here overlooking the lawn. It was hard to imagine a world as genteel as this could ever have existed.

'Beautiful isn't it?' Amrein noticed I was looking at the summer house, 'and so quaint, don't you think, the product of a more innocent era. I think that is why I appreciate it so.' We both stood in silence for a moment in front of this expensive little folly then he said, 'thank you for coming down,' as he offered me his hand and I shook it. 'I will look forward to your next visit, which I feel certain will be more timely.'

'It will be.'

He turned to look me in the eye, 'I do hope so,' he said it placidly, with a hint of the implied regret he would feel over what he would be forced to do if it wasn't. As threats go it was very low key but he used those four simple words masterfully. They left me in no doubt that another late drop would simply not be tolerated.

The journey back gave me ample time to think about our new problem. As if Cartwright's murder and the disappearance of our money, coupled with DI Clifford's personal vendetta against us, wasn't enough for one week, I now learned SOCA had got themselves a top grass in our firm. This could bring us all down. We kept on top of the law, following each new development as if we and the police were opposing superpowers in some new version of the Cold War. The Supergrass had been discredited by the abuses of the 80s, when grasses were often paid for duff info that was invariably chucked out on appeal. Lately though, they had come back into vogue, with the Met landing some high profile villains on the back of their testimony. The key was linking the word of the grass to other, more substantial evidence. That was how you got your conviction.

If a hit man, say, is caught, found guilty and handed down a longer-than-life sentence for multiple murders the police still aren't too happy, because he is basically just a hired hand. It doesn't get them any closer to the man who gave the order for the hits. The bloke who pulls the trigger, well he could be anybody and there are always plenty of others willing to fill his shoes. The police know this, so they offer the hit man a deal to rat out his boss.

One guy had a sixty-year sentence cut to four, so the story goes. If it all works out he gets a new ID and the Met get the crime boss they've been after for decades. The dubious morality of letting a hit man back on the streets looking for a job, when all he's qualified to be is a hit man, is usually forgotten in all of the euphoria.

If SOCA were after Bobby and they had a man on the inside, I had to find him and fast. I couldn't rely on Amrein to deliver that name. Even if he was really trying, it might take too long and I was sure there was something he wasn't telling me. So, we were on our own.

'What did Amrein have to say while you had your walk in the garden?' asked Finney, once he realised I wasn't going to volunteer the information.

'He wanted to know why the Drop was late.'

'And what did you tell him?'

'I said we had a little local difficulty, that it was nothing to get bent out of shape over, that everything was under control.'

Finney grunted, 'He believe you?'

'Who knows?' I said, 'maybe.'

I wasn't going to tell Finney what else Amrein had mentioned; the man SOCA had on the inside of our firm. Like I told Amrein, there were only half a dozen men with enough information to really bring Bobby down and Finney was one of them.

EIGHTEEN

....

I was expecting a sombre mood at the Cauldron and was more than a little surprised to hear the sound of raucous male laughter coming from the bar, which was closed to the public this early. We'd still got problems, big bloody problems and I wondered what was going on to make everyone so damned cheerful. I walked in to find Bobby, Jerry Lemon, Finney and Mickey Hunter all having a bottle of Newcy Brown together. Bobby spotted my incomprehension and walked over to me.

'You're back in my good books son,' he said, slapping a huge hand on my shoulder, 'for now.'

'Really?' I asked, trying not to sound pathetically grateful, 'why's that then?'

'That little tip you gave me the other day?' he said, eyes sparkling.

'What?' I asked, more than a little surprised, 'the one you said was a non-runner?'

'That's the one,' he nodded at me, then actually winked, 'well it came in didn't it, and at very long odds,' and he smiled a beatific smile, before repeating, 'very long odds,' then he patted me on the back, 'have some Geordie champagne,' He thrust a cold bottle of Broon at me and, even though I don't normally touch the stuff, particularly this early, I took a big swig.

I supposed I should have been delighted but I had mixed feelings. On the one hand I was glad that a plan I concocted for Bobby, to rob a casino that was a little less secure than it should have been, had come off. It was on the outskirts of town, in a side street, not many passers-by, and we knew they kept too much cash on the premises. Most importantly, the idiots weren't paying protection money to us, or anyone else. I figured it was prime to be turned over at the end of a busy night. We put a lot of surveillance work into that place but when I initially went to Bobby, he rejected my idea.

He must have been desperate for some extra cash by now to replace the Drop, because he had been willing to take what he had seen as too big a risk. From the way Bobby was talking, it reaped us a better-than-expected dividend. There's nothing like an earner to get you back on the right side of the boss and now he was all smiles - and the rest of the crew might even remember why I was on the payroll in the first place, now they had some money in their pockets because of me. I was an ideas man and none of them ever had an idea in their lives, except Bobby.

The thing was, even though he had given my plan the green light and set a heavy duty crew onto it, he had done it without telling me, which meant he still didn't fully trust me. It continued to trouble me even as I downed my beer and laughed along with the rest of the boys.

'I do like a successful day at the races,' laughed Bobby.

'Aye,' said Hunter, 'and here's to our very own king of the tipsters,' they raised their glasses to me.

I had to content myself that my plan had led to a successful job, with no casualties or arrests. It wasn't perfect, but it would do for now.

Bobby did get round to asking me quietly about the missing money and I answered him honestly, 'nothing conclusive yet, but we are turning over every stone, believe me.' He just nodded but didn't say another word.

I had a couple of drinks that day, more than a couple if I'm honest, as I moved from place to place trying to fathom what was going on around me. I got one of our lads to drive me around on the pretext of following up some leads but really it was just an excuse to leave Bobby, Finney and the rest celebrating on their own while I got the fuck out of it.

When I finally got back that evening, Laura had, as usual, opened a bottle of white wine. Before I met her, I only ever used to drink beer, now it was a nightly ritual to lose our stresses in the bottom of a bottle of Pinot Grigio. I chose one of our big wine glasses and poured it almost to the top, sitting down heavily on the couch.

'Bobby still giving you a hard time?' she said breezily, as if Newcastle had just lost again; another thing she didn't seem to understand the seriousness of.

'That's one way of describing it.'

Laura leaned forward in her chair, tilted her head to one side and gave me her wide-eyed empathising look.

'What's happened?'

I wasn't sure how to put it into words but then I figured I should try. There was something about her pitying, supportive look that spurred me into making an effort, 'suppose you had an idea, a good idea but your boss rejected it as… too risky… in the context of an overall business plan?'

'Right.'

'Then, because things changed, he suddenly decided that

your idea was worth the risk after all, so he went ahead with it and it worked.'

'Right,' she said, frowning, 'but that's good isn't it? If it worked I mean.'

'But…'

'There's a but?'

'There's a but. He didn't tell me about it, implementing my idea that is. Until he had actually gone ahead with it.'

'Right,' she kept saying 'right' but this time she said it doubtfully, 'I'm not sure I…'

'Which means he still doesn't fully trust me, don't you see?'

'Well,' she thought for a moment, 'not really. I mean could he not just have forgotten to tell you?'

'No.'

'It's not all bad surely? I mean, you'll get credit for this idea won't you?'

'Yes but that's not what I care about right now. It's the trust thing that's worrying me.'

'I know, I do know what you mean,' she said enthusiastically, 'it's like with the Watson case, when Thomas wouldn't hand it over to me without continuing to be involved. It was like he just didn't trust me to do a good job.'

'No,' I said, 'no, with respect to you Laura, it's not like that at all. The consequences could be very different.' I actually wanted to say 'why does it always have to be about you?' but I managed to not go down that road.

'Alright,' she said, through gritted teeth, 'if you think your boss doesn't trust you any more, here's a radical idea…'

'What?' She gave me a challenging look, 'no, seriously I'm interested, I really am, honestly. What's your radical idea?'

'Think the unthinkable,' she offered enigmatically.

I creased my eyebrows together, in what I hoped was a silent way of conveying the question, 'what the fuck are you talking about?'

'Leave.'

'Leave?'

'Yes,' she said, almost triumphantly, 'why not. If you've had enough, just leave. Go and do something else.'

'Like what?'

'I don't know. What would you like to do?'. She was acting as if I could turn up for work at an RAF base tomorrow and start flying Tornado jets instead.

'In case you haven't noticed, my Curriculum Vitae is a little unorthodox; graduated from college, worked for a notorious gangster… That's it. Somehow I don't think that's going to get me into Microsoft.'

'I'm only saying… '

'What?' I interrupted her, even though she hates that, 'what are you saying? You've used that big lawyerly brain to help me and you've come up with a whole new radical idea? Leave? Simple as that, leave?'

'Why the fuck not?' she raised her voice.

'Why the fuck not? I'll tell you why the fuck not, because I don't work for Marks & Spencer or the local council. Get real. You don't leave a job like mine. It doesn't fucking happen. Bobby won't allow it. He's not going to give me severance pay and a bloody carriage clock.'

'Why?'

'Why?' I almost screeched, 'are you fucking mental? Because I know all about him and his business. He's not going to let me go off on a gap year, is he? Don't you know anything?!'

'No!' she was still up for a fight, 'I don't know anything and why is that? Because you never tell me anything! I don't know what you do for Bobby because you keep telling me I don't want to know. I know you're not a gangster because you've told me that one over and over again but it seems you do work for one. So what does that make you then eh? Sometimes I think I don't even know you at all.'

'You didn't mind me working for a gangster when it was all about corporate hospitality and money coming in, expensive presents and holidays in Thailand. You didn't mind me working for Bobby Mahoney then. You even like the guy.'

'I do not!'

'Yes, you do. Don't deny it Laura. Wandering over to chat with him, flirting with him at his parties, laughing at his jokes, so some of that gangster glamour rubs off on you.'

'I laugh at his stupid jokes because he's your boss.'

'Bullshit. It's so you can go back to your chambers and tell everybody you've had a barbeque at Bobby Mahoney's house, the home of Newcastle's most wanted. With all of those divorce cases it's the closest you'll ever get to any real crime but believe me, it isn't so glamorous when you're stuck right in the middle of it.'

'You're a complete bastard sometimes, do you know that?' she said and she climbed off the sofa, 'you're so cold and you can't even see it.'

'Is that a fact?'

'I don't want to hear any more of this,' she said and she walked out of the room.

'For fuck's sake,' I called after her, 'is that what you tell the judge when he says something you don't like? "I don't want to hear any more of this" and then you walk out, eh!'

NINETEEN

....

I'm not some exercise Nazi but I do like to stay in shape. That morning, I did my twenty minutes on the treadmill then some weights then changed for the pool. It wasn't busy.

It was a modern place, all pristine, white tiles and new age background music that sounded like whales shagging. There were a couple of wrinkly, old blokes sitting around and a middle-aged wifey doing lengths. I'd done mine and was about to go into the sauna and sweat for ten minutes but I stopped by the side of the pool to get a drink from the water fountain. It was near the entrance to the female changing rooms and as I bent my head towards the water I saw her. As my head was at an incline, I got a view of her that started with her bare toes and rose up over her slim, tanned legs and into the white 'V' of her bikini bottoms, a little pair that just about covered her lady bits. It was enough to keep her decent but there wasn't a lot in it. Her stomach was still tanned from months of travelling abroad during the summer and her breasts swelled over her bikini top in a way that left one of the old geezers in the pool standing there with a look of undisguised longing on his face. Her long, blonde hair was tied back for the pool.

'Hello David,' she said, smiling at me like she knew exactly how good she looked.

'Sarah,' I said, resisting the temptation to say something cheesy like 'you've grown'. I just about managed to avoid sounding like Sid James and instead I said, 'haven't you got a proper swimming costume?'

She frowned at me like she didn't understand what I was talking about, but she knew alright. Sarah Mahoney had to know the effect she was having; on the middle aged bloke pretending to read by the pool as she dropped her towel on one of the loungers next to him, on the old geezer who had stopped staring at her and shuffled off out of there sharpish, in case he got a lob-on for the first time in years, and on me. She must have known the effect she had on me

I was not supposed to find Sarah Mahoney distracting. In fact an inner voice in my head was already cautioning me that even acknowledging the fact she had grown into a very hot young girl indeed was tantamount to suicide. Bobby did not want his pride and joy, his most precious possession, letched at by members of his crew. Bobby, though he makes a lot of his money out of the sex trade, would prefer it in fact if Sarah didn't have a boyfriend at all until she was at least 25, then immediately married the first nice, harmless guy who took her out. He's from the old school and what he definitely, categorically does not want is one of his closest men eyeing her up in the swimming pool. Not when he has tasked him with looking after her tonight at her big birthday party.

There is however one slight problem, something that Bobby is in fact quite unaware of. Sarah Mahoney has the hots for me, has done for a very long time. Sarah has fancied me since she was about 16 in fact, before her cute, hard-bodied figure lost all of its puppy fat. I know this because she has made it clear. As crystal. She doesn't come out and say the words exactly but she can flirt for England.

'So,' she said, as she laid her big bath towel out on a lounger, 'what you doing?'

I shrugged, 'nothing too knackering, a few lengths. I come here the same time every morning.'

'Yeah,' she said, smiling, 'dad said.'

Of course. I'd mentioned it to Bobby. He must have told her in passing and, the first chance she got, she came down here.

'So what are you doing here?' I'm not sure what I'd do if she said 'I came down here to see you' but thankfully she took the politician's tactic and answered a different question to the one I actually asked.

'Dad bought me a membership.'

'Nice birthday present.'

'It was a graduation present,' and she smiled, 'he got me the car for my 21st.'

'Oh yes, the car,' I was with him the day he picked it out for her down at the dealership, making sure it had every possible safety feature, 'happy birthday by the way.'

'Thank you.'

'Do you always get up this early for a swim on your birthday?'

'Couldn't sleep.'

I nodded and looked around us at the plush surroundings of the spa, 'not a bad gift for graduation either is it? I got a wallet when I got my degree.'

'Yeah, well, Dad was chuffed. I was the first to get one in our family.'

'Same here. Of course your old man doesn't realise they aren't worth the paper they're written on these days,'

'Oi.' she said.

'I mean, a trained monkey can get a degree in Media Studies.'

'True,' she agreed, 'but I got a first in Business Administration,' and she tilted her head to one side and gave me a shitty look like she was saying 'shove that up yer arse mate'. I have to admit it's a look that made her seem cute, pretty and endearing all at once.

'So,' I said, 'you swimming or just here to pose? I'm not sure the old guys in here can cope with the excitement.'

'At least you admit it's exciting,' she said, 'I'll go in if you'll keep me company.'

I shrugged, 'I'm not in any hurry,' I said, knowing that I should have just told her I was finished then left. It would have been a lot safer but I told myself it was okay, because the one thing I was absolutely not going to do was put my job and my life in jeopardy by fucking Bobby Mahoney's only daughter. Bobby Mahoney's gorgeous, young daughter, I thought to myself, as she sashayed ahead of me into the clear, blue water. Bobby Mahoney's gorgeous, young daughter who fancies me, I concluded, as I watched her cute little bum disappear beneath the surface. She leaned forward and was off, gliding effortlessly through the water.

We did a few lengths then swam over to the corner of the pool where they have three strong jets that you stand under. The water comes down so hard it massages your neck and back. It's almost as good as a real massage. Normally it's just relaxing. Of course it's a bit different when you have a stunning blonde in a tiny white bikini standing opposite you with water cascading down over her breasts and shoulders. The little sod, I thought, she definitely knew how bloody good she looked.

All I got from her was that Mona Lisa smile, 'how's your wife?' she asked, knowing full well that Laura and I were not married.

'Fine,' I answered, 'busy, you know.'

'Busy,' her face creased up while she pretended to contemplate this for some hidden meaning, 'poor you,' she said, like I was being neglected.

'Since I'm busy too... ' And I shrugged under the water as if it was no big deal.

'Course,' she said, like I was telling her porkies. She kneaded her neck under the water jet with her hands and this pushed her chest out. I had to force myself to look away from her breasts. The water was making her nipples hard. They were jutting out through the material, which was sticking to her like clingfilm, 'great here isn't it?'

'Yes,' I said.

'Wonder if you can hire it privately,' she said as she looked at the small collection of oldies around us, 'you know, for an hour or a morning or something.'

'Dunno,' I said, 'it would cost you.'

'Yeah,' she agreed, 'worth it though. You could go skinny dipping.'

I laughed at the notion.

'Would you,' she said, daring me, 'go skinny dipping?' and her eyes locked onto mine. They were deep and blue and inviting.

I didn't answer her for a while. 'Maybe,' I said and she smiled, 'if I was on my own,' I added.

She frowned, 'where's the fun in that?'

'Come on,' I said, 'I'll buy you a coffee.'

'We can't go yet, we've not had a smelly shower.'

'We've not had a what?' I asked.

'Follow me,' she told me as she climbed out.

She stood behind me, leaned past me and pressed the button on the shower, then pushed me gently into it until I was under the spray. 'Tell me that's not fantastic,' she challenged.

It was fantastic. I'd assumed the two open shower booths behind the pool, half-hidden by a walled enclosure, were just conventional showers, which was why I'd never been in them. It turned out they were a part of the spa experience I'd been completely unaware of. The water felt great. It was hot and bracing and smelled of something girly.

'Breathe in,' she ordered and I did, 'what's that smell like?'

'Like a tart's window box,' I told her and received a thump on my back for my troubles.

'It's ylang ylang and patchouli.'

'I think I know them. A couple of Thai hookers?' and she gave me another thump.

'Stay there,' she ordered when the water stopped automatically after a couple of minutes. She leaned forward again so she could press the other button. It was harder to reach and I could feel her left breast pressing against my back for a moment. Next thing, I was shocked by a fine spray of ice cold water.

'Jesus,' I hissed.

'What about that one?' she asked.

I breathed in, gasped more like, 'Polo mints,' I told her, barely able to say the words.

'Sort of,' she said, 'it's mint anyway. Wakes you up doesn't it?' I stepped out once it was over, 'admit you like my smelly showers,'

'Not bad,' I said, 'although I don't want to be reeking of My Ding-a-Ling and Me-Julie when I'm out with the lads tonight.'

'Ylang ylang and patchouli,' she corrected, leading me out of the way by my arm so she could get in under the hot spray she'd just activated, 'and don't wind me up. You're not out with the lads. You are coming to my party and you know it.'

'Party?' my turn to frown at her, 'what party?'

'Cruising for a bruising shit bag,' she told me.

'Oh yeah,' I said dumbly, 'now I remember. We are all off to Pizza Hut and your dad's ordered a cake with some candles. I think he's hired a clown as well.'

'Only clown there tonight will be you. We are off to Café 21, appropriately enough, for dinner, then those who aint too old to cut it, will be going clubbing.'

'Yeah, I know,' I admitted, 'your dad told me, asked me to arrange a driver for your lift home.'

'He didn't!' her little face dropped at the thought of a gnarled gangster like Finney picking her up outside some cool club, 'who is it?' I gave her an apologetic look and spread my palms in a 'little old me' gesture, 'really?' she seemed thrilled, 'honestly?'

'Fraid so.'

'Things are looking up!'

TWENTY

....

I bought Sarah a birthday breakfast and we talked a bit about college.

'Good but I was ready to leave.'

Her plans now she'd graduated.

'Haven't a clue.'

And her last boyfriend.

'Dumped him, turned out he was an arse. I've had it with boys, from now on it's only men.' She smiled at me when she said that.

Then I watched her climb into her new car and drive off, waving at me. I told myself she was a top lass and would make somebody a great girlfriend one day but it wouldn't be me. Bobby would never stand for it - and besides, there was Laura. Almost forgot about her for a moment.

There was no point in standing there like a Muppet. I still had to find Bobby's money.

'You're wearing your Paul Smith jacket?' Laura asked me, as I buttoned it up in front of the mirror. She said it as if I had just openly put a packet of condoms in my pocket right there in front of her, 'for Sarah Mahoney's 21st?' she made it sound like I was going to dig the garden in it.

'Bobby's taking us all to Café 21. I told you, got to look the part.'

Laura was sitting on the sofa, legs folded up under her, dressed in her standard uniform of shapeless, baggy fleece and ancient leggings. She used to be smart when I first met her, always dressed immaculately.

Was it my imagination or was she eyeing me suspiciously as I buttoned my best jacket in front of the mirror?

'Will you be back after the meal then?' she asked.

'No,' I was trying to sound patient, 'I'm on babysitting duty, I told you that too. I have to make sure Sarah doesn't rape or murder anyone or get roasted by the Newcastle youth team.'

'Why do you have to be the one to keep an eye on her?'

I sighed, 'because he asked me, because he trusts me with her. You could have come too, I said.'

'And I told you I have to visit mother.'

'I'm only saying, it's not like you aren't invited or anything.'

'Well,' she said, because she couldn't refute the logic of that, 'I just think it would be nice if you weren't back late tonight that's all.'

'Laura, it's her 21st birthday and she's going clubbing. How early were you home on your 21st? I have to look after her so of course I'm going to be late. Jesus!' I scooped up my keys and left her to it.

Bobby bought everybody a really nice meal at Café 21. There weren't too many of us; a little bit of family, what little he had left, a young brother who had nothing to do with the firm, an older sister, there was the birthday girl of course and three of her friends, all lasses, since the boyfriend had been given the heave-ho, Malcolm, a bloke who worked for Bobby's firm in a non-muscle capacity who'd known Sarah since she was a baby, and there was me.

'Where's the wife?' asked Sarah.

'Visiting her mum in hospital,' I said, 'the old bird's not well.' I didn't tell her I was secretly pleased Laura couldn't make it. Aside from the fact I had to concentrate on making sure Sarah was safe tonight, I really didn't fancy a whole evening of Laura moaning that it was getting late, then getting the huff with me when I poured her into a taxi and sent her off home on her own. Since we'd got back from holiday she'd not been too much fun to be around. Sure she was worried about her mother but the old lady'd been ill, on and off, for years. She was one of those thin, scrawny women, who looked like an undernourished sparrow but I'd have put money on her reaching ninety and still moaning about her health everyday along the way.

During the meal, I made a big point of drinking nothing but mineral water and I watched my manners. We then said goodbye to Bobby and the oldies and I drove the four girls off to the club in the Merc.

We fought our way through the crowd and into the roped-off VIP section I'd sorted for Sarah. It was one of our places so I made sure there was plenty of comped champagne, the decent stuff, not the house shite we bought in bulk. The bottles of Veuve had been laid out nicely for our arrival in big, silver ice buckets with their best glasses and some table decorations. All of this made me pretty popular and Sarah kissed me on the cheek, 'thanks David,' she said.

'No bother,' I told her and it wasn't. I mean I hadn't actually done any of it myself. I'd just told them to make the tables look nice.

Sarah said 'I can't believe you're not having any.'

I shrugged, 'I'm your designated driver.'

'I know, but you can have one glass,' and before I could argue she poured one and handed it to me. We were all sitting in a half moon shaped banquette set against the wall, overlooking the dance floor. We toasted Sarah's birthday and the girls proceeded to get well lashed-up. Before too long, they'd finished the champagne, so I ordered some cocktails then they hit the dance floor. They tried to drag me on there with them but I said, 'later, got to see someone right now.' Sarah did a mock pout. 'Won't take me long,' I assured her.

I then went to find Palmer, the guy I'd entrusted to discreetly watch my back all night while I was watching Sarah. He was hard to spot at first, being all of five foot eight in his socks. Palmer was a muscley Scot without an ounce of fat on him. He was a calm and soft-spoken bloke, particularly considering he was from Glasgow.

'Anything?' I asked him.

'Nah,' he shook his head, 'quiet. Got a man watching the CCTV and he's not seen anything unusual. There are no new faces that concern us and nobody's been watching you. I would know,' he would as well, he was ex special forces and very, very good, which was why I'd convinced Bobby he was worth having on the payroll. He certainly didn't look like he'd been in the SAS but you tend to find that with those guys. They are often small and not that hard looking, until it matters. I liked the fact that he didn't look like a big psycho. With Finney you could always see him coming. If you spotted him having a pint you'd know straightaway what he did for a living. Palmer meanwhile wasn't so obvious, he'd blend in anywhere and you wouldn't notice him until it was too late.

Of course, he'd have been more expensive if he had left the army voluntarily, instead of being booted out suddenly about six years ago, when he went a bit mental, but that's another story. 'Nobody's been eyeing up the girls any longer than a normal man would stare at a fit bunch of lasses like that, if you don't mind me saying it.'

I was relieved, 'I don't mind you saying it but you might not want to put it like that if Bobby's around or he'll cut your dick off.'

Palmer laughed, 'yeah, well, you aint her dad are you and you have to admit that Sarah is a tidy bit of…'

'Just do your job,' I snapped at him without meaning to.

'Sure,' he said calmly, 'I am doing it.'

'Good,' I said and left him to it. I walked away wondering why I'd reacted so strongly to some pretty mild words about Sarah and her pals. I put it down to stress.

I returned to the banquette and sat there on my own for a bit, sipping yet another mineral water, badly wanting a real drink after my one glass of champagne but knowing it wouldn't be a good idea. I reminded myself things weren't going too badly. I'd had it first hand from Palmer that his blokes had spotted nothing out of the ordinary. Sarah was having a good time and she wasn't even aware I had a crew watching her every move. Just as well, she'd have gone mad if she'd known. I just hoped no lagered-up bloke pinched her arse on the dance floor because, if I didn't get there before Palmer's lads, the silly bastard wouldn't know what hit him.

Two of Sarah's friends looked like they'd pulled, leaving Sarah and her mad mate Joanne alone in a corner of the dance floor. The last time I'd seen Joanne she was at work, standing on the bar down at Buffalo Joe's in a black bikini and a Stetson, twirling a flag and marching along, miming the words to *Amarillo* with four other girls, while the crowd in the bar went crazy; only in Newcastle.

I could still see them both from where I was sitting. I was faintly amused by the obvious effort they put into making every move seem effortless. They adopted a studied cool but every turn and wiggle looked choreographed. Why is it girls always know the moves to every dance and blokes don't have a clue? I wondered if they all went to secret practice sessions we didn't know about.

Joanne leaned forward and said something into Sarah's ear and she laughed. It was good to see her enjoying herself. Akon and Kardinal Offishall's *Dangerous* started blaring out from the speakers, an appropriate song for Sarah Mahoney if ever I'd heard one.

They piled into the back of my car, giggling like a couple of teenagers. The birthday cocktails made them braver than normal and they were pretty cheeky when they were sober. I knew I'd got to be on top form to avoid looking like a total cock in front of them.

I put Ne-yo on and turned the volume up a couple of notches for *Closer*.

'Blimey,' said Sarah, 'I thought you'd be cranking out U2 or something!'

'I spend my life in clubs, I hear this stuff more than you do.'

'Bit old for it aren't you?' asked Joanne.

'Are you walking home?' I asked her in return and she laughed. 'Can't believe you don't think I'm down with the kids…'

We passed another club that used to be an old warehouse. It had a big, metal ladder stuck to the side with thick, steel steps that zig-zagged up the side of the building and there was a ledge at the top right by the roof.

Sarah leaned forward and said, 'See that ladder… ow!' it sounded like Joanne had thumped her one, 'Jo, you total slag,' but she laughed anyway and a belt on the arm wasn't going to stop her from telling me, 'Joanne fucked a bloke at the top of that ladder!'

'I did not! You bitch!' and she was laughing as well, the two of them were like a couple of breathless hyenas behind me.

'Is that right Jo?' I asked nonchalantly, as if she had just admitted to kissing a bloke beneath Grey's Monument.

'No it fucking isn't!' she pretended to be horrified.

'Yeah,' said Sarah, 'she fucking did.'

'I did not!' and she could hardly breathe through laughing, 'if you must know I just sucked him off!'

'Oh, that's alright then,' I deadpanned and we all cracked up.

When they finally calmed down Joanne said, 'I can't believe you told him. I think I should tell him something about you now.'

'Oh I don't think so.'

'I do,' I said, genuinely intrigued.

'Ha, you see,' said Joanne, 'he wants to know.'

'Well that's fine because you don't know anything about me. Nothing recent anyway. I've been a good girl.'

'Really?' Joanne was teasing now and I was beginning to get a little sick feeling, in case she told me Sarah had been shagging some spotty student or footballer. I realised to my horror that I'd be jealous. I told myself I was just being protective of her but I wasn't sure I was really buying that argument. You can fool just about anybody but you can't fool yourself.

'Last Christmas, we had a girls' night in. We got really pissed on wine and played 'Marry him, Fuck him, Shove him off a cliff',' said Joanne.

'How does that work then?' I asked, none the wiser.

"Chelle started nominating blokes we knew and we all had to say whether we would marry them, fuck them or chuck them off a cliff,' and she giggled.

'Oh right,' I got it now.

'We went through all the boys our age, then some celebs,' then she paused, 'you don't even remember do you?' she asked Sarah who seemed blissfully unperturbed by this.

'Remember what?' she asked.

'Well, you had been on the vodka as well as the wine,' was all Joanne offered by way of explanation.

'What are you on about?' said Sarah testily.

'What you said when *his* name came up.' I couldn't see Joanne, so I don't know if she nodded in my direction but it was clear that she meant me. At this point Sarah literally gasped.

'Joanne,' she made her friend's name into a warning.

'You really can't remember can you?' she was loving Sarah's discomfort now. I must admit I was taking a pretty big interest in this myself. I was quietly confident that I'd made the 'fuck him' list not the 'shove him off the cliff' pile but either answer was going to be embarrassing for both of us.

'I don't even remember playing the game,' said Sarah a little snootily, 'I was mullered.'

'What do you think you said?' urged Joanne, oblivious to Sarah's mounting irritation.

'No idea,' replied Sarah, 'could have been any of them or all three. No offence,' the last two words were directed towards me.

'None taken,' I replied like her answer didn't matter but of course it did matter, quite a lot. I put it down to male ego.

'Want me to tell you?' giggled Joanne, making the words into a sing-song, playground style taunt.

Sarah had clearly had enough of this and wasn't going to allow herself to be embarrassed by her mate, 'I should imagine,' she began, 'knowing me and how I am when I've been on the vodka,' there was a moment's pause when she summoned up the nerve, 'I probably said that I would fuck him.' She said the last bit defiantly, daring either of us to take the piss out of her.

I got a strange, conflicting sensation of being embarrassed, chuffed and not a little bit turned-on all at once because I knew from the sudden silence that she was telling the truth.

My feeling of euphoria didn't last long however, 'no!' squealed Joanne, like it was the funniest thing, 'that's not what you said!'

Great, so when Sarah's really drunk I join the ranks of the lemmings. Shit.

Joanne continued, saying the words slowly and deliberately, 'what you actually said was, and I'm quoting here, "I'd fuck him *then* marry him, so I could fuck him some more!" Joanne started pissing herself laughing but Sarah had gone deathly quiet in the back of my car. Joanne had finally achieved the unachievable, embarrassing Sarah to the core of her being and I knew why. The M word. Marriage. Marriage wasn't cool or something you could shrug off because you were drunk, like a loose comment about a shag. Marriage was love and kids and setting up home together, for life, it was the real deal. Blimey.

Joanne finally stopped laughing, perhaps realising she'd gone a bit too far for her friend's liking. The situation needed remedying, if we were not going to have the longest, most embarrassing journey home imaginable.

Luckily we had to stop at a red light, so I could safely turn round and face them both. I glanced briefly at Sarah who looked like someone had just slapped her hard in the face. She didn't want to look at me directly. Instead I looked Joanne in the eye, put on a serious looking frown and asked her outright, 'you mean you wouldn't?'

And she roared with laughter, instantly breaking the spell. 'Eeh you cocky bastard!' she cried.

'I must be slipping,' I added for effect, before turning back and easing the car away through the green light. I could hear Sarah laughing in the back again too. I was glad I'd spared her blushes and I made a conscious effort to stop feeling so bloody chuffed with myself.

TWENTY-ONE

....

When I dropped Joanne off at her mum's house, Sarah got out of the back seat and climbed into the front passenger seat next to me. She wound down the window and called after Joanne's retreating rear, 'laters bee-yatch!'

Joanne span round and flicked the Vs up at her before calling out, 'be good you two and if you can't be good be careful!' then she did a pretty clear mime of a blow job, pushing an imaginary cock into her mouth with her hand while making the inside of her cheek bulge outwards with her tongue.

'Classy,' I said quietly as Sarah wound up the window.

'I only hang round with her 'cos she makes me look good.'

'I can see that,' I acted like the little conversation we'd just had hadn't happened, 'you enjoy yourself tonight then pet?'

She smiled happily, 'yeah, I did. It was great. You? Sorry you couldn't drink.'

'No harm in it this once. Told you, I spend my life in clubs.'

When I got her home, the gates to Bobby's house were wide open and I drove on through, parking up so she didn't have far to walk up the gravel driveway, but not right by the windows. 'Don't want to wake your dad,' I said.

'He won't be asleep,' she told me, 'not till I get in.'

I wouldn't sleep either if I was him.

'So where is it then?'

'Where's what?' I asked.

'My present,' she said, 'unless you are gonna carry on pretending you've not bought me anything for my 21st?'

'Glove compartment,' I said quietly.

Without another word she opened up the glove compartment and took out the long, thin box I'd put there at the beginning of the night. 'Mmm, it's beautifully wrapped,' then she got suspicious, 'did you get Laura to do it?'

'Why would I do that when I could just flirt with the lass in the shop until she did it for me?'

'Thoughtful,' she said and she took her time unwrapping the gold paper, opened the box and took a long look at the watch I'd bought her. It was a nice gift, just expensive enough to thrill a 21-year-old who wasn't expecting something that good, but not so extravagant that Bobby or Laura were going to want to take it in turns to beat me to a pulp for buying it. It was just the right side of innocent.

Sarah didn't say anything at first. I was about as sure as I could be that she was going to like it, so I said, 'what's the matter? Not up to much?'

'It's great and I fucking love it, thanks!' and she did and that also gave me more pleasure than it should. Sarah wrapped her arms round me and gave me a big, friendly hug that could just about be described as platonic. 'You coming in? Dad'll be chuffed if you do.'

'No he won't,' I said,

'Yes he will,' and she laughed self-consciously, 'you can have one drink with me.'

'I'm driving.'

She stuck her tongue out at me and called me boring, 'got to get home to the wife have you?' she knew how to press my buttons.

'She's not my wife,' I said uselessly, 'but I do have to get home, yes.'

'Oh-kay,' she said it in a sing-song voice and started to climb out of the car, 'thanks for my pressie, it's beautiful.'

'Not every day a girl turns 21.'

'So true,' and she was out of the car and gone, except she wasn't, because there was a blur of movement as she went round the front of the car and was suddenly standing by my window. I wound it down and she said, 'thanks pet,' and held her hands wide for another hug and when I didn't react she said, 'oh come on, give me some sugar,' in her mock-American accent. I put an arm out through the window and she wrapped her arms around me and this time the hug was for real. God she smelt so good and I knew I should let go of her, but it was way too nice.

Her voice was muffled by my shoulder but I could still make out every word when she said them back to me, 'not every day a girl turns 21,' she agreed and there was a second's hesitation, 'and I've not even had a birthday kiss… from any one.'

'A birthday kiss?' I asked, like I was a simpleton.

'Yep.'

'Right,' I said and before I could think of anything cool or dismissive or safer to say than that, she pulled her head out of my shoulder, placed her cool palms gently on either side of my face and quietly said, 'Just one,' and softly planted her lips against mine, then kissed me long and slow. And I did nothing about it, even though I knew this was the dumbest, most dangerous thing I'd probably ever done in my life. I just let her go on kissing me, even when she slid her tongue into my mouth, in fact I kissed her back, until

I forgot everything; who I was, who she was, who her dad was, somebody called Laura, everything. And just when I was liking it the most, she stopped.

'Phew,' she said, like she had enjoyed it too, 'time to say goodnight.'

'Goodnight Sarah,' I managed.

'It's true by the way,' she added, as she walked slowly away from the car, 'what Jo said.' And she laughed, loud and embarrassed like she couldn't quite believe she'd admitted it to me then she was off, walking down the gravel drive way - but not before turning back and shouting at me, 'mull that one over on the way home to your wife!'

And I did. Of course I did, I didn't think about anything else if I'm honest, which is exactly what she wanted, the distracting little bugger.

When I got home Laura was still up. She was sitting on the couch all by herself and her eyes were smudged with tears. I instantly tried to work out what I had done to cause them or, more accurately, I thought about what I had done that she knew about that could have caused them.

'What's the matter?' I said while my panicked, inner voice told me not to be such an idiot. She wasn't outside Bobby's house hiding in the bushes. She hadn't bugged my car. Had she?

'It's mum,' she said softly, 'she's dead.'

TWENTY-TWO

....

The funeral was pretty grim, even by normal standards. I always hate them but Laura and her sister seemed to be competing in the waterworks stakes and I had to play the dutiful partner of the grieving daughter, which made me feel like the proper hypocrite, as I didn't like the old girl and she never bothered to hide the fact that the feeling was mutual.

The service seemed to drag on and on and I began to feel completely trapped. There's just something I can't stand about funerals. It might sound obvious but it's the way they have of making you think about your own inevitable demise. They seem such a pointless exercise. The person doing the dying has gone and it's very sad but they are not coming back and we've got to carry on. So there's no point moping about it. Some people are comforted by funerals but I think they are a load of old bollocks. All those long-lost relatives crawling out of the woodwork, the old ones treating it like a day out, barely able to hide their glee that they are still here and they've outlived someone else. Then there's all the inane chit-chat about a good turn-out and the weather being nice on the day, as if the person in that little wooden box is aware of any of it.

Death might be an inevitability but I don't want to think about dying. Funerals always make me want to go out, get pissed and fuck somebody, just so I can prove to myself that I'm still here. Must be some sort of putting-two-fingers-up-at-death thing. I guess that's not something I should admit to but you are what you are and there's no changing it.

'I feel as if you haven't been here for me,' said Laura as she leant forward on the couch to face me. Since the funeral we'd had a number of conversations about the way Laura had been feeling. Mostly she'd been feeling bad and it turned out this was usually my fault. I was beginning to wonder if she had been secretly visiting a therapist who had urged her to 'tell your boyfriend how you feel. Make him feel shit instead'.

'But I have been here for you,' I protested. And I had. I mean, I wasn't there every night obviously. I was still trying to find out what had happened to Cartwright and Bobby's money but I wasn't on it twenty-four-seven like I should have been. I'd made sure Bobby knew Laura's mum had died and that she had gone a little bit mad as a result, so I was home quite a bit in the evenings even if I then went out again later, after she was tucked up in bed. He was okay about it, considering. Maybe it reminded him of losing his missus and how Sarah must have felt at the time. I had to tell Finney as well but they both agreed to keep it to themselves.

We'd had lots of long conversations, Laura and I, that dragged on for hours about how her mum's death was such a shock and how she had always been there for her daughter and how Laura didn't know how she was going to manage without her mother, which I didn't really get, as Laura had been an adult for some considerable time now. I couldn't really understand how her mum's death had been such a shock either, considering the years of illness she'd had. It had been a bit of a shock to me admittedly but then, I'd thought the old bird was putting it on.

'Yes,' she said, as if I had somehow proven her point, 'you've been here physically.'

'What's that supposed to mean?'

'But I don't think you are really here mentally.'

She was right. I wasn't - and with good reason. I was usually mulling over how to get myself out of the shit I was in and, to be fair to me, we had been talking about the same old stuff every night for ages. I'd made the same suggestions; take some time off work, go and see your old friends from Uni, stay with your big sister for a while? I'd also exhausted all the usual platitudes associated with bereavement. 'Perhaps it was for the best Laura, you wouldn't have wanted her to suffer Laura, she would have hated not being a hundred per cent Laura, but, after a while endlessly going through the same topic, who wouldn't let their mind wander? Blokes aren't like women. We don't want to regurgitate everything a million bloody times.

I felt a bit pissed-off at Laura for saying I was unsupportive considering what I could see every time I looked up from my sofa. On one of my bookshelves a space had been cleared for the squat china urn that contained the last remnants of Mrs Angela Cooper.

'Do you mind?' she'd asked as she'd brought her mum's ashes home from the crematorium, holding them like a little baby, 'it's only for a while.'

'Of course not,' I'd said because at that moment, she'd looked like any objection from me might very likely push her over the edge into some form of grief-related madness. So she'd moved my books and placed the urn on the shelf with great reverence. I had to stifle a grin. After all, a bookshelf was probably an appropriate place for *Angela's Ashes*.

After a while though, their presence had started to irritate me. I couldn't think of anything more morbid to have in my flat than my girlfriend's late mother's remains. Why couldn't her big sister, her dim husband and their two overweight children take the bloody urn? It was meant to be a temporary home but just how temporary is temporary? A week, a month, two years? The problem was I couldn't think of any subtle way of asking Laura, 'when do you think you'll be shifting your mother off my bookshelf then?'

I didn't want to get into another row with Laura about my lack of support so I asked, 'do you want me to stay home tomorrow night instead of going to the match?'

I'd hoped the offer of staying home would be big enough to placate her without actually having to go ahead and do it. I figured she would say something like 'that's really nice of you but you love the football, you should go.' Then I could say, 'are you really sure, I honestly don't mind missing it just this once.' If I was really lucky this might even lead to make-up sex. Any sex would have been preferable to the complete drought I was currently experiencing. Clearly funerals didn't have the same effect on Laura's libido as they did on mine.

What she actually said was, 'do you mind not going?'

Yes, I thought.

'No,' I said.

'Really?' she asked

'Course not,' I said.

Shit.

I was driving through the city on my way home when Sarah called, 'I need a hunky man,' she told me.

'Any particular reason,' I asked, 'or have your batteries gone?'

'Cheeky,' she said. 'It's a crisis.'

'Broken a nail have we?'

'No. I've got a flat tyre and I need a hunky man to rescue me. I'm a damsel in distress.'

'You're in luck, I'm doing a special offer on damsels this week. It's two for the price of one. I'll throw in a dragon slaying too if you ask me nicely.'

'Sounds like good value, trouble is... '

'Yeah.'

'I'm down at the Metro Centre,' she said, like she was wincing at the level of the favour she was asking, 'you're not by any chance passing through Gateshead on your white charger right now are you?'

'No,' I said.

'Oh.'

'But I could be.'

'I knew there was a reason why I love you.'

'You mean apart from my good looks, charm and raw sexuality?'

There was a slight pause for effect, 'has someone been telling you you're good looking?'

'Do you want this tyre changing or not?'

'Yes please!' she trilled, 'love ya.'

She told me where she was parked and I set off to the Metro Centre, a place I would normally have avoided like the plague. With its acres of shopping hell, all under one big roof, I'd normally rather have a tooth pulled than go there voluntarily.

When I pulled up beside her she climbed out of her car. She looked very good in her skinny jeans.

'Those the jeans you've been banging on about?'

'Seven Jeans,' she sang and she swayed her bum round and out at me, slapping her rump like they do in the R&B videos, 'you like?'

'They're okay.'

'Just bought 'em. Perfect fit, wore them out of the shop.'

I found that strangely sexy and I didn't even know why.

I think maybe it was because Laura would never have done something that spontaneous. I looked away from her and surveyed the problem, 'yep,' I announced solemnly, 'your diagnosis is correct, that tyre is definitely flat.'

'Thank you doctor, now are you going to change it for me?'

'Nope.'

'What? I thought this was damsel day. Am I not a damsel then?'

'Yep, you're a damsel right enough but, if I change that tyre for you, you are going to be late for the match.'

'I'm already late for the match. I've had to phone ahead so they'll save me some dinner in the box.'

'I also phoned ahead. One of my guys is on his way down here. He will take your keys, change your tyre and drive your car home for you. As soon as he gets here, I'll drive you to the match just in time for your prawn sandwiches. Your dad or Finney can run you back afterwards.'

She beamed at me, 'you think of everything,' then she sighed, 'why are all the good men taken?'

'Because there aren't that many of us and you've got to be quick to land one.'

We were inching towards the ground. The traffic had slowed to a virtual standstill from the sheer number of fans striding purposefully towards St James' Park.

'Can't believe you're not coming to the match,' she sighed.

'I know, neither can I, if I'm honest, but Laura's a bit upset about her mum, so I said I'd give it a miss.' I knew I'd have to sit there with her again in virtual silence while she sniffed and moped about her ma, like she'd done every day since the old lady'd croaked. I'd hoped she might ease up a bit after the funeral, but it actually seemed to get worse then because she didn't have any arrangements to distract her. Let's be brutally honest, her mum was old and ill and she'd had a bloody good innings. I've seen a damn sight more tragic and sudden deaths than her's I can tell you. Besides, life is for the living.

'We'll probably be shite tonight,' consoled Sarah, 'the back four wanted shooting last time and the food in the box isn't great these days. It was sausage and mash last time,' she sounded amazed. 'I mean they put "balsamic-glazed, onion gravy" on the menu, but it was still bangers and mash.'

'Slumming it eh? Count yourself lucky,' I told her, 'when I was a kid, I used to be happy calling into the Metro Café for a plate of chips on my way up to the ground. I could only dream of sausage and mash. No executive boxes back then and, if there had been, I couldn't have got in them. I was a Gallowgate-ender, standing in the rain. There wasn't even a bloody roof.'

'Must have been worth it to see Jackie Milburn though?' She told me.

'Oi, watch it you. You're not too old to go across my knee.'

'You wish!'

I dropped Sarah at the ground and wound the window down to shout, 'behave yourself,' at her as she walked off.

'Don't worry, I'm a good girl,' she called back cheerfully.

'Yeah, right,' I said but she had already turned her back and was disappearing into the crowd.

I got a real pang as the cold air hit me through the opened window. I could smell the onions frying in the burger vans nearby and I was picking up individual shouts from the crowd as this great stream of humanity, all clad in black and white stripes, ascended the stairs to the turnstiles. I was gutted to be missing the atmosphere as much as the game.

I found myself wanting to be with Sarah tonight too. She'd really developed and not just physically. She'd grown up a lot at college and what had come back was smart and funny and able to banter away with the best of them. And she was beautiful, that had to be admitted. The sixth-former with the teeth braces had long since been transformed into a babe with a cracking figure. Mustn't think like that though. The one thing I was not going to do was roll around with Bobby Mahoney's daughter - no matter how tempting it might be. I did keep having to tell myself that, over and over, ever since Sarah kissed me after her birthday party. Bobby loved his daughter more than anything, I reminded myself constantly, and the one thing he didn't want was her hooking up with a member of his crew. Bobby liked me but not *that* much. He'd got a doctor in mind for Sarah or, failing that, Prince Harry. If I told him I had nothing but the finest intentions for his daughter, there would be no cosy arm around the shoulder while he discussed me inheriting the family business. More than likely the conversation would end in a short walk off a big cliff.

I took my time getting home, calling in on Palmer to see if he had made any progress looking for our Russian friend.

'If he was in the city I'd have found him by now,' he told me.

'So he's not in the city.'

'That's about the size of it.'

'Keep looking,' I told him.

When I got home, I opened the door of my apartment to be greeted by darkness. What the fuck? Where was Laura? I turned on the light and there was a note on the coffee table telling me she'd gone to see her big sister. 'Jesus Christ,' I said aloud. I tried to remind myself they were both grief stricken, but Laura had clearly forgotten how she'd pleaded with me to give up the match so I could stay in and take care of her. It was too late to go back up there now.

I swore and went right out again. There was a Chinese restaurant over the road. It was as good a place as any to eat on your own and I could get goal updates by text message from Sarah.

After my meal, I returned to my empty flat, still feeling mightily pissed-off. I walked into the kitchen, opened the fridge and took the top off a cold beer, swigging from the bottle. I was about to sit down in the lounge but figured I'd hang my jacket up in a wardrobe first. I put the bottle of beer on the coffee table, slipped off my jacket and carried it to the bedroom. I opened the door, turned on the light and that's when the bloke hit me.

TWENTY-THREE

....

Luckily for me, it was a glancing blow or that would have been the end of me. I must have reacted just in time, raising my left arm instinctively to parry, because the heavy cosh he was carrying skidded off my forehead and he dropped it from his gloved hand. The impact was still hard enough to draw blood, rattle my brains and give me a sick feeling deep in my stomach.

My attacker was a weasel-faced, gaunt guy about my height. He didn't look like conventional muscle and if he had been I'd have been dead by now, so I figured he was there just to turn my place over. He was looking for something.

That's all I had time to think about. Weasel-face grabbed me round my neck and slammed me back through the bedroom door. Christ he was strong for such a lean guy, with a grip like a vice. He must have been a rock-climbing cat burglar. His fingers were digging into me, closing round my throat until I could barely breathe. As he forced me backwards, I grabbed his arm and tried to dislodge it but I couldn't shake it loose. It didn't help that he was pummelling my head with his free fist as he propelled me back down the hall, knocking me half-senseless in the process.

I fought back of course, hitting him a couple of times in the body and the side of the head but I couldn't get him off me and I was starting to feel the heat in my face as he was cutting off my airway. He was staring at me like he was mightily pissed-off I'd disturbed him. He must have known he had to finish me or he'd be a dead man.

He was still pushing me backwards and we ended up in the living room struggling. He knocked me right back to the far wall and I still couldn't prise him away. I was kicking out at his shins, trying to knee him in the bollocks and punching him but nothing I did seemed capable of stopping him. Eventually, he virtually lifted me off my feet and I felt the wall slam hard into my back, knocking the wind out of me. His fingers squeezed tighter round my throat. I knew I was in serious shit now. He was going to kill me if I didn't do something, and quick.

I snaked my free arm out across the wall and stretched as far as I could, desperate to reach the heavy wooden plaque with its ornately-carved elephants that we'd brought back from Thailand. I'd only nailed it up there a few days ago so I knew it had enough weight. I could give him a smack round the head that would fell anyone and then I could kill the fucker with it. I'd almost blacked out but I was an inch away from it, and he suddenly realised what I was trying to do and gripped me even tighter round the throat. I was choking so bad I couldn't extend my arm any further. It was no use, I couldn't reach it. I strained for it once more and felt the back of my fingertips graze it but again he lifted me off my feet then bumped me away from it, slamming my head against the side of the shelf nearby for good measure. I managed to get a punch into the side of his head and it was a good one. He listed slightly, off balance for a moment but kept his grip round my throat and I knew I would black out soon. In desperation, I flailed my free arm out to the opposite side and my hand connected with the only other item in the flat that I could now reach.

As my hand touched it, I pushed my other palm up under his chin and gouged my thumb into the flesh just above his Adam's apple. He shrieked in pain and loosened his grip round my throat for just a second. I pushed his arm away and butted him hard in the nose with my head, drawing blood and forcing him back just a little. He blinked as he tried to clear his head and I knew this was my only chance. I grabbed the heavy object from the shelf and, as he came rushing back at me, I twisted my body. His arm was lower than it should have been and I brought my weapon smartly across in a nice, hard, fluid arc, until it crashed into the side of his face with a sickening smash. Weasel-face screamed like I had just put twenty thousand volts through him and the urn I was holding smashed on impact into dozens of sharp pieces, sending a spray of blood into the air.

Everything seemed to move in slow motion then, including the blood that gushed all over the bastard's face and slid down the side of his head, but that too was instantly obscured by the huge cloud of ash that followed it. The late Angela Cooper seemed to hang in the air for a second before covering him. The ashes were all over his face like a swarm of insects and he went down screaming, frantically wiping his eyes. He must have been wondering what the hell I had hit him with.

That was all the energy I had left. I dropped to the floor like someone just took my batteries out and ended up propped up against the wall like a puppet with its strings cut. As the room started to spin and turn slowly black, I was vaguely aware of Weasel-face scrambling to his feet and I thought oh fuck, he is going to finish me now, he'll have all of the time in the world to do it as well and I've nowt left to give, but instead he got up unsteadily, clutching his face, screaming like he was on fire and leaking blood big style. There was a thin shard of china sticking out of the side of his face and all I could think was what a shame I didn't get the chance to wedge that into his neck. He gave one last shriek and ran from my flat.

The last thing I remembered, before I passed out, was trying to reach my mobile phone from my pocket and being dimly aware that Laura's mother had slowly fallen to the ground around me in a great big slate-grey plume of ash; thousands of her component particles now littered my carpet. It was funny; I'd have said she'd be the last person in the world to save my life.

I lost track of time or what I was supposed to be doing. Then, I didn't think about anything any more. There was just silence and a great big, comforting cloak of blackness.

When I came round, Finney was laughing at me. 'Don't worry Brains,' he said, 'you've not lost your looks,' his great, ugly mug was peering down at me and then Sarah, all concern, was at my side, a damp tea towel in her hand, which she proceeded to dab with great tenderness to my bruised and battered face. The cool water helped me to get my senses and, though it was an effort to talk, I asked them.

'How'd you find me?'

'You called me,' said Sarah. I had no recollection of this at all.

'Did I?' and I wondered why I had dialled her and not Laura or some more useful and muscular presence for the aftermath of a fight, like Finney. I put it down to delirium and she continued to look at me with the concern of a mother for a small, injured child.

'You couldn't really speak, just sort of gurgled, so I asked if you were at your flat and you said yes, then it all went quiet. I was in the car with Finney anyway. He was dropping me off at Joanne's, so we shot round here straight away.'

'You're just lucky the match was over,' said Finney, 'else you'd have waited ninety minutes for the cavalry.'

'You break the door in?' I asked.

'It was open,' he said, 'whoever did this left in a hurry and, judging by your carpet, he was bleeding like a stuck pig. What happened?'

So I told them. There didn't seem any reason not to tell the truth, all of it. Finney listened to my slightly delirious description of the fight then he looked at the mess on the living room floor. 'Well,' he said approvingly, 'looks like your mum in law come in handy.'

And then I remembered what I hit Weasel-face with. I got a slow and horrible realisation that I had used the irreplaceable ashes of my girlfriend's dead mother as a weapon and, even now, they were all over my carpet, mixed in with bits of broken china and a burglar's blood and most likely trodden right into it all by Finney's size twelves.

'Oh fuck,' I said and Finney laughed an evil laugh.

'I'd say your problems are just starting.'

Sarah was a diamond, she really was. She insisted Finney helped me to my feet and got me sitting up on the couch. She made me a cup of tea, which I sipped while I slowly came back down to planet earth. Finney rang in a brief, coded description of what had happened to me to Bobby who was apparently very relieved to hear that I was more or less okay. In a strange way, I realised that me being targeted like this might just end any lingering suspicion he might have had about me.

Only when she was sure I was not suffering from major, life-threatening concussion did Sarah transfer her attention to the mess that littered the floor of my flat and began to tidy it up for me. 'I'm sure we can sort all this out before Laura gets back,' she said doubtfully. I appreciated her lying to me like that, especially as I felt like shit. I had bruises everywhere. Even in my crap state I knew there was no chance of making this scene look any better than it did but Sarah tried, bless her.

I was beginning to think I must have done something really bad in a past life when at that point, with impeccable timing, Laura walked through the front door, keys in hand. She spotted Finney standing there then looked at me slumped on the couch and asked, 'what's the matter?' before I could answer she finally noticed Sarah kneeling on my carpet, a brush and a dustpan in hand, into which she had managed to sweep roughly a third of Laura's mother.

The noise Laura made was almost indescribable.

TWENTY-FOUR

Laura never really did calm down, not even later while she was packing her night bag and storming out on me. Obviously I did not expect her to be happy that her mum was scattered all over the carpet like a carton of Shake-n-Vac but I did expect her to listen to me while I tried to explain what had happened. I told her I'd had no choice but to fend off my attacker with the only object to hand, which just happened to be the urn, but she treated me as if I had somehow contrived this whole scene deliberately. She regarded Finney and Sarah as if they were a couple of teenage accomplices who had wrecked her parents' house during an illicit party while they were away on holiday.

'I realise you weren't there Laura,' I said in what I thought was my most reasonable tone, considering my head hurt like a bastard and my throat had almost been crushed, 'but it's not as if I had a choice of weapons.'

'That's it,' she half screamed, half sobbed at me, 'make a bloody joke out of it!'

'I wasn't,' I said, 'he almost fucking killed me.' And even completing that small sentence was a supreme effort. I didn't have the energy to fight any one else tonight, least of all Laura. If I was expecting a modicum of concern from my girlfriend it was distinctly absent. Instead she shooed Sarah away from the pile of ashes and insisted on sweeping it all up herself, then she looked around uselessly, as if she somehow expected the urn to have magically reformed so she could put the ashes back into it. Realising there was nowhere for her mother to go, Laura's bottom lip started to tremble and she seemed on the verge of a bout of cataclysmic weeping when Sarah, who had at least anticipated the problem in advance, appeared from the kitchen, clutching a large, clear plastic dish complete with a bright blue lid. The sort of thing you'd pack sandwiches into for your lunch and maybe an apple.

'I realise it's not ideal,' conceded Sarah and Laura scowled at us both.

When she finally left, with a Tupperware dish full of her mum, she told me, 'I can't stay here. I'm going back to my sister's. You can call me tomorrow.'

When she'd gone, Sarah said, 'I wouldn't call her,' and she looked me right in the eye, 'not a word about you, no concern about whether you're alright or not. That's not love,' and then she realised she was probably out of order and added quickly, 'I know, it's none of my business. I'll shut up,' but to be honest I was starting to think she might have a point, so I didn't scold her. I couldn't even be arsed to contradict her.

Sarah tried to get me to go to bed before they left but I refused. I needed to think. I had to try and work out what was happening. Who was behind this raid on my flat? What was he looking for - and why would he rather kill me than risk being caught? I assured Sarah I would be okay and I told Finney to drive her to her mate's house. He didn't argue. He'd seen men in a far worse state than me and, considering he thought I was some sort of pseudo intellectual woofter, he was probably finding the whole thing pretty amusing.

They'd been gone thirty minutes when the doorbell rang. I figured it was Laura, who'd seen the error of her ways and come back to apologise but I wasn't taking any chances. I'd already brought the gun out of its hiding place in my golf bag, a location I had chosen because there was no way Laura was ever going to look in there. I moved very slowly, very quietly from the sofa and walked over to the door. I made sure I didn't stand right behind it in case they shot-gunned me through the wood. I leaned over and peered through the eye slot then I opened the door.

'What's going on?' I asked, bemused now.

'I wanted to make sure you are okay.'

'But you know I'm okay,' I told her.

'No I don't,' Sarah explained it to me as if I was a slow learner, 'I only have your word you're okay, and you might have a concussion. You need someone with you for the night,' and she must have seen the worried look, 'don't panic. I'm not here for a shag. I don't think you're really up to that.'

'Thanks.'

'I got Finney to drop me outside Joanne's and got a cab back here as soon as he left, so you don't have to worry about him or the rest of the boys talking.'

'It's not him I'm worried about.'

'Well I won't tell dad unless you do. Now are you going to let me in or what?'

I held the door wide and she walked in. I slipped the gun back in the golf bag without her seeing it.

'You've not got any overnight things.'

'You can lend me a T-shirt,' she said, 'now sit down on that couch while I boil the kettle.' She walked off into the kitchen and, though I had wanted to be alone to work all of this out, I had to admit it was nice to see her. I was touched by her concern for my wellbeing, which was a marked contrast to my girlfriend's mood.

She made me cups of sweet tea, for energy. I never take sugar but there was something warm and comforting about them. We stayed up and talked for a while and then she told me to get my battered head down. We argued about who should get the bed and who the couch. She eventually wore me down by insisting I was an invalid who needed a proper pillow and mattress.

'I'll be fine on the couch with a blanket and a cushion,' she said.

'Well,' I admitted, 'we've got plenty of those.'

She told me she was going to watch some brain-rotting, reality TV show that I wouldn't want to bother with. She was right on that score.

Sarah went into my bedroom and came back dragging the spare duvet from the bottom of my wardrobe where I told her it would be. She'd taken off her jeans and shirt and was now wearing something of mine instead. I'd told her she could have one of my shirts, anything she liked the look of or felt comfy in but, even in my concussed state, I did a double take when I saw her.

'Christ lass,' I said, 'do you do this sort of thing deliberately?'

'What?' she asked innocently. She let the duvet cover fall out of her arms then stood straight and turned to one side like she'd just reached the end of the catwalk at a fashion show, 'I thought you'd approve.'

Of course I approved. She looked amazing, standing there in just my Newcastle shirt.

I shook my head, 'Peter Beardsley never looked that good.'

'I should hope not.'

'I'm off to bed,' I said, before I did something really stupid.

She laughed, 'night-night pet.'

My sleep was restless, filled with nightmares in which I was repeatedly attacked by faceless assassins who would never give up or drop no matter what I did to them. I finally woke, feeling like I'd been run over by a lorry, to the smell of sizzling bacon coming from my kitchen. At first I was confused. Laura never made me that kind of breakfast. She disapproved of anything that didn't come in a bowl containing nuts and inedible chunks of oats welded together. Also, she wasn't really one for cooking. For her, preparing a meal meant saying 'why don't you book us a table at… ' then inserting the name of the latest fashionable eatery that had just opened on the Quayside.

By the time I'd surfaced, Sarah had set my kitchen table with cutlery, plates and a little ovenproof dish onto which she'd piled bacon, sausages and eggs. There was toast, proper butter and a bottle of ketchup. Sarah was still wearing my Newcastle shirt but she'd put her jeans back on and I was thankful for that.

'You darling,' I said and meant it. For some reason I was starving, 'where'd you get all this?'

'There's a shop on the corner,' she gently rebuked me, 'or have you never noticed?'

'I'm vaguely aware of it.'

'Thought so, that oven looks like it's never been used.'

'I sometimes use the rings to light a cigarette.'

I sat down and grabbed a piece of toast, spread a dollop of melting butter over it and took a big bite, 'I never have time for cooking,' I said, talking with my mouth full, 'I usually eat breakfast at the gym and… ' I shrugged. I couldn't be bothered to explain that meals were taken wherever I happened to be at the time.

I ate loads and thanked her. 'Don't be daft,' she said. She was sitting bare foot on my couch a few moments later looking like she'd been living with me for weeks when a key turned in the lock and Laura walked in. When she saw Sarah in my football top her mouth literally fell open.

I have no idea what she would have said to me if Sarah hadn't been there. I will never know if she had come back to apologise, to continue the row or to leave me for good. She didn't look like she was about to beg my forgiveness, check my vital signs then shag me as a way of assuaging her guilt.

Instead she just went into one. 'Well YOU didn't waste your fucking time!' she shouted, leaving me with no idea if the *you* in question was meant to be me or Sarah or both of us. 'For fuck's sake, I've only been gone a night.'

I opened my mouth to say something like, 'Laura, it's not the way it looks,' but I realised that was such a corny line it would have been completely counterproductive. Deep down I knew it probably did look pretty bad. Laura knew, or at least sensed, that Sarah liked me and now she was sitting on my sofa, wearing my Newcastle shirt, the one with my name on the back, having just enjoyed what appeared to be, judging by the pile of dirty plates and pans in the sink, a hearty post-conjugal breakfast. The trouble was I hadn't shagged Sarah and I was starting to feel more than a little aggrieved with Laura. To use her phrase, she had not been there for me last night and Sarah had. Now she was treating me like a bad boy and I'd done fuck-all to deserve it. I didn't count the occasional fleeting thought about what Sarah looked like under my football shirt.

I was going to argue the toss but I felt indescribably weary. Watching Laura virtually foaming at the mouth as she continued to bollock Sarah, I suddenly got a vivid insight into my future; a sexless, mundane place, punctuated by meaningless rows over nothing on the way back from Ikea. I knew deep down that, if we still had something worth saving, I could have turned things around. I could have forced her to listen, told her I loved her, made her see that Sarah and I were little more than long-standing, platonic friends. I could have got her to believe me.

I was sure of it. I just didn't want to. In fact, all of a sudden, I didn't give a shit.

Sarah was fighting her corner. 'I only stayed to make sure he didn't have a concussion. That's meant to be your job, but you didn't care!'

'Don't give me that, you little slag. Do you think I don't know what's been going on? That I haven't seen the way you look at him, like you want to have his bloody babies!'

Sarah's face reddened. She looked like she was just about to explode and knock Laura out. It was time to intervene.

'Laura,' I said it very calmly and very quietly and because of that they both turned to listen to me, 'I realise you are upset but what you think has happened hasn't happened, though that's not even what's important right now.'

'What?' she asked me incredulously, 'what do you mean it's not important?'

'No,' I assured her, 'the important thing is this; if you keep calling my good friend Sarah here a slag, very soon she is going to get really tired of it. She is going to walk over there and grab you by the hair then she is going to bitch-slap you all round my apartment and throw you out.' For the second time that morning Laura's mouth gaped open. She looked at me, then she looked at Sarah who nodded at her slowly for emphasis, but I wasn't finished. 'More to the point, I'm going to do sod-all to stop her. Have you got that?'

Laura broke down then. Her body seemed to crumple, her face sagged and the tears flowed freely. I was surprised by the fact that I didn't care about her tears any more. There had been a time when I would have done anything to stop her from crying. Now I think I had become immune to them. I just wanted her to shut up and go away.

'You can come back tonight for your things, I won't be in,' I told her as she turned away from me, 'make sure you take your candles, your throws and all of your bloody cushions with you.'

Then I added for good measure, 'now fuck off out of my flat.'

When she finally stopped sobbing long enough to say something, she turned back to me and wailed, 'don't you love me any more?'

'Love you?' I asked her as if she was completely mad, 'I don't even like you!'

Laura went without another word.

TWENTY-FIVE

Sharp brought a bloke down to my flat to make an identikit drawing, so I didn't have to go into the station. He told the artist it was for my protection.

'Don't worry,' he said, 'I gave him some bullshit about you being an innocent caught up in a gangland feud.'

'I am,' I said, which made him laugh out loud though that wasn't my intention.

The artist quizzed me about every aspect of my attacker's features, as his hand skimmed over his pad. With a last confident stroke of his pencil, he finished and turned it round to show me the result. There, looking right back at me, was an unmistakeable likeness of Weasel-face. I noted with satisfaction that if you knew him you would have recognised him, except now that same face would be sporting stitches where the broken shard of urn had sliced deep into his skin.

After the identikit guy had gone, I asked Sharp, 'what next?'

'Officially, I'll be circulating his image round all the nicks in the area. On the assumption he's an outsider, I'll be concentrating on other forces. I can't see a local villain wanting to rob one of Bobby Mahoney's men,' he shrugged, 'might as well dig his own grave.'

'And unofficially?'

'I'll get a copy of the sketch and send it round that other little world we are familiar with, till one of our grasses comes up with a name to match the face. If he's out there, if he's known, we'll get him eventually.'

Sharp had the right idea. If we found anything it would more than likely be through a grass. There's a lot of shite spoken about the criminal code. People bang on about it as if the last thing any villain would ever do is grass up another crook to the police. What a load of crap that is. The city is full of informants, from the lowest dealer on the street right up to the very top. At street level, a dealer might keep himself out of nick if he informs regularly to a local DI or DS. Some of them just do it to eliminate the competition and the police are cool with that, as long as they get the arrests.

We are no different. When some cocky young fucker starts dealing blow or selling guns, sets up a brothel or starts a crew that does robberies, we get to hear about it sooner rather than later. Then we pay them a visit. If I do it, I make sure Finney is there to back me up. The message then goes out to them like a biblical prophecy. And Lo' the Lord said 'all the world shall be taxed'. The only difference being that their local lord is Bobby Mahoney and the tax in question is a percentage of their estimated earnings. If they are sensible, they pay. If they are not they get another visit from Finney. This time he is on his own or he might bring some of the other lads down with him. They always pay after the second visit, if he has left them in a fit state to do it, that is. We tax our local villains and no one should feel too sorry for them. Everyone else in the country has to pay tax and it's not as if they are declaring their income to the Inland Revenue.

Sometimes we take another tack though. From time to time, if it suits us, we will shop their whole operation to the Northumbria Police, removing our competitors at a stroke and gaining us some much-needed goodwill in the process. How do you think a corrupt cop like Sharp becomes a DS in the first place? By busting-up crews we tipped him off about.

So don't talk to me about a code. There isn't one.

It took a few days for the bruises to heal and I was wary of everybody for a while, strangers coming towards me, people walking too close behind me. For a day or two, I had Palmer watch my back from a distance but there was nothing, so I told him to stand down. I had more important things for him to be doing.

Bobby seemed to find the whole thing faintly amusing. While he took it seriously on one level - someone had the cheek to burgle my flat to try and find some dirt on us - he was pleased I had seen off my assailant and done him some damage. I was right, it did seem like he was more trusting of me after that. After all, I was hardly likely to arrange a serious beating to deflect suspicion, was I?

Finney surveyed my bruises as they changed colour, eventually settling into a sickly, jaundiced yellow and said, 'you got a comprehensive tuning there.'

'You should have seen the other guy,' I said.

'I saw the blood,' he admitted, 'turns out you were harder than I thought.' Since he'd always assumed I was soft as shit, this was a pretty back-handed compliment.

I'd been trying to steer clear of Sarah for a bit. Don't get me wrong, I had no regrets about Laura, none at all. I was just annoyed it had taken me so long to realise how barking mad she was.

Sarah texted me a few times, checking I was okay, which was nice and for the next few days I got some light-hearted messages about what she was doing, how bored she was, how daft her mates were, that sort of thing. I always replied eventually but I made out like I was well busy, which I was. Trouble was, I couldn't stop thinking about her. To tell the truth, I was beginning to crave her.

Inevitably my thoughts would come back round to Sarah and how much I wanted her. I tried to remind myself it was suicide to even contemplate shagging Bobby Mahoney's daughter but, in the end, I knew that desire, or simple plain lust, was beginning to win out over caution. Men are slaves to that kind of thinking. It can bother you all day until you eventually run out of reasons for not doing what you know you should be *not doing*. And so we do it, no matter how stupid, even if we know it will make our lives more complicated in the long run and we're very likely to regret it. We just can't help ourselves.

Fuck it. I picked up my phone and dialled.

'Hello,' a soft voice on the end of the line.

'It's me,' I told her, 'you doing anything?'

'Right now?'

'Yeah,' I said, 'right now.'

TWENTY-SIX

....

'Will I see you later?' she asked me as I was dressing. The sun was shining through the windows, bathing her bed in a bright morning light that showed just how much we'd creased her sheets the night before, but at least it helped me to find my clothes as I picked them from the floor where we'd left them. I'd made sure it was her flat we went to, so much easier to make an uncomplicated exit.

'Maybe,' I said, checking myself in the mirror. 'You at Privado?'

'Yeah, I'm working tonight,' Michelle said, 'supposed to be anyhow but... I don't know... thought I might phone in sick, you know,' and she laughed, 'you've tired me out David. I need a duvet day.'

Before she could invite me to share that duvet with her, I said, 'think of that student loan pet. Anyway you've got hours yet.'

'Guess so,' then she giggled, 'you know it was only the other day I found out what Privado means,' she told me, 'I Googled it.'

'And what does it mean?' I asked as I started to lace my shoes.

'It means "confidential friend",' she said, 'is that what we are eh? Confidential friends?'

'Yep, and let's keep it that way,' I said, then quickly added, 'the girls in there can be jealous.'

'All want you, do they?'

'I didn't say that. If you let on about us they'll soon think you are getting special treatment.'

'I am,' she told me, 'very special.'

'Good,' I said, 'got to go now though.'

'Do you have to dash off?' she sounded disappointed. 'Sorry.'

I checked I had everything; wallet, keys, phone. I didn't want to leave anything behind. I walked back over to the bed.

'Last night was good,' I told her, bending to kiss her on the lips. She liked that, accepting the kiss then almost toppling me forwards when she wrapped her arms round my neck and kissed me back, long and deep *'you* were good,' I said breaking from her embrace. For a moment, as I looked at her bare, inviting breasts, I almost climbed back in there.

'Was I?' she asked hopefully.

'Oh yeah,' and she lit up like a Christmas tree. There's never any harm in making a girl feel good about herself afterwards.

I put on my jacket, 'call you later yeah.'

'Yeah,' she brightened, 'we could do something,' she suggested.

'See you,' I said.

Sharp was leaning against the bar at Rosie's. The pub was one of our usual meeting spots because it was ideally situated on the corner of Stowell Street, right by the football ground and you could easily tell if you were being followed as you approached it. A quick glance behind you down a short, clear street and you'd pretty much know if someone was on your arse then you could just keep on walking by, meeting aborted. The pub was popular and nicely public so you could stand a few feet apart but next to each other at the bar and a casual observer might not even notice you were together. Plus, it was always a good pint in there.

Of course, if we were spotted, we would simply resort to our default position. I was a criminal source, a highly-placed grass whom Sharp had been secretively cultivating for years in an attempt to find out more about the crime boss, Bobby Mahoney. Playing the double agent was not without its danger for me but I made sure Bobby knew all about our bent copper and the fall-back plan if we were ever lifted. He had a right to know all about it. After all, the money we were paying Sharp was coming out of his coffers.

'We managed to put a face to a name,' he told me.

'And?'

He slid a folded piece of A4 sideways along the bar to me, 'it's all in there. We reckon your guy is Andrew Stone, a professional burglar from Glasgow, a regular exponent of robbery with violence. His local boys checked out his address but, surprise, surprise, he hasn't been seen there for days. Before you ask, Stone is not directly affiliated to any of the main gangs up there, including their top boys.'

We both knew he meant the Gladwells. 'A freelancer?'

'We're working on that assumption.'

'That's what I'd do if I was probing somebody else's firm, bring in an outsider, someone deniable who couldn't drop me in the shit if it went tits up. I'd use cut-outs, make sure he didn't even know who'd hired him.'

'You'd use someone from another city wouldn't you?'

'Yeah, I would.' Like me, he was wondering if the Gladwells had gotten sloppy, sending a man from their own city down to ours to stir up some trouble.

When I showed Bobby the name and last known address of Weasel-face, aka Andrew Stone, he said, 'right, well this needs sorting and sharpish. We're going up to Glasgow; you, me, Finney and Jerry. We are going to see the Gladwells.'

'What kind of visit is this one?' I asked him.

'Unannounced.'

We took the train to Edinburgh and changed for the Glasgow service. Our journey up there was uneventful, there wasn't much conversation. I was pretty sure we were all reflecting on the seriousness of calling on Arthur Gladwell, Glasgow's Top Boy, uninvited. Although I understood Bobby's reasons, it was a prospect I wasn't exactly relishing.

I stared out of the train window, looking down at the cliffs that overlooked the North Sea, which, as always, was frighteningly choppy and looked freezing cold. You wouldn't last five minutes in it. Then I realised Bobby was looking at me.

'That was a nice watch you got our Sarah for her birthday,' he said uncertainly, as if I'd bought her some crotch-less knickers and a dildo, 'she keeps going on about it,' he added, 'and you. My little girl seems to think you are the doggy's bollocks these days.' Something about the way he called her my-little-girl set alarm bells ringing.

'Bless her,' I said, as if I was talking about a nine-year-old, 'well, you know me, I got a great deal on that watch, just don't tell her eh.'

He was still looking right at me which was making me

nervous, but I was determined to hide it. I faked a yawn like we were having the most innocent conversation imaginable, 'I had to get the boss' daughter something nice for her 21st didn't I?' I told him, 'she's a good kid, you should be proud of her.'

'I am proud of her,' he said quietly, leaving me none-the-wiser as to what he was actually thinking.

We'd enquired about Arthur Gladwell and knew it was his wife's 60th birthday. He was taking her for dinner at Roganos, which was very classy, for him. I half expected a private table at a Berni Inn, steak and chips all round with a fried egg on top. He'd never lost the common touch, Arthur, because he had no idea there was any other way to go about things. Lord knows who told him about a place like Roganos.

We got word they were having their pre-dinner drinks in a nearby pub. Arthur was standing there with his missus and their four sons, all stocky like their father but slightly shorter versions of his towering frame, as if they hadn't yet earned the right to see the world from a higher perspective than him. Their other halves were there too and, if they could be classed as beautiful, it was in a heavily made-up, perma-tanned way that my late mother would have described as 'all fur coat and no knickers'.

Arthur looked surprised to see us but he hid it well. He quietly instructed his eldest boy Tommy's wife to look after the ladies at the bar while he walked over to greet us by the door, followed by his boys. They were frowning, our very presence on their patch was a massive affront to them.

There were five of them and four of us but I wasn't in the same league as Bobby, Finney and Jerry Lemon. I was praying they wouldn't want to start anything in a pub, even a dog-rough one with ancient wallpaper, and woodchip walls like this one. I sized up Arthur's lads so I could pick the softest one to lamp if it did kick off, but they were all built like steroidal bouncers. Each of them looked like he'd grown up fighting every day, encouraged by his dad, and I didn't like the odds. The eldest, Tommy, was sporting the remnants of a black eye and there was something about the way he carried himself, a little warily, that made me wonder if he might have been given it by his father.

'Arthur,' said Bobby.

'Bobby,' Arthur Gladwell nodded, 'what brings you here? I'm not aware of a meeting. It's my wife's birthday.'

'I know that,' said Bobby, 'this won't take long.'

'Fair enough.'

Bobby handed Arthur the rolled up picture of Andrew Stone. The big man unfurled it and looked at it, while we watched him for a trace of recognition. Instead he gave us a questioning look.

'Someone's coming after me and mine, Arthur,' said Bobby, 'and I need to know it's not you, not over the phone but face-to-face, man-to-man. I want you to look me in the eye and tell me it's not you Arthur. Or you can tell me that it *is* you, then we'll both know where we stand.'

'Tommy,' said Arthur, 'go to the bar and get me two glasses of that single malt from Oban.' Tommy Gladwell looked less than thrilled to be fetching Bobby his drink but he went anyway. We watched him trudge over to the bar and order and we waited for Arthur to say something.

'We've known each other for a long time Bobby,' he said finally, 'we've had our differences over the years, no one would deny that. I wouldn't call us friends but I'd say we respect each other. I've heard about your troubles - but I'm not the cause of them.'

Gladwell junior returned with the glasses and handed one to Bobby who took it silently. Arthur raised his own glass to Bobby's, they clinked them together and each took an appreciative sip, 'I don't want to go to war with you,' said Arthur, 'just as you don't want to go to war with me. I'm too old and too busy with my own patch. This city is full of Jack-the-lads, all flexing their muscles because they want a piece of what I've got. They all want to be Top Boy and I get no rest 'cos I've got to keep putting them back in their place. I think you understand that.' Bobby's eyes narrowed in recognition. Arthur took another sip of his malt, 'I don't have to swear on the lives of my grandchildren Bobby but I will if it will make you feel better.'

'No Arthur, you're telling me it isn't so and that's good enough for me.'

'Good,' said Arthur Gladwell, 'now why don't you join us for a drink, your boys too of course.'

'Thanks Arthur. I appreciate the invitation but I'll leave you to your family. It's time we were heading back.' And he drained the last dregs of the malt and handed the empty glass back to Tommy Gladwell, who took it meekly enough, though he looked like he'd rather have seen it hit the floor. Bobby and Arthur Gladwell shook hands and, at the last moment, Tommy Gladwell tried to shake Bobby's hand but Bobby was already turning his back. I don't think he was snubbing the bloke deliberately but Bobby was the kind of man who wouldn't have given a toss either way. As Bobby turned away there was an awkward moment where Tommy had his hand outstretched and there was no one there to shake it. I didn't want him to look like a complete tosser so I leaned forward, shook his hand and said, 'hope your mother has a great night.'

When we were back in the train Bobby said, 'how has he heard about my troubles?'

'Eh?' asked Finney.

'I said, how does he know about my troubles?'

'I dunno,' answered Finney. He seemed a little perturbed to be asked the question. I kept silent, assuming it was rhetorical.

We had the first class carriage to ourselves, except for a business type who was busy reading his paper.

'What did you think about that Davey?' Bobby asked me.

'Well, he's saying it has nowt to do with him and I tend to believe it.'

'You believe that fucking snake,' said Jerry Lemon, 'he'd grass on his own grandma if it suited him.'

'And so would we,' I reminded him, 'I don't know, I may be wrong but my instinct says it isn't Arthur Gladwell. He doesn't want a war right now. In fact it's the last thing he needs, though… '

'What?' asked Bobby

'He didn't say anything about Stone, when you showed him the picture. He didn't say a word.'

'Well, he would know him, a professional operator on his patch,' said Bobby.

'Yeah but he didn't deny using him, he didn't ask you what any of this had to do with him, he just didn't say anything.'

'So what you're saying is, you don't know if it's him or not?' challenged Jerry Lemon.

'Yes, that's right Jerry, that's exactly what I'm saying.'

'Then going up there was a complete waste of time,' added Jerry.

'No it wasn't!' snapped Bobby, 'if it was him, he knows we are on to him and he's been warned off. If it wasn't, well he knows we don't fuck about down here, we come up and confront people if we think they are taking the piss, so him and his boys will know that too, for future reference.'

'Sorry Bobby,' said Jerry Lemon, 'I was only saying… '

'Maybe you should do a bit less saying and a bit more thinking. Do you reckon word won't get round that we went up there to have it out with Arthur Gladwell face to face on his own patch?' Course it will. Every grass in the city will be onto it by now. We'll have been picked up on CCTV arriving at the station. That shows we'll stand, against anyone. Anyone,' Bobby stared out of the train window and he carried on addressing Jerry without even looking at him, 'why don't you do something useful for a change. Go down to the buffet car and get us all a drink.'

I was beginning to think it was worth the journey to Glasgow just to see Jerry Lemon get slapped down like that.

TWENTY-SEVEN

....

We were back to square one. We had nothing; just a photofit of a petty criminal from Glasgow and a Russian connection we didn't understand. It was doing my head in. I wasn't getting anywhere. Bobby still didn't have his money and, more importantly, I hadn't found out who was behind his 'troubles', as Arthur Gladwell so tellingly referred to them.

I was at home watching the football when the phone rang. Out of the blue, Joe Kinane called me. His happiness was in direct contrast to my mood.

'I just thought I'd give you a ring about my lad,' he told me.

'How'd he get on?'

'Beat it,' he said.

'Really?' this was more than I could have hoped for, 'that's brilliant. What happened?'

'Self-defence,' he said laughing, 'which it was of course, kind of, but that lawyer of yours was the dog's. She took the other guy apart.'

'Told you,' I said.

'Aye, well, he got a more comprehensive beating from her than he ever did from my boy. It helped that she seemed to have a lot of information about his character, stuff he wouldn't want a jury to hear. Turns out he wasn't a very nice bloke,' he said dryly.

'You don't say? Amazing what a good lawyer can turn up.'

'It is,' and he laughed, 'anyway, I just wanted to thank you for putting me onto her.'

'My pleasure mate,' I told him. I was glad he was expressing his gratitude discreetly. If anyone was listening into this, all they could accuse me of was knowing a good lawyer. 'That's in return for all the help and guidance you gave me when I was a snot-nosed kid.'

'Aye, er sorry about that like,' he said.

'Don't worry about it Joe.'

'Well, I owe you one,' he told me before he rang off, 'if I hear anything about that other thing, anything at all, I'll let you know.'

'Cheers,' I said. Maybe he would turn something up but somehow I doubted it. We had every man in our outfit on it permanently and not one of them had come up with anything worth a light.

I had never seen Sharp so rattled before. My tame DS was shitting it. It was not a good start.

'I can't meet you here,' he hissed at me after I ordered a drink a few feet from him in Rosies.

'I thought I was your major criminal source,' I said, playing his game and not looking directly at him. Instead I stared at the mirror in front of me then up at the weird assortment of ghoulish mannequin heads that were arrayed on a ledge above the bar. They didn't really fit in with all of the framed football shirts on the walls. The bar staff were busy bottling up and the pub was quiet so this nonsense was do-able but I seriously doubted if it would fool anyone for long.

'It's not funny.'

'I never said it was,' I assured him, 'where then?' I took a big gulp of my beer.

'The Angel,' he said, 'one hour - but don't be surprised if I don't show.'

'You'd better show,' I warned him and I took another large swig of beer.

He turned to face me then and he looked wild eyed, 'you don't get it, you don't know what's going on. They're everywhere, all over the station, asking questions, questions about me.'

'Who is?'

'Police Complaints Commission. They've been in with my gaffer all morning.'

'Maybe it's him they're interested in?'

'No chance, not him. He's a fucking android.'

I drained my pint, 'like I said, he sounds like heart attack material,' I told him, 'and so do you, now get a grip.' I put my empty glass down on the bar and left him to it.

By the time I'd driven out of the city, parked and trudged up to the monument with the wind whistling around my ears, I was beginning to feel mightily pissed-off. There was no sign of Sharp, so I was left standing there, hands thrust deep in my pockets, shivering under the Angel of the North, wondering what could be so important he had to see me straight away but not so urgent he couldn't just tell me about it in Rosie's.

Like most people from my city, I held a hypocritical view of the Angel. When it first appeared I thought it was an expensive and pointless monstrosity, representing the very worst excesses of modern art, two hundred tonnes of metal, part man, part aeroplane, neither one thing or another, signifying nothing. Now though, I had to admit to a grudging affection for its rusting presence. As usual, it stood tall, upright and broad-chested, like it was particularly proud of itself. I sat down between the tapered metal strips at its feet and waited, looking out at the surrounding fields under a clear blue sky. It could have been summer if it hadn't been so typically cold.

A shape in a dark raincoat emerged from the woods on my right and walked quickly towards me. There was no one else around and my first thought was Sharp had set me up for a hit. I was about to leg it when I realised the shape was him. He was out of breath by the time he reached me, 'too many fags,' he gasped.

'Was this really necessary?'

'Maybe not. But it makes me feel better. I can see people coming from here.'

I looked around. There were some figures in the field behind the monument now. 'I can see four kids and a kite,' I told him, 'I haven't got a lot of free time at the moment Sharp, what is it?'

'Something that couldn't wait.'

'I'm listening.'

'It's Jerry Lemon.'

'What about him?'

'He's dead.'

'Dead? Jerry Lemon's dead?'

'Yeah.'

'Jesus,' I said trying to take it in. It was only forty eight hours earlier that Jerry was on the train with us and now he was dead? 'What the hell happened? I'm guessing it wasn't suicide.'

'No,' he said, 'he was shot in the head'. He was still panting. I wondered how he ever caught villains, 'we got a call last night from some shit-scared anonymous pervert who'd been out by a truck stop, walking the dog, you know.'

'Eh?'

'Walking the dog,' he said again, like I was an idiot, 'only he didn't have a dog, they never do.'

'What are you going on about?'

'Dogging, he was dogging. They call it that because when we catch them they always say 'I was walking the dog' and when we say 'where is it then?' they always go 'oh, it must have run off.''

'What has dogging got to do with Jerry Lemon?'

'That's what he was doing when he was killed.'

'You're joking me.'

'No,' he assured me, 'I take it you had no idea he was into that sort of thing.'

'Course not, but then it isn't the sort of thing people usually talk about is it? I mean if you ask somebody what they did last night they usually say 'watched the match' or 'went to the pub' not 'went dogging'. Bloody hell, it's not my idea of fun either if I'm honest, standing there with a bunch of strangers all wanking over some fat, married lass while her husband watches. Jesus, his missus will be fucking devastated when she finds out.'

'Er… No… She won't.'

'What do you mean?'

'I'm afraid she was the fat, married lass and he was the husband watching all the blokes getting off. Well I assume he was, it's not like we can confirm that exactly but I don't s'pose he was just doing it for her pleasure.'

'Bloody hell. You're telling me Jerry's missus likes… ' I couldn't find the words.

'Being spunked on by strangers? Yeah, by all accounts.' He reached for another cigarette, lit it then said, 'I mean she used to like it. She's dead an' all.'

'Christ, what happened?'

'At first we thought some sicko was on the prowl, randomly shooting dogging couples. You know, a religious nutter cleaning up the city in the name of the baby Jesus or something. Then we got the name of the victim and it turned out it was Jerry

Lemon and his not-so-good lady. So, then everyone said "oh it's a gangland war".'

A gangland war? What an odd phrase. Did I live in gangland? I supposed I did, according to the tabloids. Tomorrow they'd be writing up the story of Jerry Lemon and his moll, coldly assassinated by a ruthless, underworld hit man.

'It looked like they drove in and parked up, flashed their lights in the normal secret way they are s'posed to; you know, one flash and you can watch, two you can join in, three you can take us both up the bum-hole, whatever. We have one witness who must have been even fatter and slower than your average dogger because by the time he comes out of the trees, the window was already coming down and he sees a big shaven-headed bloke step out of a car that's pulled in behind Jerry Lemon's.' It had to be one of the guys who'd gone steaming in on Barry and his lads at the bar. 'This bloke walks right up to the opened window but instead of pulling his cock out he brings a gun up and blows Jerry's head off at point blank range. His missus started screaming apparently, as you would when you get a different kind of facial from the one you were expecting, so he pops her as well.'

'Christ almighty. This witness, can we get to him? He might tell Finney a bit more than he's telling your lot.'

He shook his head, 'Anonymous. He called it in, left a description of what he had seen but wouldn't cooperate further and didn't leave his name,' he shrugged, 'who would?'

Sharp puffed away at his cigarette for a while, as if he was reflecting on the fate of Jerry Lemon. We watched as the kids walked down the mud track in front of us. They tried to fly their kite but the wind kept swooping it up high then smashing it straight back down into the ground again. Eventually Sharp said, 'I'm serious about what I was saying before. It's grim. I'm worried, really worried,' then he turned to look at me, 'you would look after me, wouldn't you? If I got sent down because of stuff we'd done together?'

'Yeah, sure. I'll send you a cake with a file in it.'

'Will you stop pissing about for five minutes? I mean it. I need to know you'll look after me, like you would if I was a proper member of the firm. You know what I'm saying.'

'Yeah,' I said, 'I know what you're saying. You're implying I'd better look after you or you'll make a deal and bring me and Bobby down with you in exchange for a lighter sentence.'

'Now hang on a minute, I wasn't… '

'Yes you were and I would do the same in your shoes but it doesn't mean I have to like it. You'll be looked after if it all goes tits-up but remember there's a flip-side to that generosity. If Bobby Mahoney thinks someone is going to betray him he doesn't mess about. Know how easy it would be to have a bent detective stabbed while he's on remand? There's people inside who would do it just for fun. Throw in a couple of grand and they'd be queuing up, a couple more would make a prison officer look the other way, they get paid even less than Detective Sergeants and we both know what people are prepared to do for money. There'd be no witnesses and about a thousand suspects. Villains in the nick don't like coppers, especially bent ones. So you better keep your lip buttoned and take what's coming to you. Getting caught and being sent down comes with the turf for dodgy detectives, but that's the least of your worries.'

Sharp had gone pale, 'I never meant anything by it, honest.'

'My guess is you're worrying about nothing. Your DI probably lamped a suspect in a past life and they put in a complaint, so stop shitting yourself and start acting like a man.'

'Yeah, yeah, that'll be it. You're right. I'm sorry.'

'You get any leads on who killed Jerry Lemon you ring me first,' I left him watching the kids, still struggling to get their kite off the ground.

I walked back to my car. Up ahead of me I could see the high rise blocks of flats from the estate nearby. They were a monument to a different kind of Tyneside. Politicians were always talking about rejuvenating the areas around Newcastle but I reckoned they were kidding us and themselves. Around the turn of a new and hopeful millennium, a housing association in North Benwell had to sell off houses for fifty pence because nobody would pay any more than that to live there. They were on a hiding to nothing.

TWENTY-EIGHT

I knew Bobby would want to hear this kind of news right away. I went straight round to his house.

'First Geordie Cartwright now Jerry Lemon,' he said in disbelief. He walked over to the drinks trolley, picked up the bottle and poured himself several fingers of scotch. He found an empty glass tumbler and held it up to me. I shook my head. I realised that lately I'd not seen him without a glass in his hand.

He took a sip of his whisky then sat down on his big old Chesterfield couch and took another mouthful.

'I've know these men for years,' he said, 'right back to when we first started out. We've been through some stuff... ' And he shook his head at the magnitude of it all, 'and now someone's killing them off, one by one, just like that.' He clicked his finger and thumb together. I thought for a second he might even be getting a tear in his eye but then his face reddened like he was fighting his emotions, his teeth set into a snarl and he growled the words, 'I want whoever is behind this dead.'

'Of course,' I said.

'But I want to look them in the eye first,' he told me, 'I want them to suffer before they die. I owe Jerry Lemon that much.'

'I think you should keep Finney with you for a while,' I told Bobby, 'until we get this sorted. I know you don't like the idea of him moving in but look at it as extra insurance.'

'I dunno,' he said then fell silent, like he was affronted by the suggestion that he, Bobby Mahoney, might actually need a little extra protection.

'Bobby, seriously, no one is saying you can't handle yourself, but we still don't know who we are up against and it's my job to keep you secure. You used to say Jerry Lemon was a hard man but they got to him. Whoever did it knows if they can get you out of the way then they've won.'

He thought about this for a long while, 'okay,' he said finally, but I could tell he still didn't like it, 'send him round - but what are you going to do for protection without Finney shadowing you?'

'I figure it's time Palmer earned his money.'

'I hope he's as good as you say he is,' Bobby told me.

'So do I.'

'Trouble is, nobody in the city knows him.' said Bobby.

'And that's just the way I like it.'

I'd thought it might be a good idea to get the two of them together, sort of like a blind date for ex-squaddies but, after a shed load of beer I was beginning to wonder if it had been such a wise move. Both of them could drink, my brother Danny and Palmer. I mean really drink.

Palmer and I had downed a few pints straight after Jerry Lemon's funeral but I didn't want to sit in my flat moping.

We'd talked to everybody we knew in the city but we were still drawing blanks. Nobody had any info on our Russians, so we had to assume they were coming into the city to attack us then melting away somewhere. I was starting to think we would have to wait for them to show themselves again. The trouble being that, every time they did, our people got hurt or killed.

We'd bumped into my brother in the Bigg Market and I just thought fuck it, let's have a beer. Now it was late and we were back in my flat, with three stubby glasses in front of us, looking at a half-empty bottle of scotch.

'I hear you were in the Paras?' asked Danny, 'before you joined the Regiment.' Like Palmer, my brother never called it the SAS, only the Regiment.

'Yeah,' said Palmer.

'How come you left then?'

'Danny,' I warned him.

'It's alright,' said Palmer, 'I'm not touchy about it. I got RTU'd.'

'Oh,' said Danny.

'Don't you want to know why?' asked Palmer. Danny shrugged, 'course you do. Everybody always does.' Danny shrugged again but this time the twinkly little smile was an admission. 'Okay, I'll tell you, since we've had a good drink up,' he sipped his whisky. 'It was nothing spectacular though, quite the reverse in fact.'

'Go on then,' said Danny, 'tell us. I could use a laugh.'

'Fuck me,' I said, 'is this how you army boys discuss each other's hardships?'

'Aye,' said Palmer, 'that's about right.' He took another sip of his drink and said, 'it was the daftest thing. Like you said, I was in the Paras, made a hundred and twelve jumps, no bother at all, never a moment's hesitation. Then one day, I was out on a routine top-up jump to keep my wings. I shuffled up to the front of the line no different to normal, but something strange happened.'

'What?' asked Danny.

'I didn't jump.'

'You didn't jump?'

'I didn't jump,' he repeated patiently.

'Why?'

'I wish I knew. To this day I can't even explain it to myself. It wasn't like I was suddenly terrified, just that I didn't want to go out the door. Not then, not that day, at that point.'

'What? You mean you had a premonition your chute wasn't going to open or something?' asked Danny, 'you thought you were going to die?'

'No, nothing so… dramatic. It was more like, out of the blue, after all those jumps, it suddenly seemed…'

'What?'

'A bloody stupid thing to be doing.'

'Christ almighty,' said Danny laughing, 'what did they do to you?'

'Made me sit down in the plane, everybody else went out. They landed the plane and I was returned to unit.'

'Just like that?' I asked. 'Could they not have given you a second chance to go?'

'Nope, that's the rule, if you don't jump,' he said, 'there are no second chances. That's the army.'

'So is that why you left?' Danny asked, 'because you were RTU'd?'

'Well, yes and no.'

Danny was laughing again, 'go on,' he urged, 'what happened?'

'It was a while after. I think by then I'd lost my love of the army and, well, me and the missus had split up and I think I was going a bit mad at that point. Then they gave me this shitty guard duty, driving round the perimeter one Friday night and, by this point, I just really didn't want to be there so… '

'What did you do?' asked Danny.

'I drove the jeep into the mess.'

'Through the door!' laughed Danny, his eyes like saucers.

'Through the plate glass, locked, double doors and right across the room,' we were all laughing now, 'I cleaned out a few tables, everybody was diving out of my way. They were having curry. I remember because I knocked over a massive pan of it, it went all over the floor.'

'You sure that was the curry?' I asked.

'Aye,' said Danny, killing himself laughing now, 'a fucking jeep's flying straight at you across the mess hall!' and he put a hand under his arse and made a long wet farting noise, 'me? I'd shit all over the floor and say "it's just the curry, honest!".'

'I bet they gave you a right kicking when the jeep finally stopped,' I said.

'There were a few harsh words exchanged,' he admitted, 'then they chucked me in a cell and before I knew it, I was out of the army.'

It didn't surprise me that Palmer had done a little time. They reckon about ten per cent of the prison population is ex-forces. Of course, you don't see that statistic on the recruitment posters.

You always need a bit of luck. I don't care who you are or how clever you think you might be, if you don't get the breaks it won't make any difference. Look at any sportsman, general, politician or rock star. They'll all tell you it started because they got a break. The next morning we finally got ours.

I was a bit hungover after my evening with Danny and Palmer, so I arrived at the gym late in the afternoon. I'd been varying my time since the attack, to make it harder for anyone to pick up my routine. I'd seen this pasty, grey-haired bloke once before while I was down there. He was sitting on a lounger by the pool while I was doing my lengths. Then another time he was in the café when I came out and I noticed he'd chosen the one seat that looked directly onto the exit door of the men's changing rooms. When I looked over he looked away.

Now he was here again. I was on one of the benches in the changing room and, as soon as I saw him, I just knew he wasn't legit. He studiously ignored me as he walked in and opened a locker, then started to undress for the pool. It was hard to explain why but it was a combination of instinct and common sense. When you walk into a public room, the first thing you do is clock who's in there already. You quickly glance at them and they look back at you, to make sure you don't represent a threat to them. It's a primeval instinct, Desmond Morris-style behaviour. We can't help ourselves then we quickly look away, so as not to challenge the other person. No one likes it if you look at them for too long. Hence the standard, it's about to kick off phrase of 'What you looking at?'

The thing is, this guy didn't do any of that. As soon as his tubby body rounded the corner, my eyes went to him automatically but he made sure he was looking the other way right from the off. I could have been a knife wielding hoody for all he knew but he just didn't take me in and that wasn't right. I'd varied my routine and this was the third time I'd clocked him. Because of that and the way he avoided looking at me, I just knew this bloke was there because of me. He was watching and he was waiting for an opportunity to set me up. He didn't look like muscle but, if he had been wanting to take me out, it was all a bit too public in here anyway. I wasn't daft like Jerry Lemon. I wasn't about to go driving into darkened truck stops to offer them an easy target.

I was ready before him, so I went to the pool but instead

of going straight into the water I sat down on a lounger. He walked in a moment later, went by me and headed for the sauna. I'd wrapped my phone up in my towel and as grey-hair disappeared into the sauna I reached for it. It was one of many pay-as-you-go phones we used and rotated, so there was less danger of it being picked up by anyone listening. I spoke to Palmer. I had to be quick so I didn't even try to talk in code.

'I'm at the gym. I want you to get one of the lads down here pronto, use one of our spare swipe keys, get into the men's changing rooms then turn over a locker for me. Number 468. Take everything, get his details. I want him checked then lifted.'

'No problem,' he said, 'a wrong 'un?'

'Looks like it.'

'I'll sort it.'

I clicked the phone shut, lay back in the lounger and waited.

I gave it forty-five minutes, swimming a few lengths, during which time our fat friend waddled from sauna to steam room to pool, then, as soon as he waded into the Jacuzzi, I left and quickly dressed. Grey-hair was on his way back in to get changed just as I was leaving. I didn't hang around to see the look on his face when he realised all we'd left him was the trunks he was standing up in.

I moved my car so that I could see everything from a distance but he wouldn't be able to spot me when he emerged. It took him ten minutes to work out what his options were. Eventually he had no choice but to kick up a fuss with the girls on the front desk, who must have been bemused by the sight of a middle aged bloke, dripping all over the floor in front of them.

Finally the big, glass doors at the front of the building slid apart and he emerged, dressed in a too tight, blue sweatshirt with the club's logo on it and a pair of grey leggings they must have retrieved from lost property. They'd found him some manky tennis shoes as well and he was hobbling along in them. He looked over to where his car had been parked and swore at the empty bay. Even from this distance I could tell he was muttering and cursing as he sloped away. He walked towards the main gate, looking like he was going to head into town.

There was a white Transit van with the council logo on it, parked just outside the main gate. I watched as he drew level with the four workers in bright orange high-visibility jackets who looked like they were just about to start digging up the road. He paid them no attention at all, until one of them stepped in his way and, before he could work out what was going on, another marched up behind him and zapped him with a Tazer. He let out a strangled gurgle as his legs gave way and they grabbed him before he hit the ground. A heartbeat later, he was in the back of the van with the doors locked behind him and they were driving away. Smooth as you like.

I'd known having our own van with the council's logo on it had been a good idea. Now I just hoped I'd given the right order. Hopefully Palmer just lifted someone who'd soon be telling us who he was working for and what was going on. Then we'd finally know who was behind the murders of Jerry Lemon and Geordie Cartwright. Either that or we were about to torture an innocent civilian on my say-so based on little more than a hunch. I tried not to think about that as I drove away.

Palmer called in and I told him to take the guy to a lock-up we used, then get Finney over to scare the hell out of him. I didn't think Bobby would mind sparing Finney if he thought it might lead to a breakthrough. I went back to the Cauldron and waited for Palmer to call me again.

When he rang, I asked him if Finney was on it. 'I've called

him a few times but he's not picking up,' he told me, his voice unconcerned. This didn't sound good to me. Finney was normally reliable when it came to that sort of thing.

'Shit,' I said.

'Don't worry,' Palmer assured me, 'you want the fear of God putting into this prick, right?'

'Yes,' I said.

'Then leave it to me.'

I waited a couple of hours at the club. I ate a meal, trying not to think about the imaginative methods Palmer was going to employ on our grey-haired stranger to get him to talk. Did I have sympathy for him? No. He'd been following me around, noting my movements. He might even have been the guy who'd told Weasel-face I'd be at the match when he broke into my apartment and almost killed me.

I'd long finished lunch when my mobile vibrated into life again. It was Palmer.

'He's copped for it,' he told me calmly, though he sounded a little out of breath, 'the whole story. You are going to want to hear this.'

'Good,' I said, 'keep him there.'

'Oh he's not going anywhere,' he assured me.

'Did he give you a name?' I asked impatiently, 'did he tell you who?'

'Yes he did,' and Palmer proceeded to tell me the whole bloody tale. I didn't say a word. I just listened. When he'd finished I thanked him and said, 'there's something else I need from you, well, from him.'

'Name it.'

'There's someone on the inside. Somebody's been handing our organisation to these bastards one bit of information at a time. They couldn't have known so much just by following us around for a few weeks. Get me a name.

Who's their man on the inside?'

'You've got it,' he said

I got straight to my feet, my heart thumping with a combination of anger, adrenalin and dread. I now knew what was going on. Our enemy finally had a face and a name. I had to get to Bobby quickly. Things were about to get rough.

TWENTY-NINE

....

On my way out of the club I dialled Bobby's mobile and it rang out. 'Pick up the phone Bobby,' I said aloud. I was walking quickly and I pressed the key for the Merc. It bleeped a couple of times to show it recognised me. I ended the call and tried to dial Finney before I reached the car. It rang eight times without any answer. I hung up and, as I did so, my phone rang.

'Hello,' I said.

'It's me,' it was Sharp, 'I've been making calls like you said and I think I've finally turned something up.' Unsurprisingly, he seemed eager to please after our last meeting.

'And?'

'A big Russian bloke with a shaved head rented a farmhouse out in the sticks. It sleeps half a dozen people and you know, I thought, how many groups of big Russian blokes can there be on their holibobs in Tyneside.'

'That's them alright.'

He gave me the address.

'Thanks,' I said, 'while you're on I need another address. It'll be easier to find but you can't give it to any one who'll want to link it back to you later, so don't use your police computer.'

There was a pause while he digested my meaning. 'Name?' he asked. I told him.

I was almost back to my car when I phoned Palmer again and gave him the address Sharp had supplied for the Russians.

'You're going to be working this weekend,' I replied.

'What's the plan boss?' he asked nonchalantly.

'Wait till I have a word with Bobby,' I told him.

'Fair enough.'

I hung up and opened the door of the car. I was about to climb in when two huge blokes suddenly appeared from nowhere. One blocked the door I was about to open and the other appeared from behind me. I hadn't heard a thing and they were on me so fast I couldn't even think about walking away. They were both big guys with shaven heads. They looked exactly like the guys who'd steamed into Benny the doorman. The same guys who'd murdered Jerry and George. I was trapped.

I knew immediately that I was fucked. I'd been stupid and careless. I was so exhilarated that I'd landed grey hair, so full of my own clever-clogs instinct that I'd parked my car in a side street by the club. That was fine in daylight, but by the time I'd walked out again it was dark and there was no one around. I'd made it easy for them.

The guy behind me pressed a gun into my side, 'get in the car,' he ordered me in heavily-accented English. He sounded Russian alright.

Instinctively I looked about me for help or some way to escape but there was no one else around and I could hardly call out. It would have been the last sound I ever made, 'don't be stupid,' he told me, 'now get in before we hurt you. You drive.'

So I got in. What option did I have?

It was all I could do to start the car, my hands were shaking so bad. My mind was racing as I tried to work out what they wanted from me, where they were taking me and what they intended to do to me when we got there.

If they planned to drive me to a remote spot and kill me like George Cartwright, I would rather at least try to get away now. Smashing the moving car into oncoming traffic or a lamp post at speed seemed about the only option left to me. I didn't fancy my chances of hurting these two like that without seriously damaging myself in the process but I knew I might not come up with a better plan. It crossed my mind that if they'd wanted me dead, they could have easily killed me in the quiet side street. So, I was still alive and I told myself that was a good thing, as I edged the car away from the club and out into the traffic.

'Don't do anything crazy,' the same guy told me, 've vont to talk, that's all.'

All very reassuring except I'd used that line myself on people Bobby wanted a little word with - and some of them had ended up face down in the Tyne with their fingers missing. The Russian said they didn't want to kill me but his word meant nothing. There really are worse things than death.

They drove me through the city and out the other side, telling me when to turn and, though they didn't explain where we were going, it worried me they hadn't bothered to blindfold me or shove me in the boot. I wondered why they weren't concerned about me knowing where I was going. Maybe I wouldn't be coming back.

The place was another disused factory. It looked lifeless, like it hadn't produced anything for months, another victim of the downturn.

There was a Porsche Cayenne with blacked-out windows

parked outside. They made me stop by a pair of big metal doors then pushed me out of the car. They took my phone and my wallet and shoved me forwards through those same doors, which clanged shut behind me. I was now in a large, windowless room, but the electricity was still connected and I blinked at the bright strip lights above me.

There, in the middle of the room, stood a familiar figure. Tommy Gladwell, Arthur Gladwell's oldest boy, was smiling at me, looking about as pleased with himself as it was possible to be. He had the other two big Russians with him. Palmer had managed to get the right story out of the bloke we'd lifted at the gym. Whatever my man from the SAS had done to him, it had worked. He had told Palmer everything and suddenly it all made sense to me; Weasel-face and the Glasgow connection, even Tommy's black eye. It wasn't tired old Arthur Gladwell, the king of his city, who'd been gunning for us. It was Tommy, his eldest lad, the prince-in-waiting who'd grown tired of the wait. He was a gangster without an empire, too impatient to stand by until his dad finally croaked. He needed his own city to run, so now he was taking ours.

'What the fuck do you want?' I asked him, though I knew the answer to that already. I was doing my best to sound hard even though I didn't feel it. I would have given every penny I had to see Finney march through those big metal doors at that moment with a shotgun, with Bobby at his side. I wondered where they were and if they had any inkling of what was going on. Was there any chance they might get here before it was too late?

'Well first I want to give you a message,' Tommy Gladwell told me cheerfully then he glanced at the Russian who'd forced me into my car, 'Vitaly,' he said simply. Without a second's pause the guy punched me so hard in the guts I doubled up rapidly and fell face first onto the ground. I went down so fast I didn't even put a hand out to stop my head from smashing into the concrete floor. I tried to get up but the Russian had hit me with such force I couldn't even move. I felt blood trickle down my forehead. The pain was like nothing I'd ever experienced before. Christ, this bloke knew what he was doing.

'That's from my lad Stone,' he told me, 'the fellah you put in hospital with a broken jaw. He's got more stitches in his face than an eiderdown,' I made a note to get even with Stone if I ever got out of this mess, which right now seemed unlikely. 'You're lucky,' said Gladwell, 'he wanted me to break your jaw and carve your face up, an eye for an eye and all that, but I told him I needed to have a little chat with you first. Maybe there'll be time for breaking jaws later.'

'You're making a big mistake,' I told him when I finally got enough breath back to speak.

'Am I?' he asked 'what do you reckon? Do you think Finney will come after me with his nail gun?' he laughed and so did his Russians.

'You won't be fucking laughing when he does,' I said and they hauled me to my feet.

'There's something I want to show you,' he said, 'come on!'

Two of them picked me up, their big hands wedged under my armpits. They moved so fast I was being dragged along, the tips of my shoes scraping against the concrete as I was propelled to the other end of the room. They were still laughing, in obvious high spirits, sure of themselves. The door up ahead was wooden and they used my head to barge it open, rattling my teeth and stunning me in the process. Inside was a smaller room, which contained a little row of offices to one side.

It was pitch dark, so they flicked on the light in the first office to illuminate the scene. At first I could barely register what it was. It looked like some big animal had been mangled at an abattoir. Then it hit me with a sudden shock of realisation and I knew, just knew, that we were lost. There was no hope for any of us.

It was Finney - or what was left of him when the Russians

had all had their fun. His eyes were open wide and staring back at me but there was no life left in them. His face had been mutilated with what looked like a serrated knife, and the flesh around the wounds was red and swollen and puffed up like he had taken a hell of a beating. His hands and legs had been fastened to the big metal chair with handcuffs around each wrist and ankle. Someone had had the foresight to cement the chair into the ground beforehand because they knew from his reputation how hard he would have fought. Christ, how he would have struggled to get at them.

It looked like he had been tortured to death at first but then I noticed the ligature around his neck, which had bitten tightly into the skin. They'd finished him off with some sort of wire garrotte. It explained the open, sightless eyes that I couldn't tear my gaze from. Someone had calmly stood behind him and tightened it round his neck until Finney finally choked to death.

I was sick on the floor then.

'Pick him up,' ordered Gladwell and I was dragged up by my arms again and taken along to the next room. This one looked like an abandoned walk-in fridge, with all of the racking taken out. They turned the light on.

'As you can see, we've been busy,' Gladwell told me. Northam was easier to recognise. They'd not messed him up nearly as much as Finney. Our bent accountant looked the same as usual in fact, except for the bullet hole in his forehead. They'd done him just like they did Geordie Cartwright. 'And it's still early,' Gladwell reminded me, 'after all, we've got all night.'

'What do you want from me?' I managed to ask, my voice a low rasp.

'I'm not sure now. When I ordered you to be picked up we didn't have the full picture but it looks like I've already got what I need. The accountant, Northam, he was very keen to cooperate, once we showed him what we'd done to Finney. We didn't have to hurt him at all, though we hurt him a bit anyway to make sure he was telling the truth. He told us all about the business, filled in the gaps for us. By the time the lads picked you up we had it all anyway. We reward people who help us and he got his reward. His worries are over.'

'Where's Bobby?'

'All in good time.'

'What have you done to Bobby?' he ignored me. It seemed he was keen to let me know how clever he'd been.

'What do you think of my boys eh?' he asked me, 'heavy duty aren't they? Took out your doormen in double-quick time. I met them in Amsterdam running guns, dope and women. We took a little of all three,' so Gladwell had no scruples about whether the women in his knocking shops were volunteers or not. Some poor, young lass leaves her village in the Ukraine looking for a better life in the west and instead ends up being raped by a dozen strangers a day with none of the money going back to her. 'And we stayed in touch,' he made them sound like old pals from Uni.

'Vitaly here was a captain in the Russian army. Do you know what the Spetsnaz is?' I nodded weakly but he told me anyway, 'Russian special forces. They are just as hard as our boys, but prepared to go that little bit further, if you know what I mean. I put that down to Chechnya. Your average Russian soldier didn't want to get sent there, not with all the atrocities the rebels were prepared to commit but my boys here? Well, it was manna from heaven to them. They loved it. When they caught one of those rebels they'd cut off his ears, his nose, his dick, while he was still alive' and he laughed. 'I'm not kidding you,' I believed him, 'then they'd leave him somewhere his mates would find him - because they knew that the greatest weapon you can have is fear. You're going to understand that by the time you leave here.'

By now I was starting to hope I'd end up like Northam and

not Finney. That seemed my best option; to tell Tommy Gladwell whatever it was he wanted to know and hope they'd had enough of inflicting pain for one day. Then it would all be over.

Gladwell wasn't finished showing off. I guess he'd been waiting a long time to show the world how clever he was. 'They were just the right people to help me take over a city. My dad wouldn't have the stomach for it. He's too old and has no ambition any more. I'm different. I'm expanding our business and you lot, well, you're in the way. My boys have been watching Bobby and his whole crew for months but we had one big problem; Finney. If we took out Bobby's enforcer and left Bobby around he'd be well on his guard wouldn't he? But we couldn't get rid of Bobby and leave Finney on the streets. No way. That would be far too dangerous. I couldn't imagine Finney seeing sense and throwing his lot in with us. No, he was too stupid for that. Trouble was, you rarely saw them together these days, Finney and Bobby. But then, lo and behold, a miracle; Finney moved into Bobby's house,' his smile was broad, 'can you imagine how we felt when we heard that? Was it your idea? I bet it was. It would have been a good one too, if your enemy was a couple of hard knocks from Glasgow but I've got five heavily-armed former members of the Spetsnaz on my payroll.'

Five? I'd seen four. I wondered where the fifth was hiding.

'What do you want from me?'

'What can you give me? Go on, convince me, tell me why I shouldn't just kill you. You might be begging me to kill you in an hour when I let these lads at you. You see, they really enjoy their work.'

I shook my head. I didn't know what the hell he wanted and I had no idea what information I could give him that he didn't already have.

'That cunt Mahoney,' he hissed it angrily, 'wouldn't even shake my hand when he came to see my father. No respect,' he told me, 'well I think he respects me now don't you?'

Tommy was pacing up and down now, tight lipped, like the memory of the humiliation was fresh in his mind, 'you shook my hand. I remember that. You were the only one who did and that is the reason you are still alive, for now.'

That gave me an insight into the man we were up against. A forty year old with the chronic lack of self-esteem you get from living your whole life in the shadow of your old man. Tommy Gladwell hadn't been allowed to order a cab without running it passed his daddy first and now he was going to take us all down. Yet I was still alive, for now, because of a handshake.

'Where's Bobby,' I asked him again, 'what have you done with him?'

'He's in there,' said Gladwell and he jerked his head towards the next room. Vitaly shoved me out of the room we were in and up against the door of the next one.

'Open it,' he ordered.

I pushed the heavy wooden door and it creaked open. I was peering into the darkness of a gloomy store room but I couldn't see anything, 'Bobby?' I called.

Silence.

Vitaly pushed me into the room and turned on the light. At first I thought the figure in the chair was dead or unconscious, the body slumped, the silver hair streaked with blood from a blow to the skull. 'Bobby?' I called again and the head slowly came up.

Bobby Mahoney had been tied to his chair just like the others. I reckoned that was the only thing keeping him upright. His head lolled back again, he looked drugged or maybe it was just the effect of the beating they'd given him.

'Bobby,' I said it again, quieter this time, willing him to say something back to me but it was all he could manage just to return my gaze.

Gladwell was at my side, 'I'm going to give you a chance

boy,' he told me, 'just one, so think fast.' Vitaly gave an order in Russian and one of his men handed Gladwell his Makarov, the Soviet era military pistol that was the weapon of choice for Eastern Europeans in our game. It was widely available on the streets of every city in Britain because it was cheap as chips.

Gladwell took out the magazine and ejected all of the bullets then he held it up so I could see and put one bullet back into the magazine before slotting it back into the gun. 'You have a choice,' he told me, 'either this bullet goes in Bobby Mahoney's brain or it goes in yours.' Bobby finally made a sound. He actually laughed. It was a big, deep, mad laugh but I was astonished by his balls nonetheless. I wish I could have been that defiant.

'What?' was all I could manage.

'Tell me,' he urged, 'I want to hear you say it,' he cocked the pistol and pressed it hard against my skull, 'him or you? Go on.'

I looked at him then I looked at Bobby, who was still laughing, like Gladwell had just said something really funny.

I didn't want to say it. I didn't want to say anything.

'Say it!' ordered Gladwell.

'Him,' I croaked the word out, too ashamed to look at Bobby.

'Good lad,' he said like it was the correct answer and he lowered the gun.

Vitaly and one of his men grabbed me and pushed me forward till I was no more than a few feet from Bobby then they released their grip. Vitaly pulled his own pistol and stood to one side of me, then pressed it against my head.

'One move,' he told me, 'one move and… ' he made a sound like a gun firing. I got the message.

Gladwell walked round to face me, standing between Bobby and me. 'I'm glad you feel that way because you are going to have to earn your life today. We both know I need

Mahoney out of the way,' he told me reasonably, 'so I want you to do it for me.'

'What?'

He couldn't be serious. He didn't really want me to do it, surely.

Tommy Gladwell pulled my arm up then he pressed the Makarov into my right hand and wrapped my fingers round the cold metal of the gun. Before he released it into my grasp, the Russian pressed his pistol harder against my head.

'One move,' he reminded me.

Gladwell stepped away and walked behind me. I was left holding the gun in my outstretched hand and it was pointing straight at Bobby. He was staring back at me, serious now. The laughter had stopped.

'Do it,' urged Gladwell, 'shoot him and walk away.'

'Fuck off,' I managed, 'you'll kill me anyway.' I was still holding the gun in my outstretched hand. I could feel the barrel of Vitaly's gun pressing into my skull and sweat forming on my forehead.

'No I won't,' he assured me, 'do this thing and we are even. I'll put you on a train to London. You have my word.'

'Your word?' I didn't believe he could be serious.

'You're basically a civilian. You're no threat to me. What the fuck are you going to do on your own - without Finney, without Mahoney, you're nothing! But, like I said, you have to earn your life. You have one round. Use it on Mahoney and live. Try and use it on us and Vitaly will drop you where you stand. But I won't wait all day son. In a moment I'll start counting down from ten and when I finish, Vitaly will kill you anyway if you haven't done what I've asked. Then he'll kill Mahoney.'

This didn't make any sense to me. None at all.

'Then why get me to shoot him?'

'Because I want to make you do it.'

'Why?'

'To prove that I can.'

'What's the point?'

'Oh fuck this,' he suddenly lost patience, 'Vitaly… '

Vitaly cocked his gun, 'No!' I shouted, quickly, 'I'll do it.' I was just desperate to buy some time. That's what I needed. Time, to think, Christ, I needed time to think.

'Ten…' said Gladwell.

'Wait,' I said, my hand shaking so badly there was a chance I'd miss, even from here. I lowered the gun just a little.

'Nine… '

'Fucking do it,' said Bobby suddenly. Those were the first words he'd spoken since I walked in the room. His voice sounded incredibly weary all of a sudden, like he was tired of the game.

'Eight…' I levelled the gun again, pointing it straight at him.

'Good lad,' said Bobby, 'you're doing me a favour,' and he actually managed a grim smile of encouragement.

'Seven… '

'Do it, they'll do it anyway,' Bobby was selling the idea to me.

'Six…'

'Get out of here, find Sarah, look after her,' so that was his reason.

'Oh, she's being looked after,' said Gladwell and the Russians laughed.

'Five.'

I tried to squeeze the trigger but I couldn't. I tried again but my arm shook. I knew I was crying now like a little girl, tears streaming down my cheeks, my face all snot and tears. I let my arm drop and the gun fell to my side. My head went down and all I could see was my shoes. Next to me Vitaly said something that sounded like he was swearing in his own language.

'You stupid cunt,' Bobby told me.

'Four.'

I tried to raise my arm again but I couldn't. I just wanted

to lie down on the floor and let them shoot me so it would all be over.

'Three…'

'Do it you spineless fucking cunt! Do it!!' Bobby was screaming at me now.

'Two… ' I raised the gun again and pointed it straight at Bobby's head.

He grinned, 'I'll see you down in hell Tommy Gladwell you fat little queer!'

'One.'

'Do it,' screamed Bobby, 'fucking do it!'

So I did. I blew Bobby Mahoney's brains out.

THIRTY

....

I couldn't take my eyes off Bobby. I couldn't tear them away from what I had just done. That's why I hadn't even realised what Tommy Gladwell had been doing while I was killing my boss. It was only when his extended arm slowly came round in a big arc towards me that I realised he was holding a mobile phone. 'Smile son,' he told me, 'you're on Candid fucking Camera,' he handed the phone to Vitaly who put it in his inside jacket pocket, 'nice phone Vitaly,' he said and then he laughed. It was a big, gleeful, triumphant laugh because he knew he had won. I didn't care about that just now. All I cared about was the fact that I had just shot Bobby Mahoney through the head - and Gladwell had filmed the whole thing on Vitaly's mobile.

I took one last look at Bobby; his head forced back by the bullet, brain matter splattered all over the white wall behind him, then they took the empty gun from me and hauled me out of the room.

'Leave a couple of your lads to deal with the bodies,' Gladwell told Vitaly, 'put them in the incinerator.'

The Russian just nodded without enthusiasm. Why did I keep getting the impression Tommy Gladwell didn't really have a clue who he was dealing with? Six months down the line, with the city under their full control, it could just as easily be Gladwell who was staring down the barrel of a Makharov, on his way to the incinerator. I couldn't imagine these guys wanting to play the hired hands for long. They looked too bloody sure of themselves. None of that really mattered though. One way or the other, I was history.

I didn't expect for one minute that Tommy Gladwell would honour his promise and let me go, even when they didn't shoot me straight away, even when I was taken from the building, bundled into the back of the Porsche Cayenne and driven away. I was vaguely aware that my car was gone but I didn't care. I still expected Gladwell to order them to pull over somewhere quiet, drag me from the car, and shoot me in the face, just like they had done to Geordie Cartwright, Jerry Lemon, and Alex Northam; just like I had done to Bobby Mahoney. As we drove back into the city I still didn't believe it. I couldn't have done it. I hadn't just murdered Bobby Mahoney in cold blood. I wasn't muscle, I wasn't a gangster, not really, but now it seemed I *was* a murderer. How the fuck had that happened?

We were getting closer and closer to the bright lights of the city and I had to stop myself from actually believing they weren't going to kill me. I tried not to even think about the possibility they might let me go because then, when they didn't, it wouldn't hurt me quite so much. I was numb, inside and out, and the quicker this hell ended then the better it would be. I played out the scene in my mind over and over; everything that was said before it happened, me firing the Makarov like I was doing it in a dream, the bullet hitting the target, smacking into Bobby's head, jerking him back, jolting his body in the chair like it was a crash test dummy and all the blood that blew up out of the back of his skull, painting the wall behind him, sending dark red splashes out over the chipped, white plaster. Jesus Christ, what had I done?

I was vaguely aware of Gladwell in the car, wittering away to the two Russians or was it to me, or perhaps he was just talking to himself. He was like some excitable child on Christmas morning who had just found out Santa's been and given him everything he ever wanted.

Gladwell was in the front passenger seat, Vitaly was in the back with me and one of his men was driving. Gladwell kept shifting about in his seat, he couldn't keep still and he was turning round to talk to us, 'did you fucking see it, did you fucking see it?' he kept asking us, 'he just stepped up to the plate and bam!' he banged his hand on the dash board in front of him, 'I give this guy, this civilian, who's never so much as punched a bloke in his life probably, a shot at the title, a once-only offer to save his life but he has to kill a bloody legend and does he take that chance? Too fucking right he does! Nooo messing! Bang! Ten seconds I tell him and he waits right till the last one and I was thinking, oh wait a minute, he's not going to do this thing, then wham,' he hit the dash board again, 'he looks Bobby Mahoney in the eye, Bobby Mahoney mind you, king of the whole city, and he slots him, cool as you like. Oh, hello man, you were awesome son! You should be in my crew. Do you want to come and work for me, do you?' they all laughed like this was a hilarious suggestion, 'anyone needs slotting, he's our Top Boy from now on, I'll get him right on it. Oh yes! You've earned this son, you really have. But tell me, for the listeners,' he held out his hand and angled his fist towards me, as if he was holding a microphone, 'what's it like to be the main man, the cock of the fucking north? How does it feel to kill a legend?' I just stared right back at him because I had absolutely nothing to say to anyone, 'no? Cat got your tongue, has it? Oh well.'

The car swung over the Redheugh bridge and followed the one-way system back round in a loop to the railway station. They parked in the short term car park outside. Gladwell, Vitaly and the driver got out and I followed them dumbly. Could it be true? Were they really going to let me go? Surely they wouldn't just put me on a train like this - but how could they kill me now in front of hundreds of people at a railway station with everything captured on CCTV? Then I remembered the Russian's little camera phone and Tommy recording Bobby Mahoney's last moments on it. They were happy to let me go because they knew I couldn't talk to anyone about this. How could I explain I ended the life of the biggest crime boss in the history of the north east? Even if the police accepted I was forced to do it under duress, there would be a big queue of people with short fuses and long memories, who would never be so understanding. Gladwell knew, as long as he had that clip on his phone he was Bank-of-England-safe, it was his insurance policy. I was in no fit state to even attempt to get it back from his Russian. It was perfect for Tommy. If anybody did try and link him to the disappearance of Bobby Mahoney, if the heat got too intense, he could make sure the powers that be received the footage of me shooting Bobby - then they'd be looking for me all over the country instead of him.

Letting me go wasn't such a risk when you thought about it. From their perspective, there was really no one left to come after them now. Even Finney was dead and I'd always thought Finney was invincible. Bullets bounced off Finney, punches had no effect, he'd faced men with knives, guns, machetes and iron bars and come away with barely a scratch. If you took on Finney you ended up dead, or in hospital or a wheelchair. Nothing could stop him. But these Spetsnaz guys managed to bring him down in a night and they weren't even out of breath.

The concourse was alive with noise, from the trains arriving and departing, from the chatter of people, from the high-pitched chirrup of the birds circling high above us. I stood under the big, old, metal clock with the Russians, while Tommy went into the ticket office. All around me, people were going about their lives and I watched them dumbly. I was aware of young couples meeting for Friday night dates. One in particular, a boy who met a girl from her train and they embraced, before linking arms then heading off into the city together. I used to be like that, lifetimes ago. They seemed normal, happy, hopeful, inhabiting a world I now realised I had left behind years ago. One which I was finally fully wrenched from tonight, at the exact moment I put a bullet through Bobby Mahoney's brain.

I killed him, me, a civilian, not a gangster. I'm not that kind of man, yet I didn't pause long before squeezing the trigger and sending a round into my boss' head. How long had it taken? All of ten seconds. I had known Bobby Mahoney since I was a kid, been tied to him for good or bad, in one form or another, for more than two decades, protected him, looked out for him, taken his money and safeguarded his interests - and his daughter loves me, of that I'm sure. Yet how long did it take me to decide to end his life when the choice was put to me? Less even than a minute to betray everything I knew, just so I could stand here like a dummy on a cold station platform. And what did I get for it? Nothing much, just my life.

I killed a man.

I killed *the* man.

But I didn't have any choice, did I? I mean, what else could I have done?

I suppose I could have called out at that point, shouted for help or the police but even in my shocked state I knew that was a really dumb idea. All the cops would be left with was a bit of CCTV footage of me being stabbed and dropped on the ground. They'd issue descriptions of some shaven-headed blokes who'd be back in Moscow before their identikit pictures appeared in the Journal. Even if they didn't kill me, how could I explain what had happened? The police might not unreasonably deduce I was the real murderer when they received the clip from Vitaly's phone. So it wasn't going to happen. They'd won, they'd got me and they knew it.

All in all, I was astonished to be alive and I was almost pathetically grateful when Gladwell came out of the ticket office holding the long, thin piece of card that represented my freedom. I had to try very hard not to sob again at that point, because I was so relieved, 'I bought you a first class ticket,' he told me, 'a little reward for killing your boss for me. I thought it would be nice to give you one last taste of the high life before you disappear for ever,' and he smiled at me, 'you know I almost envy you. You've been given a great opportunity. You can start all over again with no shite and no baggage, a clean slate. There's many a man would kill for that, son. But then I guess you did,' and he laughed again but suddenly his smile vanished. He leaned forward and told me, 'just don't come back, ever, you hear. If you do there will be no mercy from me. There's nothing here for you now, everybody you ever worked with is dead and, if they're not, they'll be working for me when the weekend's out. I'll not be hanging around just now though. After all, I'm the man who shot Billy the Kid. I'm off to collect my missus then we're away home on the late train. I'm going to have a hot bath and a nice meal when I get in. Tomorrow night my lads here will be doing the rounds. There won't be a joint in the city that won't know it's under new ownership by midnight. You got that?'

I didn't have the energy to answer him but I managed a nod and he took that as a yes. He stuffed the ticket into my jacket pocket and one of the Russians gave me back my wallet. 'No credit cards but I left you a tenner in there,' said Gladwell, 'let's see how far that gets you in London eh?' and he laughed again, 'put him on the train.'

The two Russians stood on the platform so they could see me through the window, making sure I didn't try and get off but there really was no danger of that. They waited until the electric doors hissed then thumped suddenly closed and the train started to pull away before they turned their backs. By then I couldn't have got off even if I'd wanted to and, believe me, I didn't want to. Vitaly couldn't resist lifting his hand in something between a wave and a mock salute.

It was late. I was all alone in my half of the first class carriage and I was glad of it. I slumped back in the chair and my head lolled to one side as the train went high over the Tyne, crossing the railway bridge, speeding away from the city that had been my home all my life, a place to which I knew I could never return. I was so tired I could barely muster the energy to hand over my ticket when the conductor walked through. Despite my exhaustion, the relief flooded through me. It wasn't me in that chair in a lock up with a bullet through my head, it wasn't me that had been tortured to death for the numbers of Bobby's bank accounts and it wasn't me that had been beaten unrecognisable because four ex-Spetsnaz men wanted to prove they were tougher than me. I was grateful for that. I should be grateful. I *was* grateful, definitely. But something was wrong.

I wasn't grateful enough.

All the way down as far as Durham, I kept telling myself how lucky I'd been. I'd survived a war, a war that had killed all of my comrades. Like Gladwell said, I'd been given a chance to start again, to go legit, live like a normal person. When I arrived in London, a whole new world would open up to me. I could live a life without fear. I had half convinced myself I believed all of this by the time the train pulled into Durham station, the illuminated horizon of its castle and cathedral on the hill telling me that a half hour journey had gone by in an instant, so wrapped up had I been in my thoughts.

I stayed on the train. One thing I was definitely going to do was stay on the train. Getting off it would be suicide.

I was worried though. Gladwell had footage that could get me a life sentence should he ever feel like using it. And that was only half of it. What the hell was I going to do in London, realistically? What job was I qualified for and who was going to want to take me on? My business card said I was a sales and marketing director but I wasn't. I was an ideas man for a gangster and they don't advertise those posts in the paper. Getting a job like that is about trust and being known by the man who employs you. No one in London knew or gave a fuck about me.

That idea I used to have about owning a restaurant? I knew nothing about restaurants except how to eat in them. It was a load of shite, a dream no more realistic than the one I'd had about playing for Newcastle when I was a kid. Face facts. It was never going to happen. I was going to be nothing in London, a nobody. The money I'd get from selling my flat wouldn't get me a cupboard down there. I'd end up pulling pints behind a bar or washing dishes in a hotel. Shit job, shit pay, shit life, might as well be dead, which was something I hadn't thought about when they were pointing a gun at my head.

The train pulled away once more and something began to happen to me. Somehow the fear I felt when I thought I was going to be killed or tortured started to recede. It had become more like a distant feeling and was slowly being replaced by something else. Anger.

We'd been sloppy, we'd taken our eye off the ball, we'd thought we could go on like this forever. Like every top champion that has ever lived, there came a day when we were knocked off our perch by someone else but that wasn't the only thing burning into my brain. We had been out-thought and out-fought by wee Tommy Gladwell, the unproven, first born son of Arthur Gladwell. I told myself if it had been anybody else, someone more worthy of respect, then I could have accepted it but this just wasn't right. I knew a bit about Tommy Gladwell and if he ran Newcastle there'd be no hope for anyone. Bobby knew how to be Top Boy. Hell, even I knew how to be Top Boy. I'd watched Bobby do it for years, learned it from him, given him new ideas that helped him to be the successful boss that he so obviously was. Together we knew how to keep order, we helped to keep the city ticking over. His other lieutenants weren't there to advise him, give him big ideas, work out the strategy and the tactics needed to run an empire. I was the only one who could do that for him. I'd watched him for so long. It was always just a question of judgement. You had to say the right things to the right people at the right time, keep the wheels oiled, control the men who work for you and never give them an excuse to turn against you. Easy, except I still wouldn't trust anybody from our crew, alive or dead, to do the job after Bobby. There was nobody I could work for without the risk of ending up in prison or the mortuary being way too high. I wouldn't trust anybody.

Not one.

Well, maybe one.

Jesus, after all, *I* was the man who *really* shot Billy the Kid.

And there was one more thing that clinched it. I'd tried hard not to think about her. I'd told myself there was nothing I could do, no way I could help. It was somebody else's problem now but I knew that wasn't going to work. There was no way I could just ignore it. I'd been so damn scared, I wanted to banish any thought that kept me from putting at least three hundred long miles between myself and Vitaly but I couldn't help myself because I knew I had to help her. *Sarah*.

I got off the train at Darlington.

THIRTY-ONE

....

It was starting to rain. There were some young lads standing around outside the station trying to look hard. I walked straight up to them,

'I'll give you a tenner for a use of your phone.' The lad looked at me like I was mental. I stuffed the note into his shirt pocket and I must have looked as if I'd had a very bad night because, without a word, he handed me his mobile. They all eyed me suspiciously, as if I was going to run off with his precious Nokia, 'don't worry,' I told him, 'you'll get it back.' And I turned away as I dialled Palmer.

'Jesus,' he hissed, 'where've you been? I've been ringing you for ages.'

'My phone's gone but don't worry about that. Get in your car and drive. I need you to pick me up, now.'

'Okay,' he said, 'where are you?'

'Standing outside Darlington station.'

'Darlington?' he asked, 'what are you doing there?'

'Just get here,' I snapped, 'on your way down I need you to make sure I have a car, a phone and a few hundred quid waiting for me when we get back to Newcastle. Get one of your boys to meet you with that outside my brother's place.'

'No problem,'

'And I want you to bring something with you now.'

'What?'

I kept my voice low as I told him then I rang off and threw the phone back to the young lad. I walked out of the station and down the ramp, turning the collar of my jacket up against the rain.

Palmer didn't say anything when I climbed into the car. There was plenty of time for explanations on the drive back to Newcastle. I waited till we were on the main road before I asked him.

'Did you bring it?'

'Glove compartment.'

I opened the glove box and took it out, weighed it in my hand but kept it low, out of sight, 'loaded?'

"Course,' then he gave me a look, 'not taking the piss, but have you ever fired a gun before?'

'Yep,' I told him casually, not adding how recently.

'Fair enough,' he said.

I put the Glock back in the glove compartment and closed it.

'I need to tell you what's been going on,' I told him, 'I am going to be relying on you, so you'd better be on your game.'

'Right,' he said simply. What I liked about Palmer was that he never seemed fazed about anything. It was hard to imagine a jeep through some plate glass doors. He didn't look like that sort of guy - but then I probably didn't look like a murderer.

'Tommy Gladwell and his Russians are trying to take over the city tonight,' I said.

He nodded sagely, 'and we are going to stop them?'

'Yeah,' I said resisting the temptation to add, 'we are going to try.'

'There's just one thing,' I told him, 'you know that Tommy is Arthur's boy and you know all about Arthur Gladwell?'

'That scussy wee shite. Aye, I've heard of him but he doesn't scare me if that's what's worrying you?'

'It's not that,' I said, 'it's just, you're both from Glasgow so, if that's going to be a problem, I need to know it now.'

'If it's a question of loyalty,' he said, 'Tommy Gladwell didn't put food on my table when I was cashiered out of the army. You did.'

I wasn't expecting a big speech and I didn't get one but what he'd said was good enough for me.

'In any case, Arthur Gladwell is a boil on Glasgow's arse, always has been. He won't be winning any popularity contests up there.'

Palmer had a couple of questions but it didn't take long to put him in the picture. He'd already tortured most of the story out of grey-hair, whose real name turned out to be Terry apparently, but there was one last piece of the jigsaw that I still didn't have.

'Did you get that name for me?'

'Yeah,' he said thoughtfully, 'I did.'

And when he told me who had been selling us out, I have to say that, for some reason I still can't fathom, I wasn't even a bit surprised.

I'd never been happier to experience the unmistakeable smell of tobacco and stale piss outside the flats, especially when I noticed there was a light on in Our-young-un's window. I left Palmer in the car to watch my back and wait for his man to show up with the cash, the phones and the car. I went to collect Danny. I didn't want to hang about. We needed to be gone from there as soon as. I couldn't afford to be caught in the city by Vitaly and his thugs.

I was pretty sure Danny would be okay. I couldn't see why anyone, even someone who had been tailing me for weeks, would consider my bro to be anything other than a washed-up version of his former self. He was obviously a civilian who had nothing to do with any part of Bobby Mahoney's business but, just to be sure, I had the Glock.

The bell has never worked as long as I've been coming here, so I banged on the door. No answer. I hammered again, a bit louder this time, and still he didn't come to the door. That wasn't like him. Danny wasn't a heavy sleeper even when he'd been drinking. I reached for my keys and found the spare one for the front door that I kept on the fob for emergencies. This was definitely an emergency. I told myself everything would be alright, as I opened the door, but I was already beginning to have a very bad feeling about it.

My brother could be a bit jumpy, what with his war experiences and everything, so I made sure I didn't burst in there unannounced. Instead I pushed the door wide and, before I stepped in, I called his name. No answer. The flat was quiet, the lights were on but he didn't seem to be about. I called his name again, louder this time and that's when I saw him.

Danny was sitting in his old arm chair in the lounge. Because his back was to me, the only bit of him I could actually see was his left hand, which was resting on the arm of the chair. It was quite still. My brother wasn't moving.

'Danny,' I called quietly at first, because my heart had shot up into my throat, and it was stopping the words from coming out. How could he have not heard me banging on the door? Unless…

Oh no, not him, not my brother as well.

'Danny!' I called his name louder now. After all, he could be asleep. I told myself that he could be asleep but I knew he wasn't asleep. A sleeping person would have heard me by now, 'oh Christ,' then I was running across the lino towards him. The bastards had killed my brother.

I reached the chair and in the same moment I put my palm onto his hand and leaned round to see his poor, dead face.

And he screamed.

Danny screamed. He spun towards me and grabbed me by the throat. Next thing I knew I was being lifted off the ground and I was so relieved to see his scared, startled, lovely face that I forget to be annoyed when he upended me in one instinctive, fluid movement and threw me down on the deck. Then he was standing over me, one hand tight round my throat again and the other pulled back and formed into a fist like he was about to smash my bloody face in.

'It's me, it's me,' I gurgled and at that point he seemed to snap out of whatever auto pilot he was on. His eyes narrowed in confusion and he looked at me like I'd gone mad, 'you're alive,' I said, not quite believing it myself, 'I knocked, I called your name,' I blurted out by way of explanation, 'Christ I thought they'd killed you.' And it was only then I finally realised why he didn't answer, why he couldn't hear me. There was a long, thin, white wire hanging down from his ear.

'I was listening to me iPod man!' he told me with not a little irritation, 'I said I was going to sort it,' he was shouting, as one ear piece from the iPod was still in place, the other one had fallen out. He pulled the remaining one free, 'anyway,' he asked, 'who's supposed to have killed me?'

Palmer's guy Toddy sorted me out with a BMW 7 series. He gave Danny his semi automatic. I issued instructions and they left without a fuss. Now that I had Danny with me I could leave Palmer to it.

In my pocket I still had the shabby little business card Joe Kinane had given me down at the Cronk. I reached for the new phone Palmer's man had supplied me and dialled. Kinane answered like he'd just woken up.

'I need to meet you,' I said.

He recognised my voice straight away, 'What? Right now? Where? Why?'

I didn't have time for subtlety and there was no need for it. I had to get my message across to him so he understood what was going on right away with no pauses, no questions and no fucking about. 'Bobby's dead,' I said and I waited for that to sink in.

'Jesus,' he said a moment later. 'Fuck's sake,' he added. 'I don't believe it.' He wasn't doubting me, it was a figure of speech.

'Believe it,' I told him, 'it's true. Bobby's dead and so is Finney. I've seen it with my own eyes.'

'Bloody hell,' he said as he came to terms with the fact that the man he hated more than any other was dead. I guessed that, more than any other emotion, he would feel cheated.

'Bobby Mahoney is dead,' I told him again so it would sink in, 'Finney's dead, Northam's dead. Jerry Lemon and Geordie Cartwright you know about already. They are all gone, all dead.'

'Fuck! What's happened?'

I ignored him, 'I'll explain it all to you when I see you. I need you to come to the house of a guy called Palmer who works for me. He's coming round to fetch you now, you and your sons. I'm going to need all of your boys from the gym, but tonight just bring your sons. Don't bring anybody with you who isn't family.'

'Right,' he said, 'what have you got in mind?'

'I'm offering you a deal Kinane,' I told him, 'a very good one.'

THIRTY-TWO

....

Our-young-'un and me headed west across the city. I was driving as fast as I dared but I still had to be careful because I couldn't run the risk of being pulled over by the police, not with a gun on me.

'I need to know I can rely on you,' I told Danny, 'because of what's happened, you and Palmer are just about the only people left I can trust.'

'Of course,' he sounded almost offended. 'You can rely on me man,'

'I mean it Danny. You used to say that you and your mates in the army were like brothers, you'd do anything for each other, well I'm your real brother and I need to know what you are prepared to do for me.'

He mulled that over for less than a second, 'anything, name it.'

'Even if it's dangerous.'

'Well, yeah, no sweat like.'

'Even if it means killing.'

He thought that one over for a moment. 'You wouldn't ask me unless it was the only choice. I know that. I owe everything to you man, everything. Don't know where I'd be without you but it sure as hell wouldn't be here.'

'Thanks,' I mumbled, feeling grateful and uncomfortable at the same time.

'Anyhow,' he said quietly, 'killing's not as hard as you might think.'

He was right there.

'I've never asked you this before,' I told him, 'and I wouldn't ask it now but I've got to because I'm trusting you with my life and the lives of the people who work for me. What happened to you in the Falklands that made you the way you are?'

'The way I am?' he asked as if he didn't comprehend me.

'You know what I mean,' and he fell silent for a time.

'Aye,' he said quietly, 'I know what you mean.'

'Was it at Goose Green?'

He just nodded.

'You don't have to tell me,' I admitted, 'but I have to know that, whatever it is, it won't stop you from being on top form when I need you.' I was starting to think this might have been a bad idea, that I should have left Our-young-'un in his flat and done this on my own, except I didn't know how.

'It's alright,' he said, 'I was only eighteen,' and he shook his head as if he couldn't imagine being that young in a war zone, 'eighteen but I can remember most of it like it was yesterday,' then he let out a bitter laugh, 'and I can't remember yesterday.' He leant back in his seat, against the headrest. 'When the battle started we got pinned down, they had more men and about a dozen trenches with machine guns zeroed in. We couldn't get through them and it looked like we were in the shit big style. I thought we were all going to die, I really did. Then Colonel H, he got up and led the way, went after a couple of machine guns with two of our NCOs and well, you know what happened.'

I nodded, 'that's how he got his VC,' I knew the tale of Lieutenant Colonel H Jones, Commanding Officer of 2 Para, well enough to recite it myself.

'Posthumous VC,' Danny corrected me, 'he went straight at them but the machine guns got him in the end. Bravest thing I ever saw. It was his example that got the boys up the hill that day.'

I could see how much Danny respected bravery and I was starting to get a sick feeling like he was going to admit something to me that I might not want to hear. All these years I'd took it as read that my brother was a hero who went into battle in a hail of bullets, against awful odds. I didn't think I'd be able to cope with it now if he suddenly told me he was a coward. Having one in the family was quite enough.

'So what happened?'

'I did my job,' he said, 'but I didn't do enough,' his voice faltered, 'I found cover when I had to, I went forward when the NCOs ordered me to, I fired my rifle, I even killed a man, shot him from a distance and found his body when we went forward again. He didn't look any older than me, but...'

'But what?'

'That's all,' he said, 'I didn't distinguish myself. I kept my head down when some of the others were running through the bullets. I moved after they moved. I fired after they fired, I was never the first to get up that hill. I made sure I didn't get my head blown off. I came out the other side without a scratch. We lost seventeen men. Seventeen dead and sixty four wounded and I didn't even stub my toe on a rock. When I look back on it now I sometimes feel like I wasn't really there, the fear stopped me from performing the way I know I could have, the way they'd trained me to. I should have been quicker. I should have been stronger. I should have been first.'

'Christ!' I shouted in exasperation, 'is that it?'

'What do you mean is that it?' he looked at me like I was crazy.

'I thought you'd seen something awful or done something awful. All these years I thought maybe you'd accidentally shot one of your mates, or murdered some Argie prisoners or run away or something.

'Run away?' he asked me, 'Course I didn't fucking run away. What do you take me for?'

'I don't know Danny, maybe not run away but I thought it was something worse than… well what you've just told me. Jesus, your whole life,' I couldn't comprehend him, 'you've been so messed up since then and that's all it's been about? Just because you weren't bloody Rambo?'

'I did see something awful,' he told me calmly, 'the whole battle was awful, people having their arms and legs blown off, mates from my company getting shot in the head, of course it was awful.'

'But that wasn't what kept you awake at night?' I said quietly, 'was it?'

'No,' he told me, 'you don't get it, you weren't in the army. The thing that gets you through it is your mates and the fear of letting them down. That's worse than being shit scared of dying or ending up paralysed or a vegetable. Worse than all the god-awful horror of a battle is how scared you are that you are going to let your mates down when it comes to the crunch. That's the code. I can't tell you how it feels when you are standing in the pissing rain next to one of those big, open graves full of body bags, while the padre reads out the names of your friends and all you can think of is "I could have done more",'

'Did someone say something to you?' I asked him, 'afterwards. Did someone say you'd let your mates down, that you'd not done enough?'

'No,' he said, 'no, nobody said anything, but I knew I had and that's all that matters.'

'Shit Danny, you didn't fuck up. You did your job. It's not like you dug a hole and hid in it crying. You moved, you fired your gun, you engaged the enemy and you killed one of them. You weren't Audie Murphy but Jesus man, who is? If you'd done any more they'd have been burying you on that bloody hill. You were 18 for Christ's sake. Everybody I know still thinks you're a total hero just for being there and walking through that. You didn't fuck up and you have no reason for feeling like a failure. The only thing you really feel guilty about is surviving and I can understand it, but that's just the luck of war. Thank God you weren't one of the poor bastards who didn't come back. We did. Me and ma, we thanked God.'

'I thought you were an atheist?'

'I am but back then I was only a wee bairn, so I prayed anyhow, every night.'

'I know you did and I'm grateful but I tell you there hasn't been a day when I haven't relived that bloody battle in my head and wished I'd done better, wished I'd been the soldier I know I could have been.'

I thought about this for a moment that seemed to stretch out in front of us.

'You still can be Danny,' I told him firmly, 'you still can be.'

The front door to the Gosforth mansion was hanging off its hinges when we got there. I held the gun out in front of me, in case the fifth Russian was still there with Sarah, and walked inside. Danny followed me in. I hadn't forgotten there were meant to be five of them. I'd been dialling Sarah's mobile number on and off with Palmer's phone since he picked me up outside the railway station. No answer. I was worried sick but I couldn't let that distract me. I'd be no use to her dead.

The only sign of a struggle was in the hallway; an up-ended table, the phone lying redundantly on the carpet next to it. We gave the downstairs a quick once-over and found nothing.

There wasn't a sound. I left Danny watching the door and slowly inched my way up the stairs, not bothering to call out because I didn't want to warn anyone who might still be up there keeping a guard on Sarah. I could feel my heart thumping. I'd have sworn the sound was audible it was pounding so fast.

The landing was clear, the door to Sarah's room open. It was empty, the posters from her pre-college days seeming absurdly innocent, all pop stars and cute animals.

There was a light on in what I took to be the master bedroom. I could see it beneath the crack in the door. I listened intently but heard nothing. I began to feel too vulnerable on the landing. This Russian could drop me through the door before I even saw him, but it was too late to go back now. I had to find Sarah. I took a few quick steps towards the door and kicked it open, pointing the gun out in front of me Jack Bauer-style as I stepped through.

THIRTY-THREE

....

Sarah was on the floor. She was sitting up, dressed in just a fleece and knickers like she'd been about to go to bed but there was a pair of torn leggings on the floor nearby. From the look on her face, she was in shock. And she had good reason to be judging by what else was on the floor in front of her; a big, shaven-headed, presumably Russian, bastard, lay face down and motionless. His trousers were round his knees and there was an old lock knife sticking out of his neck. The full size mirror had a big, wide arc of blood across it and more blood covered the floor. Some of it had even reached the ceiling. As I drew nearer, I realised some of it was on Sarah's face.

Good girl, I thought, and the relief flooded through me. Sarah Mahoney had never been near her old man's world, yet the minute she was cornered, her instincts kicked in and she killed rather than be killed. Talk about a chip off the old block.

It looked like the Russian had been dead a while. She must have been sitting here on her own looking at the body for hours, too shocked to move, just waiting for someone from Bobby's crew to turn up and help her but, of course, no one came. I was the only one left.

When she finally registered it was me, Sarah jumped to her feet and ran towards me. I had just enough time to move the gun before she threw her arms around me. I couldn't tell you how relieved I was that she was alive.

'Are you alright?'

'Yes.'

'Did he hurt you?' I asked.

'Tried,' she said.

We left the dead Russian where he lay and I steered her to her bedroom. I pulled an old suitcase down off of the top of the wardrobe and told her, 'pack some clothes, enough for a couple of days,' then I added, 'you've got two minutes.' I didn't want the other Russian guys turning up looking for their friend.

Sarah pulled on her jeans, stuffed some clothes and toiletries in her bag and we got out of there.

'This is my brother Danny,' I told her when we reached the bottom of the stairs.

'Good to meet you pet,' he said.

The keys to Bobby's Jag were on the floor by the phone. I picked them up and said, 'Danny, take the Beamer and follow me.' I didn't want Bobby's car sitting there in the morning. That wasn't part of my plan.

'What happened?' I asked as I roared along the driveway.

'They took dad and Finney,' she said. 'I was in my room and I heard a big bang and when I went to the top of the stairs to see what had happened the door was hanging off and there were these big blokes with shotguns - Russians or Poles?'

'Russians,' I told her. 'Was anybody else with them?'

'Yeah,' she said with anger in her voice, 'a Scottish bloke

and a fucking bitch.'

'A woman?' she nodded. So Lady Macbeth was in on the act. She'd live to regret that if I had my way. 'Did she say anything to you?'

'She told one of the guys to stay behind and watch me then she called up the stairs, telling me to come down. I could see they were dragging dad and Finney away, so I legged it into dad's office. He keeps his lock knife in a desk drawer so I opened it up and stuffed it in the pocket of my fleece. When I got back to the top of the stairs she was sneering at me from the bottom with that big lunk next to her. She said "little girls need to learn to do what they're told by their elders" then she turned to the bastard and said "keep her quiet, you can do what you like".' Sarah put her hand up to her forehead like she might be about to pass out but she managed to continue, 'I started shouting "leave me alone, my father will fucking kill you" and the bitch laughed,' Sarah shook her head, 'she just laughed, then she said "oh get over yersell hen".' It was a pretty good impression of Lady Macbeth's thick Glasgow accent.

'She left with all of the others and the guy you saw came up the stairs. I still didn't believe he was going to do it but he hit me then he tore my leggings off. When he started undoing his trousers I grabbed the knife and stabbed him.'

Sarah had been incredibly brave and very lucky. She probably only had one chance to knife the guy somewhere vital before he'd have disarmed her, raped her and most probably killed her. But she'd earned her luck.

'I didn't want to kill him,' she said quietly. 'I just wanted it to stop.'

'I know,' I said, 'you did well, you did the right thing. It was him or you.' I spoke the words like the expert on killing I had recently become.

We drove in silence for a minute while she plucked up the courage to ask me. I knew it was coming but I was dreading it.

'What about Dad?' she asked quietly.

She had a right to know about her old man. I couldn't lie to her and tell her everything was going to be alright, because it wasn't. But what was I supposed to do? Tell her the old fellah was gone because of me, tell her I killed him because I was forced into it by a Glasgow gangster, that they would have killed me too if I hadn't done it. That I had no more choice in killing Bobby than she did in topping that big Russian? It was him or me. Is that what I was supposed to tell her?

I didn't think so.

'He's gone, Sarah,' I said quietly, 'Finney too.'

She's a tough cookie Sarah and I think she half expected it would end like that for her dad one day. Maybe she'd been preparing for this moment all her life because she just nodded and said, 'thank you for telling me,' as if it was somehow a relief that I didn't try to lie to her. She started weeping silently next to me as I drove. She made no sound at all but occasionally, out of the corner of my eye, I would see her sweep her arm up to her face to wipe her eyes with the back of her hand. By the time we reached Palmer's rented house she'd dried them. I parked up and she followed me inside, her eyes red and puffy.

I realised Sarah had just had a night on a par with mine. We had both nearly died and we had both killed a man for the first time in our lives. She'd had it worse, she'd lost her beloved dad in the process.

But there was no time to think about any of that right now. We were at war.

I made Sarah go up to the spare room and wait there. I didn't want her to hear any of this. I followed her into the spare room and she sat on the edge of the bed. She looked up at me, appealing.

'I want to do something,' she said, 'I want to help you, for my dad.'

'Believe me when I say this, I knew your dad for a very long time and the last thing he would want is for me to involve you in any of this,' I told her. 'I will handle it, I promise.'

'Are you going out again tonight?' she asked, looking scared.

I nodded, 'I'll leave someone behind. He'll be downstairs all night and tomorrow. You're totally safe. Nobody knows you're here. You can stay in the room if you want.'

'I don't want you to leave me again,' she looked terrified.

'Listen to me,' I told her and I stopped her protests by putting both of my hands out and gently holding her face between them, 'I have to go and do this one thing. I have to finish it and I will be back, I promise you.'

She opened her mouth to say something but I interrupted her, 'I need you to do something for me. I need you to be brave until I sort this mess out. Then I promise I'll come back and I will never leave you alone again, I swear.' She looked like she was going to cry again, but not in the same way. This was a different emotion. Relief perhaps.

I kissed her, there in the bare, spare room of that rented house. It was a strange place for our first proper kiss but it had been a strange night. That kiss was a promise and we both made it.

Palmer's rented house could have been described as minimalist, as if the bare walls, limited furniture and an absence of family photos were some deliberate design statement. I knew differently. He was a bloke who just didn't value stuff. He had a 42-inch plasma TV on one wall to watch the football on a Sunday afternoon, a fridge full of beers and a couple of small couches to sit on but precious little else, so we just stood around in his kitchen.

Palmer had rounded them up. They were all there, just like I asked: Palmer, Toddy, Mickey Hunter, Danny, Kinane and all three of his sons.

I turned to Hunter and nodded. He put two long, bulky, black holdalls on the kitchen table and unzipped them both.

Hunter took out the weapons one by one and placed them carefully on the table. He had brought everything I'd asked for. If he had been surprised to see Kinane and his sons he didn't make a big deal out of it, just nodded in the older man's direction, then he talked us through the guns he'd brought with him.

'Four Beretta semi-automatic shotguns. From what you tell me there's no need to saw off the barrels?' He was obviously trying to find out more but I wasn't about to tell Mickey Hunter what I had planned.

'No need,' I confirmed.

'I'm grateful for that small mercy.' He held up the ammo to show us, 'don't fuck about with these, they're two and a quarter-ounce Super Magnum cartridges. They'll bring down a rampaging elephant,' and we all nodded respectfully. Kinane and his sons picked up the shotguns and started loading them like they knew what they were doing, which I didn't doubt.

'Danny,' said Hunter. My brother was paying attention alright and he even smiled when he saw what Hunter was taking out of the bag for him, 'the SLR; British Army, standard-issue, semi-automatic rifle from your time and beyond. I don't have to tell you anything about this, do I?'

'No mate,' said Danny as he picked it up, scrutinised its length closely, peered down its barrel then held it reverentially, 'you don't have to tell me anything about it.'

'Better than the SA80 any day,' said Palmer, appearing at his side, 'that won't jam in a bloody sand dune.' The two of them were gazing at the rifle like it was a picture of an old and much-loved girlfriend.

'I thought you might feel that way,' Hunter told Palmer, 'so I brought you one as well.'

'Nice one.'

'Sure you don't need anything?' Hunter asked me, 'I put another shotgun in the car, just in case.'

I shook my head. I was happier with the Glock and less likely to blow my own foot off with it.

Hunter handed me the long, thin black bag, 'and you asked for this.'

'Thanks,' I said taking it from him without another word.

'You going to war?' asked Hunter, a little nervously.

'Maybe,' he was still fishing. I jerked my head so he would follow me out of the kitchen where we couldn't be heard. More importantly it would separate him from the others and he wouldn't be able to hear me speaking to them later. 'I need you to stay here with Toddy. Don't go anywhere. Keep your phone handy.'

'No sweat,' he said, though he did look a bit worried, 'I wasn't planning to leave the country or anything.'

'Make sure you don't,' I told him. Then I gave him a smile like he was my best mate.

I returned to the front room and I didn't waste any time. I went through it all; what happened to Bobby, Finney and Northam and who was behind it - except I left out the bit about me shooting Bobby, but you can't blame me for that. I then told them what we were going to do about it. There weren't many questions. They all knew we were in the shit and if we didn't act now, we'd lose the city for good.

We left Hunter and Toddy with Sarah. Danny and Palmer went in one car with two of Kinane's sons. Kinane and his eldest came with me. Kinane sat up front while I drove.

'I always thought I'd have the chance to sort it out,' Kinane said, 'you know, me and Bobby, even after all this time. We fell out over nowt really, pride more than anything. We were both stubborn fuckers, always were,' he sounded almost affectionate, 'these Russian tossers have robbed me of that and they are going to pay.' I was glad he was angry and so confident. I wasn't. 'Even Finney,' he continued, 'I mean, he was a cunt and everything but he didn't deserve that. It's no way to go is it?'

'No,' I said, 'it's no way to go.'

I didn't want to talk about it. I didn't want to talk about anything. Soon we'd be at the farm house.

What is it about certain nationalities and drinking? I mean, Geordies like a drink as much as the next man but they don't go about it with the fervour of some countries. It's not their religion. If they have one at all it's football not drink. The Irish are different. They sink booze like they are trying to fill a deep, despairing void in their lives.

With the Russians, I'd always assumed they drank because there was sod all to do under the communists but they've been free of them for years, so it has to be something deeper than that, otherwise they'd have stopped when the wall came down and everyone got cable. It's more like a national pastime to them. I dated a Russian girl once. She taught me a phrase 'Do Dna'. The Russians say it to each other when they raise a glass. It means 'to the bottom'. No half measures with these guys.

So it was no great surprise to me when Palmer reported back, 'they make party,' he said in a joke Russian accent, 'slugging back the vodka. Guess they thought with Bobby and Finney out of the way, it was all over.'

'Then we'll leave them to it,' I said, 'until the morning, nice and early.'

I'd always known it would be handy having an ex-special forces guy on our team. I don't know anyone else who would have calmly climbed from his car and walked across the fields in the pitch darkness to that farmhouse, watching close enough to see those sickos glugging back their vodka, then cheerfully reported back to me.

We left while it was still dark, Palmer leading the way, crouched low and moving silently across the fields to the farm house. The rest of us followed on behind, me wincing at every sound we made. By now I could have sworn Vitaly and his mates were capable of hearing every blade of grass we trampled.

There wasn't much moon but if they'd bothered with sentries they'd have seen dark shapes breaking the horizon behind us and we would never have got close enough. Luckily for us, they must have thought their job was all but done. I never took my eyes off that farmhouse as it gradually drew nearer, its slate-grey walls growing bigger with every step.

We had to resist the temptation to run, knowing we needed to be silent. Instead we followed Palmer's lead, walking slowly and fanning out, so we didn't make one big, easy target.

The last thirty yards or so were the worst, out in the open with no cover to dive behind, knowing all it would take was some pissed-up Ivan stumbling out of the farmhouse for a piss or a cig and it would all be over. As soon as his mates heard him screaming blue murder, we wouldn't have a chance in the open.

I could hear my own breathing, which sounded incredibly loud to me in my overwrought state, my breath coming out in plumes of white in front of me against the cold air. My heart was thumping in my chest again. What if I had messed this up? What if Palmer wasn't half as good as we both thought he was and the Russians were better? We'd be dead that's what - and if we were really lucky it would be quick. But if we weren't... Christ I was scared.

We made it to the relative cover of the hedge and stopped, hunching down low. Palmer held up his hand and we all froze, quiet as we could be, while he had a listen. The farmhouse was silent. Maybe they were asleep already. Was it too much to hope that they'd all passed out drunk in there? Probably.

Palmer patted Danny quietly on the shoulder and pointed

to a gap in the bushes a few yards along from where we were. Danny nodded and moved silently away towards his firing point. I'd never seen him so alert before.

Kinane and his boys knew what to do. Palmer had given them their instructions and, thankfully, the big man had deferred to the former soldier's experience in these matters. Kinane and his sons got to their feet and walked round the hedge into the open farmyard. I watched them make their way with exaggerated care across the wide open space. Christ, this was worse than crossing the field. A little sliver of light coming out of the farmhouse illuminated a section of the land they were forced to cross. They were moving like children playing a game of Simon Says, pulling their feet up higher than normal, then placing their boots down on the gravel with a gentleness I'd have thought impossible of such big men. Even so, their footsteps were clearly audible in the silence of the night. Surely they'd be heard before they made it to the other side?

Then I heard a noise, a loud grating, piercing sound from within the house that made me start. Someone was shouting. They'd been spotted.

I shot a glance at the house, expecting the door to fly open and armed men to rush out at any second. I made a move for my gun and Palmer placed his hand firmly on mine to prevent me from doing something stupid. I looked back to the farm yard and saw Kinane standing there, poised somewhere between standing firm, ready to fire his gun, and getting ready to leg it. His hand was in the air in warning, keeping his sons from shooting at shadows or panicking into a sprint.

I still couldn't place the sound. It was a shout, but was it really one of alarm? I could feel the sweat dripping from my armpits down my torso, cold and wet. I didn't dare to even blink, in case I missed something that would have cost me my life.

Then there was another shout and another. It sounded like a quarrel. There was a slight pause which felt like an eternity, and then a final shout that was halfway between mocking and challenging. A second later, voices were raised again but this time in raucous, mirth-filled laughter. The Russkies had been having a laugh, a bit of banter from one man to the other, then someone had cracked a joke and they all fell about. They were winding each other up. I couldn't fucking believe it. I thought I was going to drop down dead from the tension of it all. Even Palmer raised an eyebrow and exhaled in relief.

I glanced back at Kinane. He was still rooted to the spot. He looked round at his sons, nodded slowly and lowered his hand. He then walked the rest of the way across the farmyard with his boys following dutifully behind him, still clutching their shotguns. It had to be said they were disciplined; as good as any bunch of trained squaddies. Eventually, and not before time, they reached their position and disappeared from view.

Palmer nodded at me and I knew what that meant. It was our turn. I was glad Danny was in place to cover us and I was mightily relieved Kinane and his sons had made it, but now there was no dodging it. We had to cross that farm yard too; a big, open expanse of gravel that looked about the size of a football pitch to me now and we had to do it without making a sound. Worse than that, we had to get right up to the farmhouse itself, leaving just the width of a wall between us and men who liked to cut people into pieces for fun.

I took a deep breath, tried to forget that I wanted to be sick again and stood up. I followed Palmer as he made his way round the hedge. He paused to make sure the front door wasn't about to be opened at any moment and we stepped out into the farmyard. We walked with excruciating slowness across the gravel drive way, closer to the building than Kinane and his sons, but only because we had no choice. The wind was blowing in the trees above us, I could feel the gravel under my feet and hear the slight scrunch-scrunch as my shoes settled on them with every step. My eyes were glued to the door of that farmhouse, though I knew that wouldn't do me any good. If it opened, I was a dead man.

We were nearly there, so close I started to feel a wave of exultation. I could see the end of the building, the far gable wall we would disappear behind. Only another few steps; then it happened.

I took a step and felt a loosening of the pressure around my waist. Before I could do anything about it, the gun I was carrying there started to slip from my belt. Panicked, I snatched at it, desperate to prevent it from hitting the gravel where it would have made enough noise on impact for everyone in the farmhouse to hear, even if it didn't go off in the process. How to describe something so terrible, so heart-wrenching, that happens to you in a millisecond? My right palm went instinctively across to snatch at the gun but it didn't get there in time. Instead it flailed at the metal, caught it a glancing blow and deflected it to the left. Terrified, I grabbed at it desperately with my other hand but only proceeded to do the same thing, half-catching the gun as it fell but unable to prevent it from slipping through my grasp like a wet cricket ball. Palmer spun round in time to see the Glock drop from my hand and head in a downward trajectory towards the gravel, certain to give away our presence as soon as it hit the ground.

I don't know how I did it and I don't really want to think about how close we came to disaster but, at the last available second, I stuck my foot out. It was an entirely instinctive gesture but I managed to get the top of my foot under the gun just before it crashed to the ground. The effect was a bit like trapping a football, much of the speed was taken out of the falling gun as it bounced off the top of my foot and with a nerve shredding bump it fell off my toes and onto the gravel.

The sound was audible, but not half as bad as it would have been if I hadn't interrupted the Glock's fall with my shoe. I froze, my foot still hanging pointlessly in the air. Palmer raised his SLR and pointed it at the door, ready to drop anyone who burst through it.

We gave it a second then another.

Nothing. No sound from inside. Jesus Christ, we were off the hook.

Palmer nodded for me to pick up the gun. I wasted no time in obeying him and we both edged slowly to the far wall of the building then disappeared around it. We went down on our haunches and kept back in the shadows. I could just about see his face and I gave him a look that I hoped would appear apologetic. He just nodded like he understood but he looked like a ghost. It seemed I had managed to shit him up almost as badly as I had myself.

We weren't about to go bursting in on them. We didn't know what Vitaly and his mates were doing right now, how alert they were and how much weaponry they had nearby. To take men like these on we'd have to do it on our own terms.

All we could do now was wait until it got light. That's when it would happen. I looked at the dark sky around me and wondered how many of us would still be alive when night came around once more.

THIRTY-FOUR

We'd been waiting for hours, crouched down, in silence, freezing our bollocks off, trying not to think about what would happen if it all went wrong

It was just after eight in the morning when the Russians finally got their act together. We heard the latch on the door snap back and started, immediately going on the alert. Both Palmer and I had our guns ready. We listened intently as the door swung open, squeaking on its hinges, and low muffled voices reached us as they trudged out of the farmhouse. We were out of sight but knew we'd be able to see their backs in a moment as they walked across the farm yard towards their car. I was praying the others were as wide awake and alert as we were.

Seeing nothing amiss, they ambled towards the blacked-out Porsche Cayenne that was parked some way from their front door. It must have made a lot of sense to them to have somewhere isolated to lie low after hitting our organisation, but being this far from the city had its disadvantages, as they were about to find out. We knew they'd all be armed but we didn't want to give them time to reach for weapons.

We'd worked out the crossfire in advance, thanks to Palmer's recce the night before. We waited till they had almost reached the car then I shouted. That was the signal. What happened next was a blur. I saw the Russians spin round towards us in surprise, then Kinane and his sons stepped out from behind a skip with their shotguns raised. They didn't hang about, they just let them have it. At the same time, my brother opened up from behind the hedge. Palmer and me, we were behind their backs, blind-siding them as we stepped out from the side of the farmhouse.

We'd been waiting a long time in the cold but it was worth it to see the looks of comprehension on their dumb faces. They had just enough time to work out what was going to happen to them before we let loose but no time to react to it. The noise was incredible. Where all had been deathly quiet, there was a sudden explosion of gunfire and shouting. They were shouting because they were dying. We were shouting because we were killing them. The bodies twitched and were thrown about as they took the shotgun blasts from Kinane and his sons, the rifle bullets my brother was letting loose at a hell of a rate and all the rounds from the automatic pistol and the SLR Palmer and I were pumping into them. The glass from the nearby car's windows popped and burst, the metal of the bodywork sang as the bullets bounced through it and the tyres sagged, making the Porsche Cayenne sink into the mud, as if the car itself was dying along with them.

When we'd finished hitting them they were a mess. There was blood everywhere. A fly couldn't have escaped the carnage. When the boys stopped firing, I walked up to the Russians, who were lying where they'd stood a moment ago, and put a round into each of their heads, just to make sure. I didn't really need to do it but I wanted to. It made me feel better after what they'd done to me. The last man to take one of my bullets was Vitaly. He didn't look so cocky now though. I did it for Cartwright, who'd been executed without mercy on a cold factory floor, I did it for Finney who'd been taken without a shot being fired then tortured to death while the Russian guys laughed at him. I did it for Bobby and, of course, Sarah. Most of all, I did it for me.

'You're a long way from home,' I told Vitaly's shocked and open, lifeless eyes, before I put a round right between them.

After I shot him, I put my gloved hand into his inside jacket pocket and pulled out his mobile phone, then I walked away from his body. Above me, panicked crows cawed manically as they flew out of the trees all around us.

I checked Vitaly's sent messages - and there was nothing recent. I then went into his video files and found the footage I was looking for. I made sure nobody else was next to me when I watched it. It was indistinct, the light in the warehouse insufficient to show us up clearly. All I could make out was a grey, grainy image of a man, who may or may not have been me, standing there with a gun in his hand and another pointed at his head. At least, if anybody did see it, they'd realise I was being forced into it. I watched as I raised the gun and fired. The camera angle moved and a large, grey haired man, who may or may not have been Bobby Mahoney, but could just as easily have been Santa Claus, slumped in the chair. The film halted. It all looked fuzzy and confused, like a bad dream. I didn't feel as sick as I thought I would. I deleted the file.

Palmer came out of the house carrying a holdall. He unzipped it, peered inside and walked up to me, angling the bag so I could see what it contained.

'This what you've been looking for?' he asked me.

The bag contained a large amount of money. There was no time to stand and count it but I was willing to bet that most of it was still there. Gladwell must have been using this as a down-payment for Vitaly's services. We'd finally found the Drop.

Strange to think that it didn't really matter that much now, not in the long run.

We threw the bodies in the car while Kinane's lads went back to the main road to fetch our vehicles, then we took cans of petrol and poured it all over them. We torched the Porsche and it went up in seconds. I threw Vitaly's mobile through the window into the heart of the flames, then we got out of there quick. As we were driving through the gate, their car exploded.

THIRTY-FIVE

....

When Tommy Gladwell finally stepped out of his home he looked like a man with a world of trouble on his shoulders, and who could blame him? He'd risked everything on one massive gamble, one big throw of the dice that actually seemed to have paid off. He owned a city. It was all his.

Then he had left his Russian muscle behind to stamp his authority on his new empire and he'd gone home to wait for their call.

And waited. And waited.

I could only guess how he must have felt when Vitaly didn't make that call. All that agonising must have taken its toll; what could have gone wrong, who was to blame, had he been double-crossed? By now, he would be seeing enemies everywhere. Tommy Gladwell must have been living in a permanent state of fear and anxiety, which would explain the bodyguards.

His missus was already in the car when Tommy came out of their home and one of the bodyguards was holding the car door open for his boss' arrival while the other scanned the horizon for potential threats, but Our-young-'un and Palmer were too far back behind the bushes to be spotted. I was next to them, keeping low. We'd left Kinane and his boys out of this one. There was no reason to be mob handed for what we had in mind and we knew it would be harder for his bodyguards to spot just the three of us.

That was the drawback of living in a nice, big fuck-off country mansion. If Gladwell had still been a scussy wee shite from the tenements of Glasgow, like his old man, he would have settled for his father's idea of heaven; three former council houses next to each other, all knocked in together to make one big monument to bad taste. But Gladwell and his missus had grander ideas, which is why he had grounds and a big clump of trees and bushes just inside the gated walls of his huge house. It was ideal for our purpose. That big house was about to cost Tommy a lot more than he ever could have imagined when he was buying it.

Danny dropped Gladwell's first bodyguard smoothly and, as he hit the floor, Palmer took out the second. Before the bloke could even react he was on the ground too, collapsed in a heap on the gravel driveway. Neither of them was getting up again. Got to hand it to our Our-young-'un, he was still a cracking shot and Palmer looked like he did this kind of thing every day of the week.

Gladwell just froze in shock. He was peering out towards us in disbelief, because the men he'd entrusted his life to were both dead and he'd only just walked out of his own front door. He'd got a good inkling he was going to be next but he couldn't see us, so he didn't know what to do. He couldn't even run, because it all happened too fast.

The next thing, Palmer put a bullet right into his leg, just above the knee and Gladwell went down wailing and shouting. His missus was clambering back out of the car and screaming blue murder, shouting, 'Tommy, Tommy!' at the top of her voice - but no one was going to hear her out here, miles from anywhere.

My brother paused for a second and looked up just long enough for me to nod at him. 'Do her,' I told him. Tommy Gladwell's missus was still screaming like a fish wife, frantic to save her husband. The next shot took her right in the chest, which finally put an end to her caterwauling.

I watched her body twist and fall back against the front side panel of their big BMW. I didn't give a fuck for her, because of what she had said to Sarah when she left her alone with that Russian.

Gladwell was trying to make sense of what had happened to him, trying to crawl but he was having a problem because of the bullet in his leg. His arm was stretched out despairingly towards his wife, even though he must have known by now it was hopeless. I patted Our-young-'un on the shoulder, climbed to my feet and walked calmly out of the bushes towards him, carrying the small black bag Hunter had given me. Palmer and Danny followed.

I crossed the land between us before Gladwell could drag his fat bulk to his wife and I called out to him. 'Time to pay what's owed Tommy,' he turned his head to see me then. I swear I will never forget the look of amazement on his stupid face.

'You?' he managed to splutter and it was clear he thought he had about as much chance of being attacked by the ghost of Mother Theresa, than of being gunned down outside his own home by me.

'That's right,' I reached into the bag and slowly, deliberately pulled out the long, flat case then I slid the razor sharp machete free and showed it to him. Instinctively he tried to get to his feet and run, so scared that he'd forgotten his legs didn't work any more. There was a look of plain terror on his chubby face. I made sure I held the machete high so he could see the edge and I marched right up to him. He somehow managed to slide himself round until he was slumped on his back, propped up against the rear door of the car. 'You killed my wife, you bastard,' he half screamed, half sobbed at me.

'Mmm, not yet,' I said, 'looks like she is just about to breathe her last though,' I was no doctor but I reckoned I had that diagnosis just about nailed. Even though Lady Macbeth was technically still alive, the last few breaths were coming out of her now, slow and hoarse.

I got right up to her, knelt down on one knee and was close enough to almost whisper in her ear. 'I've got a message for you from Bobby Mahoney's daughter,' there was the slightest glimmer of recognition in her eyes, "get over yourself Hen".'

Then I watched her die right in front of me.

'Your wife's dead Gladwell,' I told him, 'so now I guess it's your turn'

'Fuck you,' he said but the defiance was unconvincing. He was sobbing and there was a pool of piss all around him.

'I want you to know this isn't going to be quick,' I told him, 'not after what you did to Bobby and Finney. I'm going to take my time and it's going to hurt you like you can't imagine.' I shoved the point of the machete's blade right up under his chin. 'And when I'm done, I'm going to cut your fucking head off, then I'm going to chuck your bodies in with the pigs and they're going to eat you. There'll be no fancy funeral for you two.'

And he started to beg, 'you can't do this. You can't do this to me,' Who was he to start giving orders, the state he was in? 'I let you live. I let you live!'

'Yeah you did, and that was your second mistake,' I told him, 'your first was trying to take over our city. I'm not going to let you live, you sick piece of shit. Begging and pleading is just a waste of breath but you can do it if you want to,' he was shaking his head, 'now I'm going to get started and I'm not going to stop no matter how hard you scream,' he was screaming already. I'd never seen a man so shit-scared in all my life and he had good cause, because I meant every word. 'Bobby Mahoney said he'd see you down in hell - so let's not keep him waiting too long.'

I got started with the machete then and wee Tommy Gladwell screamed and screamed like you wouldn't believe.

THIRTY-SIX

....

We didn't talk much after that. There was nothing to be said. It was over and we were done - well, almost.

I called ahead and we got Hunter and Kinane to meet us just south of the border. We took the four bodies out of the boots of our cars. They'd been wrapped in thick, plastic sheeting and we quickly transferred them to the back of Hunter's old van.

'Just make sure you don't get stopped for speeding,' I told Hunter.

'No danger,' he said, 'do I know them?' before adding, 'just curious like?'

'You know one of them,' I said. 'It's Arthur Gladwell's eldest, Tommy.'

'Fucking hell.'

'Which is why you are going to make bloody sure they disappear for good.'

'I'll take them up to the pig farm.'

It was the obvious destination. Pigs can eat anything. If you need to get rid of flesh and bone, pigs are the best thing when you don't want to leave a trace.

'There is one other thing I want from you,' I said. 'It's messy though.'

'Right.'

I told him and he looked a bit sick but he nodded anyway, 'I guess you know what you are doing. Jesus, how come we are at war with the Gladwells all of a sudden?'

It was time to tell Hunter what was going on, now that security was no longer an issue. He deserved to know it all if he was going to get rid of the bodies for me. When I'd finished the story he looked like everybody else who'd suddenly learned that Bobby and Finney had been killed; stunned, like the sky had somehow fallen in and nothing would ever be the same again.

'So, are we in the clear now then?' he sounded doubtful.

'There'll be no more bother from Tommy or his Russian muscle,' I assured him, 'I'll handle Arthur Gladwell.'

'Christ, he'll be on the warpath.'

'You let me worry about that.'

Before he got behind the wheel of his van, Mickey Hunter did a strange thing. He turned back, came towards me and shook my hand respectfully then he said, 'well done,' he looked a little surprised like he wanted to add, 'I never knew you had it in you,' and that would have been fair enough because neither did I.

'When you're rid of the bodies go home and wait for me to contact you,' I told him.

Seeing Hunter shake my hand, Kinane came over and did it too, 'it was a good job,' he said then he glanced towards his sons, giving them their cue. They came over and, one by one, they shook my hand too. Danny walked by and patted me on the back, as if I had just seen off the school bully all by myself and he was proud of me. Palmer watched all the handshakes from some way off. He leaned back against his car and started whistling the theme tune to *The Godfather*.

Hunter left first, taking the lorry, with the four bodies in the back, off to the pig farm like he'd promised. Kinane and his lads took a car and followed, to give him a hand and make sure he did what he was told. Palmer, Danny and me headed off in the other one. As we climbed in Palmer started whistling again. This time it was 'Hail to the chief'.

'Knock it off,' I told him.

We were nearly back in Newcastle when Our-young-'un said, 'so, that's it then.'

'Not quite,' I told him, 'I've got to go and see someone.'

Palmer asked, 'do you want me to come with you?'

'No, I'm going to do this one myself. Danny can watch my back. If he sees you, he'll know and I want to talk to him first,' I explained. 'I want a reason.'

Palmer nodded like he understood. 'Whatever reason he gives, it won't be enough.'

'All the same,' I said, 'I want to hear it from him,' that wasn't the only reason. This was a complicated mixture of honour and my authority all rolled into one. I was about to see the man who'd made this all happen. The one responsible for all the god-awful shit we'd had to wade through. It was only right and proper that the new boss sorted it all out, drawing a line under everything so we could finally move on.

'Careful,' cautioned Palmer, 'wouldn't want it to go tits up after all this.'

'No reason it should,' I said, 'it's not as if he's expecting me.'

'What if he *is* suspicious?'

'I've still got the Glock.'

THIRTY-SEVEN

I wasn't sure whether to knock on the door. If he wasn't expecting me, he'd be as meek as a lamb, if he was, then I was as likely to be met by a shotgun blast as a cup of tea, but he didn't strike me as the kind of man who kept guns lying around the house. As I was deliberating this, I caught a glimpse of movement out of the corner of my eye, a face at the window.

It was Miller - and he looked scared.

And then he was gone.

From the look on his face there was no way he was opening the door to me. Any last doubts I'd had about Miller disappeared in an instant. It was him all right. Palmer had got the right name.

I pulled out the Glock and legged it down the side of the farm house. Miller must not have been expecting to see me again after Friday night, so now he knew something had gone wrong. I was looking ahead as I ran, hoping to get a shot at him as he flew out of his back door, so I didn't realise I was too close to the metal dustbin that stood against the wall. My knee connected with its edge as I ran by and I cried out as it knocked me off balance and I fell face first onto the ground. He must have been keeping bricks in there or something 'cos it was as solid as rock but I didn't care about that right now, because all of a sudden there was Miller up ahead of me.

He moved pretty fast for an older guy. He must have torn through his house and out the back door because he'd almost reached his studio already. I was still moving when I aimed and I was going to let loose a shot but, before I could, he threw open the door to the studio and disappeared inside.

I had about a second to think it through. I could take my time and wait. I could go back and get Danny who was in the car outside, but I'd already told him I would handle it. I had my reasons for that and they had nothing to do with ego. There were times when the guy giving the orders had to earn the right to give them. Cutting up Gladwell was one of them, this was another. Plus, I didn't want to lose momentum or give Miller the chance to grab a gun and find a nice safe spot to hide behind and phone the police. I tore after him, wrenched the door open and pointed my gun straight ahead, half expecting him to be standing there doing the same thing. I knew I'd have to be quick and accurate or he'd do for me before I could get him in my sights.

Nothing.

Just silence in the dark corridor and those bloody photographer's lamps shining brightly up ahead of me like searchlights, casting strange deep shadows, anyone of which could have been hiding Miller. I edged my way slowly forward, keeping the gun pointed straight ahead of me. I had no idea what to expect. I hadn't a clue what he kept in here.

There'd be a gun somewhere no doubt, knowing his line of work, but was it a .38 or a Kalashnikov? I was sweating because I knew that, in here, anything could happen. I could be outgunned, outthought and out of my depth but I pressed on regardless. Our-young-'un always used to say about the Paras: they kept moving, always forward, always pressing, so they didn't lose momentum.

'You sold us all out Miller,' I called, hoping I sounded a lot harder than I felt. 'I know it and you know it, so I'm coming for you now.' His answer? A bullet that he sent my way from god knows where. It ricocheted then echoed in the tight confines of the metal studio, creating a din that made my ears ring. This was the first time I'd been shot at and I tried to stay calm. I told myself he couldn't possibly hit me from wherever he was hiding, or I'd have seen him by now.

Knowing Miller, he'd most likely have a Colt or a Browning, something non-flashy, old school. My heart was thumping again. The gun felt loose in my sweating palm and I was scared I was going to drop it. I was so close to finishing all this, to taking out the guy who had given Gladwell all the information he needed about our firm, then it would be over - and that was the scary part. I felt like those soldiers who knew the war was nearly finished, the enemy had surrendered and they'd won but they'd still got streets and houses to clear and they didn't want to get shot by some mad housewife or deranged grandad.

'The gun isn't going to help you Miller. Not after what you did,' I was slowly edging my way along the corridor towards the bright lights, 'Geordie Cartwright was a soft touch, with his debts and the promise of some easy cash, wasn't he? You sold him out to Tommy Gladwell but the Russians are all dead and so is Tommy. Now you're fucked and you know it. There's nowhere to go from here but down,' Another shot hit the wall to my left so I was thinking he had to be somewhere to my right, but it was a big place and he had the advantage. If I was going to get to him I'd have to come out of this narrow corridor and then I'd be an easy target. I remembered the layout and prayed he hadn't changed things around since I was last there. I went down low, lying flat on the ground, then I bent my arm round the corner and fired once. The noise of my gun going off was deafening in here. It couldn't be long before some distant neighbour of his called the police. Danny must have heard the shots and he'd be wondering what to do. I'd told him to stay outside but it would be just like him to burst through the door to save me. I didn't want him killed because of my stupidity.

Miller answered my round with two more harmless shots and I gambled he'd want to conserve what was left of his ammo. I climbed into a sprinter's stance, kept low and launched myself forward, all the time expecting a third shot. I must have caught him by surprise because I made it behind the big metal girder before he could fire again and I was safe, for now, as long as I didn't move.

I was better off here than in the corridor but he still had the advantage. He knew my location and I hadn't a clue where he was. If I had a plan at this point I didn't know it myself. I was just hoping I could somehow draw him out, get him to betray his position with another shot and finish him. I wasn't a bad shot but that was against paper targets on a firing range, not a living person who could move and shoot back. I was about to swing out an arm and fire again when something happened that completely threw me. Abruptly, all the lights went out.

Fuck. It was pitch black, so dark I could no longer even see the gun I was holding in front of me. The bloody windows must have all been blocked up with blackout blinds, so his nuddy girls got some privacy while he took their picture, and now he'd thrown the switch.

I heard a noise and strained my ears to work it out. Miller was moving. He knew where I was. He knew the room and I didn't. I could hear him slowly edging his way round to get me and there was nothing I could do about it. I was starting to feel panicked.

The sounds he was making were so slight I couldn't place him and I knew I didn't have long. In a few seconds he would be right on top of me. He could fire at me from point-blank range and I wouldn't even see him. There was nothing I could do because I couldn't even see the bastard.

Desperately I thrust my hand into my pocket, grabbed my mobile phone and jabbed at it. It gave off a little light from the screen but I had to risk that. The phone took its time before it gave up the feature I was looking for. I scrolled down the contacts book quickly, sweat making my hand clammy. I found the name I was looking for and dialled.

It turned out he was right by me, even closer than I thought. The sound of his mobile phone going off in his jacket pocket was deafening in the silence of the studio.

As last words go his weren't particularly memorable, just 'shit, fuck!' as he scrambled to silence it. As he reached the phone he must have known it was me that was dialling him. I like to think he had a millisecond to realise I'd outwitted him before I aimed the gun straight at the noise and sent four shots rapidly in his direction.

When the sound finally died down, there was a sort of strangled gurgle coming from the floor. I had to make sure he was no longer a threat to me. I walked carefully towards the nearest wall, pointing the gun in Miller's direction before feeling around behind me until I found the thick blackout blinds. I wrenched one of them right off the wall and the moonlight shone down onto him.

Miller was lying face up, trying to cough out the blood from his shattered lungs as it filled his airways, the dark stain spreading all over his chest, proof that I had hit him more than once. His gun lay harmlessly on the ground a few feet from him. I walked over and trod on it, whilst aiming my gun at him, then kicked it to one side. I made sure he could see me.

'Why did you do it Miller?' I asked a man who had once been a big part of my extended, dysfunctional family, 'tell me it wasn't just for the money.'

He opened his mouth and it looked like he was trying to speak but the only thing that came out was more blood. He was choking on it.

I didn't say anything else. I knew I was never going to get his story now. He was too far gone. Miller couldn't have explained his treachery if he'd wanted to, he couldn't even get the words out. So I put it down to good, old-fashioned greed.

Miller had always said he was an atheist. I knew he didn't believe in anything after this life but oblivion. Sure enough, he looked terrified as he died.

THIRTY-EIGHT

....

When we got back to Palmer's house, I went straight up to Sarah's room. She was lying in bed but awake. She looked mightily relieved to see me. When she sat up, the covers slipped off her shoulders a little. It looked like she wasn't wearing anything beneath them.

'Is it over?' she asked.

'Yes,' I said.

'You finished it?'

'I finished it.'

'Good.'

'Are you alright?' she looked tired but relieved.

'I will be,' she said, 'one day.'

There was an awkward moment while both of us waited for the other to fill the silence.

'Do you want anything?' I asked.

She nodded, 'I want you to climb in here and hold me.'

'Sarah, are you sure.'

'Yes,'

She pulled back the covers. I was right. She wasn't wearing anything. I took off my clothes and climbed in next to her.

I walked into the lock-up with Palmer. His guys had been standing guard over grey-hair in shifts all this time. He looked rough; scared and stressed, cold and hungry, still wearing the horrible clothes they'd given him down the gym. When he saw me he tried to look down at the ground.

'Look at me,' I ordered and he raised his head slowly, his eyes screwed up like he expected to be shot at any moment, 'it's over and you lost,' I told him. 'Gladwell is dead and so is the she-devil.'

'Oh god,' he croaked.

'His bodyguards are both dead too and the Russians, all of them. Bobby Mahoney was too good for you. He has seen you all off. He's put all of your mates in the ground.'

'It wasn't my idea,' he was sobbing now and shaking his head.

'What wasn't?'

'Coming down here. It was Tommy's.'

'Just obeying orders were you?'

'Aye,' he was nodding like a lunatic as if that might make me understand him better.

'You were just a soldier, I s'pose?'

'That's right.'

'What am I supposed to do with a captured soldier Terry? No POW camps in Newcastle mate, haven't you heard?'

'Please… '

'I don't think so. I reckon you've had your chips.'

It was a prearranged signal for Palmer to pull out his gun then make a big show of loading a magazine and cocking it.'

'No,' the tears were flowing now.

'I think we have to say goodnight now Terry.' I told him.

'You don't have to… ' he pleaded.

My mobile rang noisily in my pocket. I'd turned the volume up to its highest level. I gave an exasperated sigh and answered it, 'hello?'

'Is that the gay advice line?' trilled Our-young-'un. 'I think me little brother might be a bender,' he hung up laughing.

'Bobby,' I said, trying not to laugh too, 'yes, I'm here with him now, that's right,' then I made a point of looking up into Terry's fear-filled eyes, 'I'm just about to take care of it.'

'Jesus Christ,' hissed Terry as he suddenly rediscovered his religion.

'What?' I asked the disconnected phone in disbelief, 'are you sure about that Bobby?' then I paused to let the ghost of Bobby Mahoney issue me some instructions, 'well, if you say so. You're the boss.'

I hung up and was greeted by Terry's expectant gaze.

'Want me to do him now?' asked Palmer and he pressed the gun right up against the bloke's temple. Terry moaned something indecipherable and shut his eyes tightly.

'Look at me Terry,' I told him but he was too scared to open his eyes, 'you'd better look at me Terry or I'll get irritated and he will shoot you anyway.' Terry slowly opened his eyes like it was a supreme effort, he was trying not to blink with the gun pressed up against his head like that.

I smiled at him, 'looks like it's your lucky day old son,' and he stared at me as if he didn't dare believe it was true, 'Bobby wants you to go home,' I said, 'with a message.'

It suited me for the Gladwells to think Bobby was still alive, the victor in this latest war. It added to the myth of the invincible Bobby Mahoney, always one step ahead of his rivals, always coming out on top - and it took the heat away from me. Bobby was high profile. He was like one of those generals in the American Civil War, riding through the massed ranks of his troops on a bright white charger with a feather plume in his hat, so they could all see him and cheer, which is fine until one day when someone from the other side notices and takes a pot shot at you. I needed a figurehead to hide behind, someone who could take all of the hatred and retribution that would be heaped on him by the Gladwell brothers and Tommy's father. Who better than a dead man?

I told Terry to go and see Gladwell senior personally to let him know that Bobby had killed his son and regained control of his city, and would take a very dim view if there was any further interference in his business. It was unlikely Tommy Gladwell would have had the inclination to tell anyone that Bobby was dead. It would have been too dangerous until he had full control of the city.

We made it clear that Bobby would no longer be based in Newcastle so there was no point trying to find him there. Bobby had gone abroad, somewhere nice and hot, but we didn't narrow it down. From there, he would continue to pull all of the strings, issuing instructions through a network of trusted associates.

When it was all finally over we went to see Amrein. I drove down to Shepperton early with Palmer and Kinane. We stayed over the night before our appointment.

It was a convivial meeting, relaxed almost, under the circumstances. We sat down together around Amrein's table. It was a sunny day and the birds were chirruping away outside, oblivious to our recent troubles. We had a light lunch with a bit of small talk; the economy, the trials and tribulations facing the entrepreneurial businessman in these days of a chastened global financial system. Then we came down to business.

Using the bare facts of what had occurred, I went through the whole tale; how Tommy Gladwell had tried and failed to step out of his old man's shadow, how he had almost been lucky enough to get to Bobby Mahoney, had even managed to kill the legendary Finney. How we had been forced into putting together a new crew and how, finally, we had taken back our city and restored order, leaving Bobby in charge just as before, only stronger.

'I'm impressed,' Amrein said quietly and he looked it. 'And the Gladwell boy, his friends?' he asked, sounding like a headmaster asking after a former pupil.

'Gone.'

'Mmm,' he pondered this for a moment, 'is that likely to cause you further problems, an escalation of hostilities perhaps?'

'Nothing we can't handle,' I told him.

'I'm sure,' he smiled benignly.

I put the bag on the table in front of him and said, 'I've brought the Drop down early since you were good enough to see us at short notice and we've upped it, by ten per cent,' that surprised him. 'We like to think we will be doing business together for a very long time,' I explained, 'if things go well between us then it will be the same amount each time from now on.' He tried hard but failed to hide the fact that he was pleased. I was relaxed about it because I knew Kinane's sons would have arrived at the Sunnydale estate by now, 'though we obviously expect you to earn it.'

'Of course,' he smiled like he couldn't quite believe my cheek, but you could tell he was a happy man.

'There is one other thing,' I said.

He held his hands out expansively, 'how can I help,'

I nodded towards the French windows, 'mind if we take a walk?'

'Certainly,' he rose and the bodyguard opened them. The two of us walked out into the garden together, crossing the great expanse of manicured lawn, the lush green symbol of Amrein's success and he let me talk, sensing I had a matter of some delicacy to raise that I would come to in my own time.

'You've done well for yourself,' I said, 'a beautiful house, priceless connections, all the influence that large sums of protection money can buy, which is why Bobby Mahoney has used you all these years and never complained about the price, not once, because he knew what he was getting out of the deal.'

Amrein nodded, 'peace of mind,' he said.

'Peace of mind,' I emphasised, 'there's a lot to be said for it,' we were half way across the lawn now, almost at the summer house, but he hadn't noticed anything different.

'And that's why we want to continue with a long-standing relationship that will be mutually beneficial and lucrative.'

'You won't hear any argument from me,' and he gave me that same disarming smile he'd given me weeks ago when he had warned us to sort out the mess back home.

'I respect you,' I told him. 'We listened to your advice, got our house in order, showed the world that a few guys from Russian Special Forces and a jock with delusions of grandeur aren't enough to knock us off our perch - but Bobby Mahoney isn't happy with you.'

'What?' He seemed genuinely taken aback. I'd lulled him with the quiet words and the increased payments.

'Because he trusted you completely,' I stopped and turned to face him and noted the faint glimmer of fear in his eyes. I'd timed it to perfection because we were almost at the summer house.

'I'm not sure I follow,' he said weakly.

'He thought that, because he had worked with you for years and put money into your bank account time and time again, you would never give your blessing to the next wannabe gangster who came to you with a half-baked plan to take over his city. But I know that you did give Tommy Gladwell your blessing.'

'That's ridiculous.'

'Is it? Tommy Gladwell may have been a fool but he was a fool from the old school. He knew how things worked. Because of his old man, he knew all about the Drop. He knew who you were and how you operated. He wasn't so stupid he wouldn't come and see you first with his business plan because he'd know if you were against him right from the start he'd have no chance. You weren't going to sit back and let our money slip through your fingers. What did he promise you, eh? A nice big chunk of wedge for yourself, with none of it kicked upstairs? It would have to be that or you wouldn't run the risk of losing our business, but your employers wouldn't see it that way, would they? The whole point of our arrangement is that you are supposed to be on our side and they know that. You have gone decidedly off-piste Amrein, I must say.'

He was looking well rattled by this stage, 'that's crazy. I don't know who's been… '

'Shut up.' I put my hand firmly on his shoulder then and he couldn't help it, he looked out of the corner of his eye, searching in vain for his bodyguard, knowing he'd been a fool, suckered by the friendly lunch, the amiable chit-chat from the deferential young man and the increased Drop. Now he knew he'd been conned. I could end him here before his bodyguard got anywhere near him. For all he knew, Kinane and Palmer had killed his guys already. 'Don't shit yourself Amrein, I'm not going to kill you. If I was I wouldn't waste my breath talking to you like this, I'd just do it. I'm planning to work with you. I just want to make sure you never forget who you are dealing with, ever. I'm a bit sharper than you think, see. Anyone ever comes to you again wanting to take over our business, you send them packing without any encouragement, then you call me and tell me all about it, straight away, no delays or I'll hold it against you later,' he didn't interrupt. 'If you don't, I'll win anyway because I know my city and I'm cleverer than all of the others. When we've won and they're dead, there'll be no more Drop. I'll leave you to explain that to the people you kick the money upstairs to. If they don't kill you, I'll come looking for you,' I gripped his shoulder more firmly and leant in close, 'and Amrein, I will find you, wherever you go.'

He had gone pale and there was a light sheen of sweat on his forehead.

'You got that?' I demanded.

'Of course,' he swallowed before he said it. He looked well nervous. I knew he prided himself on keeping a good distance from anything bloody. Like a general, he gave out the orders that lead to men dying but he never had to do it himself or witness any of it. I used to be like that myself I supposed. What had Jerry Lemon called me? A plastic gangster, so I knew the impact violence and fear can have on a man like Amrein.

'Good,' I nodded my satisfaction, released my grip from his shoulder and actually patted him on the cheek, like he'd been a good little boy listening to Daddy. 'I'm glad you feel that way,' I concluded, 'because I wouldn't want to see you end up like him,' and I nodded towards the summer house.

Amrein peered at the summer house, trying to work out what I was on about. He walked a little closer, squinting into the sunshine through those wire framed spectacles. It took him a moment or two to make out the dark shadow through the glass. Then I heard him shout 'Jesus Christ!'

'One last thing,' I told him, 'that story you gave me about having a man in HUMINT who knew we had somebody ratting to SOCA but not who it was. That was bullshit. I didn't buy it then and I don't buy it now. If he knew we had a rat he'd know who it was. You kept the name back to make me go looking for him. To distract me, while Gladwell was coming after us.'

I wasn't certain but it looked like a little dark patch had formed on the groin of his expensively tailored trousers.

'I want that name and I want the proof. Let's call it a gesture of good faith. You've got one week.'

I walked away then, back across that enormous lawn with the birds chirruping happily in the trees above me, leaving Amrein still staring at the summer house where Tommy Gladwell's severed head sat neatly on the sill, peering back at him through the window.

THIRTY-NINE

....

I phoned Arthur Gladwell on the morning of his son's memorial service. 'How did you get this number?' he asked me. He sounded in a state.

'Doesn't matter how I got it. Do you know who you are talking to?' We'd not met that often and he was unlikely to remember my voice.

There was a long pause before he finally admitted, 'No.'

'No but I know everything about you. It's Tommy's memorial today but you've got other sons, daughters, grandchildren... ' He didn't utter a word while I told him the names and addresses of everyone that was near and dear to him, right down to the nursery his youngest grandchild went to four mornings a week. I had to hand it to Sharp. He'd done a thorough job.

'How do you want to end this?' he asked me when I was done, his voice breaking.

'It's already over. I just want to make sure you understand that. Your son's dead because he was stupid. He thought he could come down here and take over a long established concern but Bobby wasn't having it. Stay out of our city Gladwell - or we'll kill your whole family, including the grandbairns, and no one will ever find your body either. Understand?'

'Yes,' he said softly.

And I hung up.

It was a German Shepherd that finally found the body. A bloke out walking his dog told the police and his local paper that the dead man had a badly scarred face and a needle sticking out of his arm. Everyone agreed it was just another sad but unsurprising case of a junkie, so far out of it he'd taken too much for his poor little body to cope with. The newspapers duly reported the death of a career-criminal called Andrew Stone, a professional burglar who had accidentally killed himself with heroin. They did include a quote from a so-called friend who swore blind that Stone had never touched heroin before. This friend even suspected foul play, but the tone of the article made it clear the reporter didn't believe such a far-fetched theory. The gist of the article being, it was never too late to become an addict and the results were almost always tragic. Andrew Stone's death was just another senseless, drug related tragedy in the squalid tenements of Glasgow.

A week later, Amrein delivered the name we were looking for, along with incontrovertible, documented proof lifted from the files of SOCA itself; the name of our rat.

I looked at it and did a double take, then I felt a little surge of relief. At least we were spared another execution. Northam, our harmless, little bent accountant was going to shop us all. Apparently he had failed to keep up with the times and SOCA managed to trace some of his dodgy international cash transfers, as they went from an uncaring bank in Luxembourg to a blind-eye-turning clearing house in the Caymans and finally arrived, laundered more times than a whore-house bed-sheet, into an account run by every criminal's favourite accomplice in Geneva. You've got to love the Swiss. If their bank accounts were good enough for the Nazis then, they were good enough for us. A bank that welcomes Herman Goering is hardly going to blanch at the prospect of Bobby Mahoney as a client.

Trouble was, the investigators were getting a little smarter and we should have kept up. Once they were able to prove to Northam he was ruined, he rolled over like he was having his tummy tickled, offering to tell them everything; names, dates, places and amounts, everything a judge and jury could ask for. He'd have sent us all down to save his own arse. Fucking accountants.

And to think I'd even felt sorry for him lying there with a bullet in his brain. It turned out Tommy Gladwell just saved me a job. Finding another accountant wasn't going to be hard. They were ten a penny, especially bent ones. I just had to make sure the next one was more scared of me than the law.

Well, there would be no trials now, what with the chief witness for the prosecution disappearing like that. It made me realise that if, Tommy Gladwell hadn't come along we would have carried on obliviously for a few more months, until the fateful day when we were all nicked. It made you think.

A couple of days later, I read a lead article in *The Times* about the Serious Organised Crime Agency and its woeful record since its inception at great public cost. The British FBI had completely failed in its quest to bring to justice the country's top 130 'crime lords', including Bobby. The article cited a top heavy management structure, overburdened bureaucracy and inefficient systems, leading to collapsing morale and an exodus of officers. It was nice to know we were not the only ones with troubles.

There was a period of transition. The word had to slowly get round that the personnel may have changed but the organisation was intact, rejuvenated in fact, by new blood. I made sure the people who mattered all knew where the authority now lay to do business with us.

The new organisation was tighter and more ruthless. Our whole outlook was geared around making sure that what was done to Bobby and Finney could never happen to us. We increased the muscle, used Kinane and his sons, plus the boys from their gym. They weren't greedy and they owed me for elevating them; most of the time they seemed pretty grateful just to be out of the wilderness.

I gave a lot of responsibility to Palmer. After all, he'd come good against the Russians so I owed him and he showed no signs of wanting to be boss. He didn't need the hassle - but then I used to say that too, so I would be keeping a closer eye on him in future.

Before I left, he told me, 'there's a rumour doing the rounds that Jerry Lemon underestimated you. Word on the street is you had him killed because he showed you up in front of everybody down at the snooker hall. They say you are not a man to be fucked with.'

I did nothing to contradict that rumour.

I also gave more responsibility to Hunter, because he'd done well when I'd needed him and he knew where the bodies were buried, or at least where the pigs lived that ate the bodies. I made sure all of these men had plenty of money in their pockets, and jobs that made them feel like a face around town. I paid better than Bobby. It was my insurance against the kind of resentful, blind ambition that brought down Bobby Mahoney after nearly thirty years as king of the Midden.

It made my brother. Whatever self respect he'd lost on that battlefield, he got back when I put him in charge of some of our dirty laundry. People started seeing him round the city in our clubs and casinos but this time he'd had a haircut and a shave, was dressed in a smart jacket and he laid off the sauce. He tidied himself up big style and the next time he was in one of our lap dancing bars, the girls were throwing themselves at him because they knew he was my brother. I even persuaded him to move out of his shit hole of a flat and take over my old apartment. After all, I wouldn't be needing it where I was going.

If they needed advice we used web phones, so much more secure than mobiles or landlines, or someone flew out to see me. Kinane, Palmer, Hunter and Danny took it in turns so the authorities wouldn't become too suspicious of any frequent flyers. I came back to Newcastle from time to time to oversee things but it was deliberately infrequent and it became less and less over time. I'd set the thing up and told them what to do, how to handle themselves with the police, other villains, our employees, everything. If they did what I told them it would be sweet and the money would continue to roll in, just so long as they remembered my cut, same time every month, regular as clockwork. Another Drop that was never to be forgotten.

Before I left the country, Detective Inspector Clifford hauled me in for a chat. I went voluntarily with my solicitor. She sat next to me in the interview room. We were complying with a request to assist the police with their enquiries. I'm afraid I wasn't much help.

'I am obviously aware that Bobby Mahoney has disappeared,' I told Clifford and his tape recorder, 'and it is deeply upsetting to me that my former employer, a respectable businessman after all, has vanished into thin air like this, but I have heard that hundreds of people go missing every year for no apparent reason.'

'You're trying to tell me that Bobby Mahoney has cracked up, lost the plot and gone walkabout?' asked Clifford, while Sharp sat stone-faced beside him. Nothing ever came from that Police Complaints Commission visit. It wasn't even about Sharp. Like I'd told him, he'd been worrying about nothing.

'I think it just goes to show how little you really know anyone,' I said. 'Have you called the homeless hostels in London, just in case? It might be a good place to start?'

'Are you taking the piss?'

'Inspector, my client has attended this interview voluntarily,' my solicitor reminded him, 'he is merely trying to assist you in your missing person's enquiry.'

'It's not a missing persons enquiry, it's a murder investigation.' His face was turning puce again, 'one of the rumours doing the rounds on the streets of this fair city is that Bobby Mahoney is in fact dead and that a person or persons unknown is now running his empire.'

'Indeed, well, where is the body?' asked my solicitor and Inspector Clifford looked even more irritated.

He turned his disparaging gaze back onto me. 'So, what are you going to do, now that your employer has apparently fucked off?'

'I am in the fortunate position that Mister Mahoney's daughter is overseeing the family business for now, until we have news of his safe whereabouts. She has asked me to remain as Group Sales and Marketing Director, in the medium term, to assist her.'

'Sales and M... ' he clenched his teeth and shook his head, 'so I take it you have no knowledge of another missing person's case we are working on?'

'I'd be glad to help of course but I'm not sure how... .'

'A gangster from Glasgow called Tommy Gladwell, his wife and two bodyguards have also mysteriously vanished into thin air around the same time that Bobby Mahoney went AWOL. The difference being, we found blood on the ground outside his home.'

'I can't help you there Inspector. I'm afraid I've never met any gangsters, let alone one from Glasgow.'

The Inspector took a deep breath and I got the impression it was only the presence of my eminently respectable, female solicitor that was keeping him from leaning over and smashing my face into the table.

'Perhaps I can get your opinion on a little matter closer to home then,' he persisted. 'How about the violent turf war that has erupted on the Sunnydale estate?'

'Oh, this I do know all about,' I assured him.

'You do?' he seemed surprised.

'Yes, after all it has been on the front pages of both *The Evening Chronicle* and *The Journal*, a dreadful business. I believe it involved the abduction and murder of some established heroin dealers. The reporter from *The Journal* said you suspected some sort of vigilante group?'

'Do we fuck,' he hissed, 'it was your lot. We are not bloody stupid.'

At this point my solicitor interjected, 'can I once again remind you that my client is a company director who has never even been charged with, much less convicted of, any crime.'

'Might I remind you Miss,' DI Clifford hissed through gritted teeth, 'that I am very much aware of your client and his role within the so-called Gallowgate Leisure Group.'

At this point I wanted to say 'if you're so clever Inspector, how is it that I've got your right hand man on my payroll and you haven't even worked that out, but I obviously thought better of it. He turned his attention back to me. He leaned forward so that he was stretching right over the desk, deliberately invading my personal space, 'I suppose you are going to try and convince me you have never even heard of a man called Vitaly Litchenko?'

'Oh yes, I have heard of him' I said calmly and DI Clifford frowned in surprise. I could see Sharp looking a little nervous at this point, 'doesn't he play for Chelsea?'

I was almost at my car when DI Clifford caught up with me. He sounded excitable.

'I want you to know something, off the record,' he told me, 'with no solicitors around. This is just between you and me. I want you to be aware that I know what's going on. I just can't prove it yet but I'm going to.'

'Really,' I said trying to look unconcerned.

'Yes I do,' he told me, 'Bobby Mahoney isn't dead. He's very much alive. He just used a war with that piss ant, little pretend gangster from Glasgow to get the fuck out of it. I know Tommy Gladwell. I know all about him and he didn't have the brains to mastermind a takeover of this city. Bobby killed him, his wife and their bodyguards and they probably deserved it too, the bloody fools. Bobby's abroad somewhere but he's still running things. I know it and I won't rest until I prove he's alive and bring him back here in handcuffs. You tell him this from me. He can run but he can't hide!' I tried to look a little bit sideswiped by this outburst and it worked. 'I knew it!' he said triumphantly, 'I'm right. Go on, admit it, just between us.'

I paused then, waiting for as long as I could before answering him, watching his piggy little eyes glaze with expectation.

'I don't know what you're talking about,' I told him as I climbed into my car. I closed the door on his indignant face and started the engine.

'I will find him,' he called through the glass, 'I will!'

'Give my regards to Lord Lucan while you're at it,' I muttered to myself as I drove sharply away.

EPILOGUE

....

L ook at him. Go on, look. Take a good, long look. Scary isn't
he; standing there by the swimming pool, five feet eight
inches of muscular, killing machine and about as hard as granite.

Not a big guy but he's a Gurkha, ex-British Army, Palmer
put me on to them. Him and his mates don't come cheap but
they are worth it because they have a very important job to do,
the most important there is. They are keeping me alive.

He won't leave my side today and his mates are patrolling
the grounds of my new home right now; a huge, luxurious,
state-of-the-art, all-mod-cons, gated compound, not a stone's
throw from the Hua Hin resort where I took Laura on holiday,
about a lifetime ago now. Funny how things work out isn't it?

Sarah comes out of our house looking beautiful in her
tiny, little, white bikini and he doesn't even notice her as she
pads past him in her bare feet, hips rolling. At least he pretends

not to, doesn't even give her a look, not even a quick, furtive, sidelong glance as she flips her pert, little arse up in the air into a perfect dive before disappearing beneath the cool, clear water. Instead he just stands there, that big fuck-off Kalashnikov slung on his shoulder, staring straight ahead like a tin soldier. He can't be human. I mean if you can't enjoy a sight like that you're not alive, not really. But me? I'm just glad he is so dedicated, so focused, so completely in the zone, concentrating on nothing more than keeping me breathing, just so long as I keep on paying.

And he is loyal, which helps in my business. Like I told you, loyalty is a rare and underestimated commodity these days. At least it is in my game. You want my opinion? You can't put a price on loyalty.

And my tin soldier and his mates are loyal.

At least, I fucking hope they are…

THE END

Howard Linskey on **'What's your perfect writing environment'** and **'What is your actual one like?'**

Howard's debut novel *The Drop* was one of the top reads of 2011 according to the *Times*. Originally from Newcastle, he has gained many fans for his excellent portrayal of the North East's seedy underbelly of crime.

'I write straight onto a laptop. Life's too short to write long-hand then transcribe it all onto a computer screen like I used to,' he says. 'I have a desk by a window in a ground floor room of my house. I've done a lot of writing there but I have probably written just as many words sitting on the sofa, laptop perched on my knee, while family members watch TV in the background. I get used to writing wherever and whenever I can – coffee bars and even pubs – if I can find a quiet corner away from everyone. I play five-a-side football and if I arrive with 20 minutes to spare before kick-off, I'll sit in my car and write. The words might be rough, need editing and may even be discarded at the eleventh hour during the final edit, but as I nail down another chapter involving my gangsters, bent coppers and assorted Geordie low-lifes, I know that if I just keep going, one day there will be a finished novel with my name on it. I completed the latest one (*The Damage*) last night in fact, and I can tell you it's a damned nice feeling.'

crimefictionlover.com